a tale of two houses

Defy the Stars, book 1

Susan Harris

A TALE OF TWO HOUSES
Copyright ©2019 Susan Harris
All rights reserved.
Printed in the United States of America
First Edition: August 2019

CLEAN TEEN PUBLISHING
WWW.CLEANTEENPUBLISHING.COM

Summary: Julian Montgomery is the reluctant Prince of House Montgomery and Rowan Cambridge is in no rush to become the Queen of House Cambridge. Both long for freedom from their birthright obligations. When fate throws these two star-crossed lovers together, it sends them on a collision course with destiny that neither of them could have predicted. If you think you know how this story ends - think again!

ISBN: 978-1-63422-355-3 (paperback)
ISBN: 978-1-63422-354-6 (e-book)
Cover Design by: Marya Heidel
Typography by: Courtney Knight
Editing by: Kelly Risser

Young Adult Fiction / Fairy Tales & Folklore / Adaptations
Young Adult Fiction / Fantasy / Wizards & Witches
Young Adult Fiction / Paranormal, Occult & Supernatural
Young Adult Fiction / Royalty

For more information about our content disclosure, please utilize the QR code above with your smart phone or visit us at www.CleanTeenPublishing.com

These violent delights have violent ends
And in their triumph die, like fire and powder,
Which, as they kiss, consume.

Romeo and Juliet
William Shakespeare

A Tale of Two Houses is dedicated
to Melanie Newton,
Without your encouragement, this book would
not have been possible.
And by encouragement, I mean all those times
you told me I had to write this book and would
not take no for an answer!
You are the best kind of friend and I am so very
lucky to know you.

Prologue

MANY, MANY YEARS AGO, A DISAGREEMENT BETWEEN the royal house of witches split the coven into two royal lineages, House Cambridge and House Montgomery. The rivalry between the two covens caused bloodshed, tore families apart and divided the country. Those without magic were forced to choose a side and became casualties of a war where no one would be victorious.

The armies of House Cambridge and House Montgomery clashed over and over again, leaving bodies of the innocent in their wake. Only those with the strongest of magic survived. Thunder boomed and lightening ripped through the skies. The gods did not favor the war and took matters into their own hands.

When a royal prince of House Montgomery struck down a favored child of one of the human encampments, the dying girl cried out, using the magic that saturated the air, and the seeping blood made the curse so much more binding.

"Both of your houses will never know peace. You will know nothing but sorrow. Only when love is possible, will you all be set free."

The gods heard the cry of the dying girl and accepted her blood sacrifice.

Time passed by, and the houses still warred.

The young girl's curse was all but forgotten.

Until now.

chapter one
julian

"EN GARDE!"

The warning cry rang out as I heaved another sigh, already bored with today's training session. I never fully understood why Father wanted me to learn to wield a sword, when my magic would be the thing that swayed a fight. After all, I was the only child of the eldest son of the head of the Montgomery witches; my magic was limitless.

Summoning the wind that blew a gentle breeze across my skin, the overly long strands of my hair falling into my face, I dangled my sword in the air, closing my eyes to the clash of metal as one of my best friends, Tobias, grunted, dodging the blade as it toyed with him. Inside my mind, I could see Tobias clear as water, striking left and right, but unable to stand up to the might of magic and metal.

"Julian!" My father's voice dragged a sense of dread through me, causing the hair on the back of my neck to stand to attention. Instantly, I opened my eyes, releasing the control I had over the wind and reached out my hand to clasp the hilt of the blade. Knowing that my father watched me did nothing to ease the tension coiled inside me, for war was coming and we Montgomerys were a bloodthirsty bunch, apparently.

Tobias gave me a small smile, inclining his head just a tad before he came at me. If it came down to a sword-on-sword fight, Tobias would out maneuver me within minutes. A magical dud, a Null, a person who comes from a magical line yet fails to have any in their blood, Tobias had proven himself to be indispensable with weapons, and it was predicated he would be my army's general, when I became head of the family that is.

That thought was enough to distract me, and sure enough, Tobias did something applause worthy with his feet, and my back hit the sand with enough force to wring a groan from me as pain blossomed in my back. Blowing out a breath, I pushed the stray strands of hair from my face and lashed out with my magic. Not much, but I sculpted a hand out of the grains of sand, reached out and yanked Tobias down by the ankle.

Tobias met the same fate as I, yet he convulsed with laughter. Taking a few moments, Tobias nip-upped, reaching out a hand to help me up. When we were both on our feet, we spared a glance in my father's direction. He scowled at our boyish behavior. When I was younger, I wondered if I was even Malcolm Montgomery's child, for we looked naught alike. I had my mother's fair hair, a coppery gold sort of color that Tobias teased me would have looked better on a girl. My father was dark haired with pale features and a hard face that came from years of leadership. He was battle worn, judging by the scars on his arms and torso. He had these dark, dark eyes that were not quite brown… but not black either.

My eyes were a royal blue, according to my mother,

and my skin held a tinge of tan from days playing in the desert sand. One night, when my father had a drop too much to drink, he told me that it was due to my mother's tainted bloodline, that her family had once been part of the Nulls, or human colonies, that divided up the two lands. The next morning, he pretended the words had never fallen from his lips, yet I always remembered.

Tobias stood next to me, hands clasped behind his back, feet slightly apart; the perfect soldier stance. I sheathed my sword into the strap on my back and boldly faced my father.

"Julian, you will never stay alive when the war comes if you continue to shirk your lessons."

"The war has been coming since I was a boy, Father. I'm pretty sure I will be an old man, and we will still be awaiting the war."

A rumble of thunder sounded in the distance, the only indication that my father was angered by my words. The Montgomery witches controlled the elements in varying degrees. My father could control the weather, while I could manipulate the elements, like creating a hand from the grains of sand that suffocated our desert home or forcing the air to hold my sword.

With a sharp turn, my father vanished from the balcony he had been standing upon as Tobias nudged me with his shoulder. "Damn, Jules, you will do just about anything to piss him off."

I grinned at Tobias. "Sure, why would I need to defend myself if I have the coven's best swordsman at my side? If you fall in battle, if someone has the audacity to strike you down, then I'm dead anyway."

Tobias made to reply, pausing when a group of young

women our age came out of the schoolhouse, giggling once they spotted me and Tobias, their eyes wandering over us as they passed by.

"Hi, Tobias. Hey, Julian."

Tobias bowed at the waist and rolled out his arm in a sweeping gesture. "Ladies, we are honored to be noticed by such beautiful women. Come, spare a thought for us. We are sore from sparring and need a kiss to strengthen us."

The girls burst into fits of laughter, as my face heated. I had never been good around girls, and no matter how many times Tobias had dragged me to one party or another, I usually slipped away when my cheeks flamed at a suggestion or two. Tobias, more often than not, was surrounded by woman at these parties. I heard the women speaking about Toby, his rich hazel eyes and mahogany colored hair, skin tanned from the desert sun, much like most of our kin, and a smile that promised mischief. They spoke of how a man as good looking as Toby could not be as dangerous as the stories that were told. But Toby was dangerous, even for someone with no magic.

As was the man who strode toward then, the woman breaking apart to let Mercuree pass by.

My other best friend, Mercuree, got his name from the silver of his hair and his matching eyes. When his mother had given birth to him, he had opened his eyes from the onset, eyes of silver mercury holding hers. His parents claim that they saw an intelligence in his eyes and refused to cut his hair, in fear of some long-told legend about a fierce warrior who lost his strength when his hair had been cut. Mercuree's hair was braided down his back.

To those who did not know him, Mercy, as he was

affectionately known, was a scary SOB. Dressed in the same military outfit that Tobias wore, black pants and embroidered short sleeved tunic that showed off the various tattoos that wound up the spy master's arms. His waist tended to be weighed down with various knives and daggers, and today was no different. His face was stern, for he rarely smiled, except with those he trusted. Mercy walked with the shadows and called them his friends.

The girls scattered as Mercy came to stand in front of them, his thick arms folded over his chest. I always wondered how a man, just seventeen like myself and Tobias, but with such a striking appearance, managed to become a spymaster. Yet when I asked Mercy this, he gave me the smile he normally reserved for those whose last sight was his eyes and shrugged.

"Have mercy on me, Mercy! You've scared all the women away."

I chuckled as Mercy simply raised a silver eyebrow. "I'm surprised there are any women left to scare away, Toby. I would have been certain that you would have sampled them all by now."

Tobias gasped and pretended to look offended, while I shook my head. "I assure you, my dearest Mercuree, with Jules here being so shy and reserved, and you…who knows what perversions you have, it will take me a while to make my way through the women of Montgomery."

I felt my cheeks flame again in embarrassment. Tobias slapped his knee, and his laughter boomed throughout the courtyard. I huffed out a breath and began to head back toward the castle wall, hesitating when Tobias called after me.

My friend clasped a hand on my shoulder, smiling as

he said. "I'm sorry, Jules, you know I'm only joking."

I shoved Tobias away with a laugh. "Of course. How else would you distract yourself from your womanizing ways?"

Mercy, Tobias and I fell into step with each other as we strode down toward the entrance to the wing that separated my quarters from my parents. When I had been old enough, I had requested to be placed there, with Tobias and Mercy, so that we could train and form a bond that no war could break. My father, always the military man, could not argue with my reasoning, but I knew he was secretly pleased to be rid of me.

When my mother had given birth to me, by all accounts my father was deliriously happy. Yet over time, when his only son seemed happier to have his nose within a book rather than learning to wield a sword, rumors of Malcolm Montgomery's distaste for his only child spread around the desert faster than wildfire.

And that resentment had continued to grow, when my mother failed to conceive another child, thus leaving the fate of the Montgomery witches in the hands of the reluctant prince, as Toby liked to call me.

It would be my duty to wage war on the Cambridge witches when the time came, to avenge whatever long forgotten slight the Montgomery witches had imparted on us. The desert isles of Montgomery land would go up against the rainforest plains of Cambridge. If we met in the middle, and those without magic happen to be caught between, I wasn't sure if I could stomach the bloodshed, the senseless violence, and the unnecessary loss of life.

Pushing open the heavy wooden door, I unhooked my sword from my back and set it down on the dining table.

In comparison to the grandeur and pageantry of the main residence, this very torrent was meant to be a servant's quarters, but it had been abandoned years ago when an army barracks had been constructed on the outskirts of the territory.

At fifteen years of age, Tobias and I had not known what to do with an entire building to ourselves, yet we had made it home. The torrent consisted of four floors, a winding staircase leading up and up to the rooftop. Mercy had come home from a three-month spy mission and demanded the top floor for himself.

Not that either myself or Toby argued with him. Most nights, Mercy could be found perched among the embrasure of the tower, his silver hair glinting against the pale moonlight. The work that Mercy did for his father meant that the spymaster rarely slept, the shadows he could blend with on occasion seemed to seep into his dreams and plague his thoughts. Both Toby and I had heard him awaken with a yell or two, and then the snick of his door when he made his way up to the not-so-comfortable humidity of the desert.

Hoisting himself up on the counter beside the sink, Toby banged his legs against the cupboard, earning a stern glare from Mercy. I flopped down into the wooden chair, pushing the boots off my feet and almost groaning at the pleasure I got from the relief in my tired soles. It might only be noon, yet Toby and I had been up as soon as the sun rose, running drills and training. After lunch, we both would be expected to return to the task at hand; preparing for the war that never came.

"I need to ask a favor of you both."

Mercy's baritone voice, quiet but full of authority,

stopped Toby from his childish banging and held our attention. Mercy rarely asked anything from us, and when he did, much like with the third-floor bedroom, Toby and I never refused him.

When we were children, the three of us gravitated toward each other for the same reason; we were all social pariah. Tobias had it the worst, being the son of a magic wielder with none of his own. Avoidance, like the boy had a disease that the noble families could catch, happened to be something that I was also more than familiar with, being the unwanted son of their illustrious king.

I had yet to come into my full power and use my abilities to ward off attacks, and on the day when a group of older boys had cornered Toby, striking at him with all kinds of magic, I had been unable to stop them. Then Mercuree had appeared.

The small, pale skinned boy, with hair so silver it looked like paint, had stepped out of the shadows and taken down the assailants before I could even blink. We had all heard of the boy who could bleed into shadows, yet I had never laid eyes on him until that day.

When the group of boys scrambled away, Mercy held out his hand to help Tobias up, to which my childhood friend hugged the other boy, whose back went stiff as a board. As Toby tried to thank him, Mercy stepped back into the shadows.

After that day, Toby had made it his life's mission to track down and befriend Mercuree, the boy who seemed to have no friends. When Toby became so efficient a swordsman, no one would spar with him but me. Until one day, Mercy came out of the shadows, twin blades twirling, and we three had been inseparable since then.

We waited in silence as Mercy rested a hip against the doorframe. When he knew he had our full attention, he nodded his head and spoke. "I have a mission that I need you to accompany me on. If it were like any other job, I would slip in and out, but the security at this place will be immense, and I need to get inside through proper channels."

Toby clapped his hands together, and his face lit up in childish glee. "So, we finally get to go on a mission! You have made all my birthdays come at once."

Mercuree snorted. "Well, Toby, it is not your help I need, but that of the future head of House Montgomery. It is the Crowned Prince I require; you can simply stay at home."

Toby clasped a hand over his chest, his face widening in mock horror.

"What do you need of me, Mercy?"

I tried to lessen the sound of despair in my voice, the burden of being heir to the throne weighed consistently on my shoulders.

"I need simply for you to attend a party with me as yourself, but not. Get me in the door, stay until I have gotten what I need, and we shall be away before anyone realizes we were ever there, apart from those who welcomed us in the door."

Leaning back in the chair, I cracked my knuckles to ease some of the tension in my bones. "You know I cannot refuse you, Mercy. So, put Toby out of his misery and tell us what you need us to do."

Rolling his eyes, Mercy spoke with a small smile playing on his lips. "There is an exclusive party next week, during the Samhain festival, that only those of royal lineage and extremely important invited guests can attend. It will mean a trek across the desert and into the mundane lands. There is a masquerade ball, right in the middle of the neutral zone. We go in, you two party, and then we get out. I will do as I have to do. And then we can come home."

Turning his silver eyes on me, Mercy continued. "It will mean a week away from here, something I have already cleared with your father. We would leave on Wednesday, attend the party on Saturday, and return home on Monday so as not to arouse suspicion. It was I who suggested that the three of us attend, as men rather than a small army. Your father hesitated for only a moment before agreeing. I told him I would not go without either of you."

I knew what Mercy was hinting at; my father had wanted his shadow and his sword to go it alone and leave me to my own devices. But Mercuree was my father's best commodity, his best asset, and he would do nothing to sully that relationship.

"So, we shall go to the ball, and dance, and drink, and be merry. We shall see the wondrous women that do not have the desert in their hair, the taste of it on their skin. Mercuree will do what he does best, and maybe, dearest Julian, you might even find a woman worthy of your time."

"We both know, Toby, that where my heart lies, is of no matter to me."

"It is not where your heart lies that matters, Jules, but your—"

"Tobias!" I growled, heat creeping into my cheeks.

Toby chuckled as Mercy shook his head. I closed my eyes, my heart suddenly excited to get out of the desert and away from my father. To cross the desert lands, to have the weight of being Malcolm Montgomery's heir gone, even for a brief period, would be like heaven.

I had heard of the grassy fields of the Null lands, seen pictures of the turquoise waters that surrounded the coast. To see it up close, to dip my toes into the water instead of trudging through sand, would be such an opportunity.

Perhaps, I could just be Julian for a few days.

chapter
two
rowan

THE TREES WHISPERED A WARNING OF THE INCOMING storm, the branches swaying slightly, the leaves touching my cheek as I waited, perched high in the tree, for my target to venture into the clearing. Though I had been lying in wait for a couple of hours, my muscles had yet to give me any bother, perhaps due to the fact this was not the first time I had found myself crouched in a tree.

My lush green cape camouflaged me amongst the foliage of the trees, the rich dark of my pants and tunic helping me blend in well, making me the perfect hunter. The hood of my cape rested on my head, my eyes focused and my stance balanced. No one would see me hidden up here among the trees, and that was precisely what I liked.

A droplet of water plopped down, causing me to crinkle my nose ever so slightly. However, that movement did not stay my hand, the bow crooked and my arrow poised to fire as soon as the opportunity arose. There were days upon days like this within my mother's territory, for despite the overabundance of green, the sun barely shone. On days when it did, the sun fought to break through the clouds, a brief moment of heat upon my skin before it was gone.

If I were not the sovereign's daughter, and therefore heir to the Cambridge crown and country, then I could daydream about spending a time within Montgomery lands, where the sun shone and the air was heated even after dusk. But, alas, I was indeed heir to the throne, and far from the queen my mother yearned for me to be.

Expelling a breath as quietly as possible, I remembered my mother's face when she learned that my magical talents erred toward that of my father, a man who died before I was born. The excitement in her eyes as little toddler me spent an hour searching for a toy she had hidden on me for not acting very princess-like. Having gotten an imprint of the toy, I managed to track it down within a record amount of time.

Imagine Kendra Cambridge's face when her only daughter turned out to have within her bones, tracker magic. Kendra herself had the ability to foresee all outcomes of battle and decide on a strategic plan of action, and that indeed made her a powerful ruler. But along with her mother's battle readiness, Kendra had charisma interwoven in her DNA, which had been passed down throughout generations of matriarchal leaders.

I lacked the charisma or the grace to be half the leader my mother was. Smiling and being bowed to frayed on my nerves, and I never lingered at social events for long. I shied away from dresses and jewels, happier to climb among the trees with dirt on my face, than sit still for a moment as maids fussed over my hair. I spoke my mind, and much to my mother's chagrin, could not hold my tongue for long enough to almost avoid political niceties.

While I was the best huntress my mother had in her

arsenal, I was not the princess to rule a kingdom.

Mayhap, had my father lived, and my mother had been blessed with a second child, then I would have been able to abdicate the throne to another of my kin. But Sovereign of the Cambridge Coven had always been female, so even if my father had lived, and they had a son, I would still be cursed to lead an entire country with no desire to do so.

If I was fortunate to be granted one wish, then I would wish to spend all of my days in the comfort of this forest, among the trees and the animals, who did not look upon me as a future ruler, but as another who dwelled within this leafy refuge.

Out of the thick foliage, a lone buck strode into the clearing. I had tracked it about a mile back, strutting around with the rest of the herd, and I felt it when he drifted away from the rest of them, allowing me to scale the tree and hunker down until he passed underneath. The buck bent his head, eating the plentiful grass that grew on the forest floor. I poised the arrow, aimed right at the spot where it would pierce through the lung and liver.

The buck took a step forward, and I took a breath before I let loose the arrow.

"Rowan!"

The buck bolted at the sound of my name being wailed through the forest, my arrow missing him and hitting the base of a tree as he fled the clearing. I growled in frustration, rising from my crouch to grab hold of the branch above my head, grasping my bow in my free hand, my frown deepening as my best friend thundered into the clearing, my name on her lips.

"Rowan Cambridge, I did not traipse out here for the

good of my health. Come down from wherever you are hiding and out of this creepy forest."

I might have missed my target, but Emilee could always make me smile. The daughter of my mother's first advisor, Emilee and I had spent much time together in the nursey, and yet being forced together did nothing to prevent the bond that formed between them. We were polar opposites, Emilee and I. Emilee always knew exactly what to say, and when to say it. A beautiful girl whose smile lit up a party, I was always of the mind that had Emilee been born a Cambridge instead of me, the fate of the coven might not be so bleak.

Hands perched on her curvy hips, Emilee flipped her long chestnut braid over her shoulder as she scanned the forest bed, grunting in frustration. Her aura always shone so bright, like the sunshine I longed to bask in, and I would slit the throat of any who tried to snuff out that brightness.

As if sensing my eyes on her, Emilee shifted her big eyes upwards. "Rowan, get your ass down here right now."

Steadying my boots on the edge of the branch, I stepped off, ignoring Emilee's shriek as I freefell downward, the adrenaline in my veins making me grin, the air slapping against my face until my feet touched solid ground. I landed with one hand in front of the other, braced on wet earth.

"You have a death wish, Rowan Cambridge."

"Then it's lucky I always land on my feet."

"Yeah," Emilee snorted, running a hand over the bodice of her dress. "Like a mangy cat."

I began to stride across the forest floor, Emilee hot on my heels. "What has you trampling through the forest and stomping about with the grace of a baby elephant?"

I ducked as Emilee made to slap me, my best friend shaking her head. "Your mother sent me to collect you."

"And if I don't come?"

"I've been asked to persuade you."

The frown that marred my friend's face showed the conflict that came with her powers; like a siren, Emilee could persuade you to do anything she pleased, convincing you that it was the most wonderful thing in the world. She in herself was a valuable commodity, for having someone tell you that they should fight beside you and make it your destiny in life.

Her mother had yet to call on Emilee to use her magic as such, yet the bright, beautiful girl could ask you to do anything and you would do it, just to see her smile. She did not need magic to do that; Emilee could do that without a breath of magic.

I shuddered to think what my mother would do to deploy Emilee should the Montgomery's muster courage and bring the war to us. All I understood growing up was that the hatred between the two covens spanned centuries of bad blood, and frankly, I think the two covens warred because we could not remember why we initially fell out. Now, we could not halt this foolish war because of it.

"It's okay, Emilee. Let us go see what Mother wants with me."

We slipped into a comfortable silence, my smile returning as I watched Emilee try and traverse her way along the forest bed, tripping over fallen branches and squealing every time something furry crossed her path. She detested having to leave the confines of the castle walls to come in search of me, yet Kendra Cambridge knew that I could have remained hidden in the forest for a long time. None of her soldiers would have found me, and I would always show myself for Emilee.

Dark had begun to settle in as we stepped out from the comfort of the forest and came to look down upon the townland. Rows and rows of dwellings lined the ground, hidden well from any scouts by the canopy of thick trees. I pulled my hood further over my head, returning the bows from the citizens who greeted me.

As the future sovereign, the witches of the Cambridge Coven held a loyal sense of respect for me, but I never felt deserving of it. The townsfolk also greeted Emilee with warm words and easy smiles. I wish I had the capacity to be as friendly and warm, but in all of my sixteen years, I did not have it in me. It was as if that piece was missing inside me.

When we managed to cross the homes of those who I would eventually rule without having to engage in any awkward conversations with the villagers, we strode into the marketplace, a bustling hub of activity that I loved. The marketplace was open almost from dawn to dusk, with many vendors remaining open into the early hours. From breads to livestock, from herbs to weapons, anything could be bought and sold here.

I maneuvered Emilee in the direction I wanted to go, veering toward the masons and armorers. The soldiers spent most of their off-duty time here, and sometimes, when I wanted nothing more but to be invisible, I joined them, lurking in the shadows with those who were more like-minded. I had asked my mother if I could train with the army, if one day I could face the wrath of the Montgomery witches with the other soldiers. She had laughed, stating that one day, I would get the chance to fight with the soldiers, but I would be trained by private tutors.

However, I still managed to come down to the area known as the Dredge and best a soldier or two with a sword and, once or twice, my fist. Here was a place that I felt comfortable; here was a place that I felt at home. The people who greeted me here and smiled did not see Rowan Cambridge, future sovereign of the Cambridge Coven. They saw Rowan, master archer and huntress. They expected nothing from me other than loyalty, and I returned that favor.

A huge crowd had gathered as a vendor displayed his finest weaponry. The man, Lawrence Reinhart, known by most as The Friar because of his unwavering faith, happened to be my father's best friend. He had fought beside my father on the day he died fighting the Montgomery witches. My mother refused to speak much of my father, yet with The Friar, I got glimpses into the parent I might have had, had it not been for this blasted war.

People mooned over the works of art that The Friar was infamous for, the blades so sharp that he guaranteed them to remain sharp year after year. Emilee sighed as I dodged between the gathered crowds, ducking under arms and slipping around willing buyers. I wandered behind the vendor's table and pressed a kiss to The Friar's cheek, ignoring the eyes on me as I lifted myself up onto a barrel and waited.

My eyes drifted over to Emilee, who had forgotten my detour and was now batting those big blue eyes at a soldier who had bent his head down to whisper in her ear. Glancing down at my fingernails and the dirt caked in them after a day well spent in the forest, I wished that I was as striking as my mother or as beautiful as Emilee. My face, no doubt streaked with dirt, was nothing to boast about, and even my tangle of wild midnight colored hair was something I could not control, which was why it was braided down my back.

Sighing at my foolish thoughts, I dangled my legs, kicking the heels of my well-worn boots against the wooden barrel. Soon enough, the man I was waiting for finished up his dealings and handed over instructions to his apprentice before he beckoned me into his tent.

"I have no deer for you today, Friar." I admitted as I pulled down my hood. "Unfortunately, Mother sent Emilee into the forest, and that girl does not move quietly. I'll get some more tomorrow."

"Worry not, Little Tree. It is not your responsibility to feed this old man."

"Old my foot." I scoffed. "You could still show those new recruits a few things, even with an arm tied behind your back."

Resting himself against one of the weapon chests, The Friar ruffled my hair as he sat down beside me. "You always know what to say to make this old man smile."

With a shake of my head, I folded my arms across my chest, even as Emilee called my name from outside the tent. I reached under my cape, pulling out the rabbit I had caught before Emilee had come to disturb the tranquility of my hunt. I set the rabbit down on the table.

"Sorry it's not much."

"Rowan, I make good money selling my weapons. It is not your responsibility to hunt for me."

"I know," I said with a shrug. "We both know hunting and tracking is in my DNA, but my mother would never eat something I caught or even acknowledge it. Knowing that the death of an animal was put to good use eases the pain of not hunting. Plus, I get to bug you for all the cool toys."

The Friar chuckled, a gigantic grin spreading out over his face. "Thank you for the rabbit. Come see me in two days, and I'll have a new toy for you."

I went up on my toes and kissed his cheek again before I darted out of the tent, grabbed Emilee and headed for the castle entrance.

At first glance, the castle was not much to behold, its stone structure seeming out of place with the greenery. The gates were guarded by two sentries, each bowing his head as I entered, but their eyes roamed over Emilee as she smiled. I could see the outline of my mother's silhouette from the window overlooking the courtyard.

Crossing over the threshold, I slipped out of my emerald cloak and crooked it on a hook just inside the doorway. I heard the maids utter curses as I raced up the stone steps, my mud ridden boots leaving a trail in my wake. I hesitated outside the door until Emilee arrived. She nudged my shoulder as the door opened, and we were both ushered inside the room.

Kendra Cambridge stood with her hands linked together, her head held high, the glint of the crown that adorned her head glinting like glass against the moonlight. Many said that we looked alike, but I could never pull off regal like my mother. Her dress was the same emerald color as my cape, with elegant stones and gems embroidered on the bodice. Her hair, the same shade of black as my own, was pinned up in an elaborate style, one that would have taken her assistants a good hour to perfect.

Her skin was a pale kiss of white, one that seemed even more pronounced by the blush of red on her lips. To all who laid eyes on her, Kendra was the epitome of a queen, but behind that pretty face and regal expression, Kendra also held an intelligence that shocked most who did not know her.

"Rowan, Emilee, come here. I have a task for you."

Surprised, we inched closer, taking the chairs that my mother indicated for us to sit on. Emilee sat down on her chair, tucking one ankle behind the other, whereas I slouched in my chair, slinging a leg over the arm.

"I've been looking for you all day, Rowan. I should have known exactly where you would have been."

"If you knew where I was, Mother, then why waste all day looking for me?" The words fell from my lips before I could stop them, the glare from my mother causing my stomach to drop to my feet.

Ignoring my insolent remarks, she turned to Emilee with a warm smile. "Emilee, dear, I have been invited to a party in the neutral zone, but I'm afraid I cannot attend. There are rumors that a convoy from the Montgomery Coven will be there, perhaps even the crowned prince. I would like you to travel to the Samhain celebrations and gather some information by any means necessary."

Pride filled Emilee's expression. "I am honored to serve, your Majesty."

My mother inclined her head. "Good. As it is a very prestigious ball that you will attend, I have the best tailors readying to create a gown to your taste. And one for Rowan."

My jaw dropped as Emilee glanced at me before returning her eyes to her sovereign. I shook my head, straightened in my chair and held my mother's gaze. "We both know that I am not someone you should volunteer for social events. I'll cause a political nightmare. Mother, please. There must be a dozen other courtesans that you could send with Emilee."

The look in my mother's eyes told me that this was one event that I would not be getting out of. She lifted a hand to her face and tapped her chin. "Who better to send in to make sure Emilee remains unharmed but her best friend. Someone trained to protect her. Emilee will try and lure out the crowned prince, and Rowan you will play the part of protector."

I couldn't argue with her on that, because despite my mother dropping this in our laps, I would trust no one but myself with Emilee's safety. My mother damn well knew it.

A triumphant smile crept over Kendra's lips as victory was won.

"And Rowan, there is one more part that I need you to play."

I considered her earlier words, and closed my eyes, wishing I could close my ears as well so that I would not her the words spoken by the sovereign of the Cambridge witches.

"I need for you to play the part of princess as well."

Well…this day sucked.

chapter
three
julian

WE LEFT THE CONFINES OF THE CASTLE BEHIND US shortly before dawn, the sun a splendid shade of burnt orange against a fading navy backdrop. The vast journey ahead of us shimmered under the sun's glare, the sand stretching out for miles and miles, as if there would be no end to it. Sand clung to my skin, the grains kicked up by the gait of our horses as they made short work of the distance that would take us farther and farther from Montgomery territory. As soon as the castle became nothing but a shadowy outline of the place we had journeyed from, the tightness in my chest seemed to evaporate, leaving me with an overwhelming sense of calm.

Mercy fell into his usual silence, but perhaps that was due to the continuous ramblings of Toby as he replayed for us every minute detail of the bed he had crawled out of in the early hours, the biggest grin on his handsome face. Mercy, who simply rolled his eyes and edged his horse onward, had this inapt ability to drown out our best friend. Unfortunately, Mercy had not divulged his secret upon me.

"This girl, I mean, Jules, she was insatiable. There was

this thing that she did with her-"

I held up my hand, shaking my head as Toby pursed his lips, pretending to scowl, but the light never once dimmed in his eyes. I cast my eyes forward, the giddiness of freedom seemingly affecting my horse as the stallion whined. I inhaled a breath and expelled it, trying to regain some resemblance of calm, yet I could not stop the racing of my heart.

A little after dusk yesterday, my father had summoned me to him, and like all of his subjects, I went when I was called. The castle itself, a stone structure bound together by magic and sand, was a magnificent sight to behold. Logic prevailed that a structure of this mass should not have been possible on top of a foundation of silk-like sand, however, Montgomery Castle had been standing for more than a century and would continue to do so after I became one with the sand.

Tapestries of battles won and kings long gone adorned the slate stones, intricate works of art that made me flinch, as one day, someone would be commissioned to stitch my portrait into fabric, forever immortalized as a ruler of the coven. My boots pounded against the stone floor, the sound reverberating inside my skull as I held my head high, ignoring the hurried bows as I passed, ignoring the blatant whispers of "reluctant prince" and sniggers.

I lifted my eyes to glare at a pair of guards, an expression I learned from Tobias, and the whispering halted, eyes lowering out of respect. Not for me, I assumed. Two sentries stood outside the throne room door, elder men who had served my father for decades. I paused outside the door, huffing out a breath before the wooden door was heaved open. I forced myself to stride into the room.

When I was a child, this had been a massive place where my father sat me upon his knee and held audiences and meetings. I spent time running around and playing hide and seek with Toby. When it became obvious that I lacked the will to be what my father wanted me to be, a king with a thirst for war like him, the time spent in the throne room, and time spent with my father, became less and less.

My father lounged on his throne, although on him, the position did not seem sloppy; only regal. Malcolm Montgomery was dressed in a similar uniform to the one I wore, yet the gold stitched into his was actual gold, not just stitching. The crown atop his head looked heavy, the gemstones twinkling under the torches blazing behind the throne.

As the wooden doors closed behind me, I strode toward my father until I came to the end of the raised dais, dropped to one knee and with a hand fisted over my heart, I bowed my head. I stayed there on bended knee for almost a minute until my father gave me permission to rise. When I did, I stood with feet apart, my hands behind my back and lifted my gaze to his.

I fought hard not to swallow my fear, as dark eyes made my pulse race, and my mouth run dry. And I fought hard not to look away, because looking away when you are a prince is seen as a weakness; and Malcolm Montgomery hated weakness.

"Have you any questions before you embark on this mission, Julian?"

"No, sir."

"Good," my father said with a nod. "The shadow has

his own task to complete, you and the null have another mission."

I held back a wince as my father referred to Toby in his non-magical designation, and I simply stood my ground and waited for him to continue.

Leaning to the left, my father rested his elbow on the arm of the throne, tapping his chin. "Even though you will not officially be attending the Samhain solstice as Prince Julian, there will be people there who will know who you are. I expect you to act with decorum and princelike behavior at all times."

"Yes, sir."

My father studied me for a moment, then continued, his dark eyes not so much as blinking. "While the shadow is doing what he does best, I need you to try and locate something very special for me, son. Do you think you can do that?"

I blinked in surprise, for it had been a long time since my father had called me son. I gave a small bow of my head and listened carefully as my father explained to me what he had in mind.

"I had heard, through my shadow, that a delegation from House Cambridge would also be attending the party, in search of the same item that the shadow seeks. I need you to flush out the delegation and distract them from their task. It would also appear that the heir to House Cambridge will also be in attendance. I need you to make sure she does not leave with the item."

I redistribute my weight, simply for something to do. "How am I to distract her?"

My father smirked. "You're not a bad looking boy, Julian. I'm sure you can think of ways. If not, then simply kill her. No heir makes it easier for me to remain the more powerful of the two covens."

Even if that heir is me…

I did not need my father to speak the words, his actions over the years was enough for me to jump to my own conclusions.

But, faced with it…could I kill the girl in cold blood?

My mask of indifference must have slipped, for anger began to show in my father's eyes. "If you do not have the stomach for it, boy, then have the null do it. Tobias is who you have chosen to lead your future army. Let it be him that gets his hands dirty."

"But, it is against the rules of engagement to attack while on neutral ground." I said with a splutter, our rules of war, of treaty, fragile at best.

"Then ensure that you do not get caught."

Having given me my orders, my father and king dismissed me with the wave of his hand, only halting my retreat when he uttered my name.

"Do not disgrace me, Julian."

Or else.

I bowed my head respectfully, then hurriedly escaped the mounting pressure that was building inside my head. Not only was I uncertain if I could kill a girl who was in the exact position I was, born into royalty with no choice, but I was also uncertain if I could order Toby to do it. It was no secret that Mercy had blood on his hands, that my father's shadow had taken a life at a young age. But Toby, despite his skill and strength, had yet to be battle tested, and if I ordered him to kill, I would be forced to watch the light flicker out in his eyes until he was as damaged as Mercy.

I had barely arrived back at my home when a servant knocked on the door, delivering a package from my father. The young girl left the package on the counter, then bowed deep before she exited. For an eternity I stared at the parcel, unsure whether or not to open it. Curiosity won out as I unfolded the brown paper parcel. My fingers danced across the collar of the new uniform. The black pants were the same as the ones I wore day in, day out, yet the short-sleeved tunic was embroidered with the same gold as my father's, the Montgomery crest stitched into the black material in a blood red thread. I set the tunic on the counter, catching the pin that had been hidden inside the cape and studied it. The pin was carved out of gold and fashioned into a sword fasten that would hold the cloak together over the uniform.

This was a uniform fit for a member of the royal family. This was a reminder of who I was and which blood flowed in my veins. This was my father's noose around my neck from a vast distance. But I had little choice but to adorn myself with my father's gift.

There was not a note inside the package, but I could hear my father's words as if he were standing beside me. *Do not forget who you are.*

When the knock came this morning signaling that our horses were ready, I had already been standing in front of the mirror staring at myself. With the new uniform on, I looked ever the prince, my sandy hair slicked back out of my eyes, my cloak fastened with the pin. The expression looking back at me seemed like a stranger.

Casting aside the unease in my stomach, I forced myself to stride out the door, unable to stop the blush from creeping to my face when a gasp resounded from the few people who were there to see us off. Both Toby and Mercy, standing beside their own horses, bowed low at the waist, and heat crept higher on my face.

Ignoring the stares, because it was not as if these people had never seen me before, it just so happened that I was not dressed like a prince on those occasions. I headed straight for my horse, Blitz, a black stallion who moved like lightening across the sand. Reaching into my pocket, I took out a slice of apple and held it up to the horse's mouth, patting him on the nose before I moved to get astride him.

Only when I had mounted Blitz did Toby and Mercy follow my lead, our belongings already strapped to the horses, and we urged them forth. I could feel my father's gaze as we ventured out the castle gate and past the villages that surrounded the castle, through the community that lived on the outskirts of our walled keep.

"Earth to Jules, come in Julian."

I blinked away thoughts of my father as I turned my attention to Tobias. His hazel eyes watched me as if he was trying to figure out what was going on inside my head. Mercy had slipped away from us, his hair glinting in the sunshine like a light reflecting off glass.

"Sorry, Toby, I was miles away."

"Thank the gods your horse is a smart animal. He's been steering the way for a good while now. Mercy says we can travel another hour or so before we need to set up camp for the night."

I nodded, trying to stop my fears from showing on my face, but Toby knew me better than I knew myself at times.

"I heard your dad sent for you last night. I assume

your broody face has something to do with that."

I slowed the horse into a trot, reaching into the saddlebags for my flask of water and taking a sip before I corked it and put it away. "Malcolm wanted to remind me that I am indeed a prince. And with that comes responsibilities. He gave me a mission of my own."

Toby motioned for me to go on, an eagerness on his face. He knew wherever I went, he followed, and despite his allegiance to me, all Toby wanted to do was prove to our king that he was a valuable member of the Montgomery coven.

"He told me that I would not be the only heir at this party. He said the Cambridge heir would be present and after the same thing as Mercy. And that I was to either seduce her, kill her, or get you to kill her. I had planned on telling him you'd have more luck seducing her but considering how much of a disappointment I already am, I couldn't sink any lower."

Toby's expression darkened as he frowned before stating. "If you kill her and the Cambridge coven finds out that you slew her under the laws of safe passage, then you would be a marked man, Jules."

"That is why Father advised me not to get caught."

Letting loose a barrage of swear words, Toby shook his head. "I will do it. My death means nothing, Jules. In comparison to you, my death means nothing."

I slowed my horse further. "Your death would mean something to me, Tobias. Do not forget that it would mean something to me."

"And me."

We both nearly fell off our horses as Mercy came up behind us, having been ahead of us for a long while. I could have sworn a ghost of a smile plucked at his lips. I hated it when Mercy was able to sneak up on us.

Tobias rolled his eyes as he said, "Now that I know at least two people will miss me gravely when I am dead, can we move on from talk of death and talk about how Julian is supposed to seduce the future queen of the Cambridge coven without turning the color of beetroot when she smiles at him?"

My cheeks heated again, dragging a chuckle from Mercy and a rapturous burst of laughter from Toby, who was still smiling an hour later when Mercy indicated that we stop for the evening. We pitched our tents, and Mercy lit a fire. We fed and watered the horses; the animals barely even broke a sweat in the heat. Like us, they were raised in the blazing heat of the desert sun, and the heat never bothered us. We ate a hearty meal of bread and cheeses that had been packed for us, keeping more rations for another stop tomorrow.

"We should reach a tavern by tomorrow evening, just on the edges of the null territory. There have been rooms booked for us there under the royal name. We can rest the horses and have a proper night sleep. I must meet an informant there after midnight. Then we go onto the keep of the high lord of null territory, where an entire wing has been requested for us to stay. No doubt, the Cambridge heir will be residing within the mansion as well."

Tobias stretched out in the sand, tossing a knife up and down in the air. He caught the blade while looking into the embers of the fire. "Perhaps I should just sneak into her bedchambers during the night and slit her throat. Make it quick. Then it would be a kindness."

"Is it a kindness to die because of your name?" I

snapped, feeling sorry for the daughter of my hated enemy. "Perhaps you should slit my throat while I sleep and call it a kindness."

Silence carried around the camp fire as Mercy sighed and Toby just glared at me. "Don't be ridiculous, Jules. We are at war, are we not? If this escalates, then many a folk will die. Would you chastise me for wanting the majority to be on their side, rather than ours?"

"I would rather there not be a war, Toby. I would prefer that innocent people not be collateral damage for a war that no one seems to remember the reasons as to why it began."

Toby heaved out a breath. "Sentimentality will get you killed, Jules. This romantic notion that we can all hold hands and be best friends will get you killed."

I shrugged my shoulders, getting up from my seat in the sand as I replied, "Then so be it. I would rather die, thinking for myself, than killing for a war I was born into and never chose."

Toby made to speak, but Mercy hushed him with a withering glare. I swept open the door to the tent and flopped down on the rolled out sleeping bag. Turning so that I faced away from the other two beds that would soon be occupied. I knew that I shouldn't have snapped at Toby, but I was tired of people expecting me to be my father, expecting me to be as bloodthirsty as he was.

I closed my eyes and thought about the pampered princess that was going to be on show for the Cambridge coven. This would be some poor defenseless girl who only understood daily hair and make-up classes. I heard that the leader of the Cambridge witches was her mother, but rumors were rife that she was a mere figurehead, that the real power was with the General of their army.

How was I supposed to take a defenseless girl's life simply because of her last name? What was a name anyways? A useless indication of a bloodline.

Those questions kept me tossing and turning for an age, until I eventually fell into a fitful sleep, long before Mercy and Toby came inside.

chapter
four
rowan

"This was not how I expected we would make the journey to the neutral zone." Emilee grumbled as we galloped through the forest at a steady pace. I answered her question with a grin that only furthered the scowl on her lips.

"Well," I began. "It was not as if we would travel in a carriage made of gold, surrounded by my soldiers, and dressed up as pretty little princesses now, would we? I know mother intends for people to know that I am a princess by the hideous gowns and crown she insured were packed. However, we are still on a mission where stealth is a requirement."

"A carriage still would have been nice, Rowan."

I patted the neck of my mare, a brilliant white horse that had been mine since the day I stepped foot in the stables and this majestic beast had sided up to me, nudging my face with her nose. Rhiannon and I had been inseparable since then. We had spent many a day escaping from our village and rushing through the forest, a blur of magnificent white and black.

A chuckle sounded over my shoulder, making me roll

my eyes at the unexpected guest who had been awaiting atop his own mount this morning when I had steered Rhiannon out of the stables. Of course, Emilee had grinned madly when my cousin Paris awaited us, informing me that my mother had decided that we needed an escort to ensure our safety.

To say that statement ruffled my feathers would be an understatement.

Six-foot-tall, with chiseled features, hair the color of the bark of a tree, and eyes of the warmest green, Paris was gorgeous, and he knew it, the cockiness in his gait warranted. But Paris's presence annoyed me on so many levels, especially since he was the man my mother wanted me to marry, in order to preserve the royal bloodline.

I had never envisioned that I would marry, yet having the option taking away from me altogether in order to continue a cycle I wanted no part in meant that I ignored Paris and his advances with the same stubborn inclination that I used against my mother.

It was not that I had not kissed a boy before. I had. There were plenty of boys that were interested in a sullen princess. When on my sixteenth birthday, my mother announced that I was to be promised to Paris on my twentieth birthday, Paris had made sure, through veiled threats and bloodied faces, that no boy showed any interest in me going forward.

And now my escape from the forest was marred by the Paris-shaped noose around my neck. I pointedly ignored him, urging Rhiannon into a faster gait. The wind whipped my hair into my face, dirt kicked up from the power of the mare's hooves, the trees blurring as we galloped, weaving in and out of them, and I closed my eyes, imagining that this was what it felt like to be free. If I could see a future free from crowns and vengeance and war, then I would happily see out the end of my life as a forest dweller, choosing to stay in the forest, but also choosing something other than my mother's ruling fist.

The blood in my veins denied me the chance.

I heard a very feminine giggle come through the trees, and I rubbed my temples. Surely Emilee could see that Paris flirted with her in an attempt to get my attention, as he had with every single girl of age within the coven. While I had been branded with a huge 'hands off' tattoo, Paris was free to bed as many as he wanted, and my mother said it was all done in order to please me, as my consort. The thought of me and Paris lying together made my stomach revolt.

My thoughts went back to when Paris had first attempted to ensure that I was reminded that I was his at one of the parties Emilee had dragged me to, and I remembered why I hated him so much.

The fire crackled in the darkness, the beauty of the night not lost on me as the stars twinkled against the backdrop of a navy sky, the moon glinting like glass in the babbling brook that flowed by the fire. I sat by the edge of the bank by myself, inhaling the smoke and scents of the forest, having spent most of the night ignoring Emilee's pleas to come and dance.

I heard the crunch of branches as someone came up behind me, but barely spared a glance in their direction, knowing full well that Paris had strayed from the blonde twins that had been glued to his side for the night.

Flopping down beside me, Paris nudged me with his shoulder, the smell of ale soaked into his skin. He slung an arm around my shoulder, and I quickly slipped out of his embrace.

"Aw, Ro, why do you have to be so mean?"

"I am not mean, Paris, I simply don't like you."

To my horror, he laughed, as if I had said the funniest thing in the world. He leaned in as if he meant to kiss my cheek, and I shoved him away. His expression quickly turned dark, the copious amount of ale consumed bringing out his nature. He grabbed my face in his hands, and I struggled to get free, reaching for the blade tucked into my belt, his warm breath against my skin.

"When we are married, I will rid you of that spirit, Rowan. No woman of mine will make a fool of me."

Paris pressed his lips hard against mine. Bile creeping up my throat, I reached out and tried to push him off me, but Paris was stronger than me. I yanked the blade from my belt and pressed the tip of it against his throat.

Had he not been drunk, I was under no illusion that Paris would not have wrestled the knife from my hands, but I pressed harder when his tongue tried to invade my mouth. Blood began to trickle down his throat, and Paris had stumbled back.

I leapt to my feet at the same time Paris did. By now, the entire party had turned to watch us, as my lips curled into a snarl. Paris leered at me, wiping the blood from the shallow graze on his throat.

"Touch me again and lose an appendage." I growled.

"Your mother gave me free reign to touch you when she declared you were mine."

Aware of my audience, I stepped into Paris and whispered. "I will not hesitate to drive a dagger into your chest if you so much as sneeze in my direction, Paris. Accidents happen all the time under the watchful gaze of mother nature. I would hate for you to fall and break your neck before we were to wed."

"Just like your father, eh?"

Even as a child, I had heard the murmurers and whispers that my father's death had not been an honorable death, that an accident had befallen him, murdered by my mother's jealous lover, and my mother had never denied the rumor, for it made her even more ruthless and dangerous. After all, she had gotten what she wanted out of him, a daughter to rule when she was ashes in the dirt.

Rage tinged my senses, my fist clenching and coiling, my knuckles connecting with Paris' face, the crunch of bone as his broke, blood gushing from the wound. He howled, and a dark part of me rejoiced in it, welcomed the power that burned inside me.

Paris' friends came over to assist him, keeping their eyes from meeting mine. I tucked the blade back into my belt, smoothed the hair from my face, and let a smile curl at my lips.

"You would do well to remember, Paris, that despite all that I appear to be, I am still Kendra Cambridge's daughter. I will not hesitate to cut off your hand if you so much as graze a finger against my shoulder. I have four years before I have to stomach you. If you want the chance to be consort, make sure you stay out of my way, or some unfortunate accident may befall you. Do we understand each other?

Paris didn't say anything, simply sneered in my direction as his comrades escorted him away from the fire. The party officially ended after that. As I stormed away from the campsite, the other teens stepped out of my way. I trudged past Emilee and slipped into the forest, my green cape flapping in the flurry of my movement.

Emilee never invited me to a party after the incident, and I was eternally grateful. I spent four days in the forest alone, hunting and living off the land until my mother sent an armed guard in search of me. Well, considering they had been sent two days into my self-imposed exile and I managed to evade them for two days, my mother was extremely infuriated when one of the guards had all but dragged me into the throne room, a hand firmly grasping my shoulder.

Hair in knots, dirt smearing my face, and my body smelling of days of being unwashed apart from time spent walking in the rain, my mother had sent me off to be cleaned up before she lectured me on my treatment of the golden boy. I rolled my eyes, telling my mother that I would never marry, especially if it were Paris. I explained what he had done, what he had said, forgoing the snide remark he had made about my father.

Kendra simply waved me off and advised me to be less prickly around my future husband. I advised her to keep Paris away from me, or he might lose the value he held if I cut off a certain piece of his anatomy, should he dare touch me without permission again. My mother told me idle threats were unwarranted. My response to her that it was not a threat, but a promise earned me a clatter to my face.

It also resulted in me being locked in my bedroom for a week, an armed guard standing outside my door, unable to flee into the forest as I would on a regular basis. After that, Paris was never left alone with me, yet, I considered that it was for his protection rather than mine.

Rhiannon had halted to lap up some water from a small stream, just on the slope of a hill that overlooked the border where my mother's territory ended and the neutral zone began. I had often wandered to the edge of the territory and glanced down at the village on the southern part of the territory, wondering what it would have been like to have been born without magic, without royal blood in my veins. It was a dream that kept me awake at night, one that would never come to fruition.

Emilee and Paris emerged into the clearing. He brushed his knuckles against Emilee's cheek, but his eyes never strayed from mine. Emilee glanced from me to Paris, then urged her horse forward, coming to a stop beside me.

The sun began to set, night having crept in while I was remembering the past. Emilee pulled her cloak around her, pointing to the flurry of lights that shone from the distance.

"Is that the village where we will stay for the night?"

I nodded. "We have two rooms booked for the evening. Tomorrow we will travel to the center of the neutral territory. The horses can rest. Hopefully, once the masquerade ball is done, we can be gone from there as soon as possible."

"Rowan, I assume you and I will be sharing?" Paris stated in an amused tone. "Or does Emilee want to keep me warm tonight?"

Emilee ducked her head, ignoring the blatant suggestion. I didn't bother even sparing Paris a glance.

"I'll be sharing with Emilee. Feel free to find some poor tavern wench to keep you warm. Perhaps, I will get lucky and some vengeful lover will put a knife in your chest and save me the trouble. Oh, how I would rejoice."

I pressed my heels into Rhiannon, and the horse stepped over the stream. We headed down the incline of the hill, with Emilee on our heels. As we came to flatter ground, I pulled the hood of my cloak up to conceal my face, which was well known to this region. I felt Emilee and Paris' presence, but ensured that I kept moving forward.

As night happened to be just settling in, the village was still bustling, people getting ready to shut up shop for the evening and head home to their loving families. Everywhere I turned, people were smiling and talking. When I was younger, I expected that those without magic would be miserable, but I never saw a sad or lonely face in the crowds. Their auras were all shiny bright colors, sparkling in my field of vision.

Steering Rhiannon through the narrow streets, the townsfolk began to realize that the horses were thoroughbred, and that the beautiful people who followed the hooded girl were so stunning that magic had to be involved.

A young boy of about nine or ten, pushing a cart of fruit and vegetables away from a market stall, glanced up from under his peak cap, stumbled at the sight of Rhiannon. The cart tipped over, sending fruit and vegetables sprawling across the cobbled stone.

The poor boy cried out, his face aghast at the spoiled produce that could no longer be sold. But some items were still salvageable. Without a second thought, I jumped down from astride Rhiannon and dropped to my knees, the hood slipping in the rushed movement.

I ignored the gasp of the people as my face was revealed. I picked up some carrots and gave a cheeky wink to the ginger haired boy. "Give them a rinse, and the carrots will be as good as new, don't you think?"

The boy took the carrots from my outstretched hand, blushing furiously as he scooped up the fallen fruit and vegetables. I plucked a slightly bruised apple from the ground, gave it a quick wipe of my cloak, before I lifted it to my lips and bit into it.

"Delicious." I grinned, reaching into my cloak and pulling out a few gold coins. "Give me a few of the ones that you won't be able to resell."

"But M'lady, those are all bruises and battered. I must give you the ones that are not damaged."

I picked up another apple, cleaned it like the other one, and held it up to Rhiannon, who munched hungrily at the crisp fruit.

"Just because something is bruised does not mean it is useless. Those with bruises inside or out often make the best people."

A considerable crowd had gathered now, a few stopping to help the child gather up the fallen food. When the boy was ready to leave, I handed him the gold coins, which he tried to decline, but with a quick raise of my eyebrows, he pocketed the gold, bowed, and handed over a bag brimming with apples, which I promptly placed in one of the saddlebags.

I held out my hand and introduced myself to the young boy, ignoring all the inquisitive eyes on me and the smirk plastered all over an unhelpful Paris' lips.

"My name is Rowan. It is very nice to meet you."

The ginger haired boy grasped my hand and shook it. "Callum, M'lady."

I adjusted his cap and winked again before saying. "Remember what I said, Callum. And should you ever fancy a trip into the rainforest, bring me some apples and come and visit me."

I swung up onto Rhiannon and strode passed Callum and his cart, Emilee coming up to walk beside me.

"That has to be the queenliest thing I have ever seen you do. By the gods, Rowan, those people were amazed by you."

"Perhaps, if she were actually more like a queen within her kingdom and less like one of the street urchins here, her people would consider her a more suitable heir to the throne."

Wishing I could fire one of Callum's apples at Paris' head, I chose to speak to Emilee only. "It wasn't queenly, Em. It was simply humane. We spooked him. His week's wages probably would have been forfeited due to the spoiled fruit. I only paid him in kind. I was simply being a human being, not a queen."

Emilee gave me a cunning grin. "If you say so. But I have no doubt that the tale of the Cambridge heir on her knees picking up dirty fruit from the ground will be weaved into a legend. That boy will always remember your kindness."

I chose not to answer, the inn we would be resting in for the night coming into sight. A stable man stood out in the night air awaiting our arrival. Paris edged his way in front of me, his horrid beast of a horse huffing in Rhiannon's face. He slid off his horse with the elegance of the snake he was and began to make demands of the stable hand. I gritted my teeth and snapped. "Paris, leave the man be. Or else your poor beast might end up with a thorn in his hoof, instead of the one riding on his back."

I jumped down to the ground, gave Rhiannon a rub down her nose, removed the saddlebags and handed the reigns to the stable hand, giving my thanks as he took them and guided Rhiannon into the stable. I turned to Emilee, holding out my hand to help her down, my best friend less used to travelling a great distance on horseback, no doubt her limbs were stiffer than mine or even Paris'. Once Emilee stood on solid ground, the stable hand took her horse into the barn, and I suppressed a grin that he had all but ignored Paris since his demands.

"My backside aches like nobody's business. I can't wait for a long soak in a bath." Emilee groaned.

"I'd quite happily join you, Emilee, and massage your tired muscles."

I stuck two fingers in my throat and pretended to be sick. Picking up the saddlebags, I tossed them over my shoulder, gave Emilee a little shove into the inn just in case my best friend was silly enough to consider taking Paris up on his offer. With a glance at Paris over my shoulder, I gave him a smirk.

"Emilee has kings and noblemen asking for her hand, eager to warm her bed. Why would she be silly enough to bed someone even the future queen can't stomach?"

Leaving Paris standing there, his growl of anger sparked satisfaction in my bones. Emilee waited for me at the reception of the inn, shaking her head in dismay.

"You are playing with fire, Rowan. It's going to get you burned."

Ignoring my friend's warning, I nudged her shoulder before turning to the woman behind the desk at the inn.

"We have two rooms booked, and we need one fit for a princess. He'll be coming inside shortly. The two of us are fine once you have a tub."

The bewildered expression of the woman who knew exactly who I was sent Emilee into a fit of rapturous laughter. And soon enough, I joined her.

chapter
five
julian

I WOKE TO THE SCREAMS OF TERRIFIED PEOPLE, MY FEET touching the cold stone floor as I grabbed for my sword and rushed toward the door. Flinging it open, I stepped over the bloodied body of one of my sentries, the hallway awash with crimson, my bare feet slipping as I made my way down toward the loudest cries for help.

As I descended the staircase, a soldier baring the Cambridge family crest came at me, his sword raised to drive the tip through my chest and into my heart. I held out my hand, clenched my fist and used the air circulating his body to halt the oxygen going to his brain. The soldier slumped to the ground before he could let loose a cry.

Stepping over the body, I didn't bother to hide myself from them, I simply carved a path through them, using my magic and my sword, ignoring the slain bodies of those of my coven who had died within my castle walls. I heard a shriek of anguish from the throne room, snapped the necks of the two Cambridge witches who dared stand sentry outside of it, and entered with my head held high.

A contingent of Cambridge witches stood around my throne, a hooded figure lazing atop my throne with blatant disrespect. My eyes wandered over to where two soldiers knelt before the throne, the unmistakable glint of silver hair catching my eye. Two soldiers off to the side made to come toward me, but as I smiled, blood staining my cheeks, and lifted my right hand, the figure seated on my throne whistled, and the soldiers retreated.

"That is the wisest thing you have done all evening." I said, my voice calm, but my tone strong. "Release my men or I will drain the room of air and smile as you all suffocate to death."

A soft feminine chuckle rang in my ears. "Are you so cruel that you would sacrifice your most loyal soldiers in order to kill me?"

Her voice was distorted, like I could hear it under water, but I answered her regardless. "This is war. Sacrifice is inevitable. If the sands come calling, then they would happily die a warrior's death. But the moment they die, the Cambridge line will be wiped out. All it takes is a wave of my hand."

"Perhaps, I should take that hand from you? See how well your magic works without the appendage."

"I would very much like to see you try."

I watched as an overzealous soldier struck out with his blade, drawing a line across Tobias' throat, a steady stream of blood gushing down his throat as eyes of the darkest hazel lost the life in. My best friend clutched his throat, and I dropped my sword, closed my eyes, and dragged my arms up, commanding the air from the room.

When I opened my eyes again, all but the Cambridge heir were dead. The young woman was gasping for breath having slumped down off my throne, and now was lying in a heap on the dais as I walked up and stood over her. I titled my head to the side, wondering why I no longer felt any emotions, why the deaths bothered me little, and all I wanted was to watch the life drain out of this wench's eyes.

"We could have saved them, Julian. We could save them all."

I lifted my bloodied foot, rested it on her throat. I pressed down hard, listened as the bones cracked and death came to claim her.

"I am not a savior, I am a king."

"Jules."

A hand touched my shoulder and I leapt up, clutching a blade, eyes wild. I could still smell the coppery scent of blood, feel the lack of empathy in my bones for others, and the total contempt for the Cambridge witches. My hands shook as I lifted my gaze expecting to see an enemy but coming face to face with eyes of purest silver.

Mercy held out his hands in a submissive gesture, and I shakily sheathed the blade. I wet my lips, making to apologize, when Mercy shook his head.

"We never apologize for the nightmares, Julian. I would like to think that the nightmares are our mind's way of letting us know that we are still somewhat mortal, that if we are haunted by things in our dreams, and wake up fearful, then we are not entirely monsters from the deeds that we have done. It is only when you awaken from a nightmare and feel absolutely nothing that an apology is warranted."

Ducking out of the tent, Mercy let me gather myself before I had to face Toby, the vision of him slit by the throat still making my stomach coil. Perhaps I should listen to Mercy, for he had more nightmares than most, and I for one would not consider him a monster.

Stepping out of the tent, I accepted a warm mug from Mercy and did as instructed as he motioned for me to sit by the small fire as he cooked. One of the things people did not know about Mercy was that he was an extremely talented cook, and we would often wake to the smell of breads, pastries, and other culinary delights, especially when he returned from a rather difficult spying task.

I gobbled down the meal, some sort of egg mixture, ignoring the queasy turn in my stomach, and a silent Tobias seated across from me. Mercy glanced from me to him, and as I lifted my shoulders, he sighed and began dismantling the tent.

After a rather tense breakfast, we cleared the campsite, prepared the horses and continued on our journey under a veil of silence. We were both stubborn, Toby and I, and neither of us would be the first to break the ice or offer an apology. Even though we rarely fell out, over less trivial stuff anyway, one day we would just start talking and the offense would be forgotten.

Toby cantered his horse off ahead, Mercy choosing to travel beside me. He waited until Toby was somewhat out of earshot, and then he looked at me with an expression that made me want to squirm.

"Would you like to tell me about your nightmare?"

"Not especially," I replied with a sigh.

"I cannot force you to tell me, for I know that I am not the most talkative of us. But it is not your burden to carry alone, Julian. The fate of the covens is not your cross to bear."

I patted Blitz on the neck as I replied, "Isn't it? When I am king, if I live that long, then it will be on me, when the time comes, to wage war. If not me, then it is a burden I must put on my children, should I have them. I want out of this vicious cycle, Mercy."

"If you are unhappy with the way the future is unfolding, then change it. Maybe not today, nor tomorrow, but one day soon, it will be only you who can shape how the world will be. If it is not what you had hoped for, then make it so. You have the power to carve your own destiny. Never forget that."

Mercy edged his horse forward, leaving me to my own thoughts. It had not escaped my mind that the nightmare had been a vision of a future I had seen, if it was a manifestation of a power my maternal grandmother had. It had been told, in legend, that my grandmother's dreams had halted many an attack, even one on my life when I was a baby.

But those visions had driven her to madness, her ramblings soon too incoherent to decipher. She had vanished from the castle, and I was told she had died.

My head snapped up as it seemed that Mercy and Toby were having words, and I assumed Mercy had been telling Toby to make the first move and speak. Toby brushed him off, and I sighed, wishing that we had never left the castle at all.

A short time later, sooner than expected, the isolated tavern came into view. We left the desert behind us, and the stark contrast of barren desert and weather-stricken sand created a sudden drop in temperature that made me shiver. As we sheltered our horses in the adjoining stable, Mercy went in to get our rooms, leaving Tobias and I waiting alone.

After a few minutes of non-verbal communication, us both glancing at each other and then adverting our eyes when we caught the other looking, Toby threw his hands in the air, and strode off toward a door where music, song, and chatter sounded. Rather than be left standing by myself, I followed after him, regretting it the moment the tavern's alehouse fell silent, and I realized I was still dressed like a member of the royal family.

My heart raced, and my palms began to sweat. Retreating now would show weakness, but I wasn't certain that I could simply stride to the other side of the bar, head held high, and sit down beside Toby. I glanced around the alehouse, a compact room smaller than my father's throne room, littered with wooden benches, stools, and patrons who looked less impressed by my status than I was.

Heat began to creep up my neck and color my cheeks. As if sensing my discomfort and suddenly realizing that the music had stopped, Tobias glanced up, muttered something under his breath and yelled. "Julian, come sit your ass down over here. You're making the poor patrons uncomfortable."

I chuckled, rolling my eyes and put one foot in front of the other, until I was beside Toby, who pushed a high stool out and patted the seat. "Sit down, your highness. It's not a throne, but it sure is comfortable."

I laughed some more, perching myself on the seat as the music struck up again, and the bustle and din of the alehouse continued. Leaning into a little, I muttered a thank you to Toby, who grinned, lifted his already half empty glass, and advised me that the next round was mine.

Drinking ale had never appealed to me, it was something that I found myself doing simply to fill the time at parties that Tobias dragged me to. I drank just enough to feel it, yet not enough to get so drunk I made a show of myself. I indicated for the barman, a burly human who eyed us suspiciously, to bring us two more.

"I only said what I said, Jules, to try and keep you safe. It is my job to keep you breathing, is it not?"

The barman set our drinks down in front of us, and I lifted the glass, taking a sip of the liquid. This was not like any ale I had tasted before. It was a splendid taste, like sunshine in a glass, and the warmth that rushed through my veins reminded me of the midday sun. I licked my lips as Toby grinned.

Glancing at my oldest friend, I set my glass down and said, "If you lose who you are, my brother, under the guise of keeping me alive, then what is it all worth? I could not bear it if this war cost me you, as you are now."

"I wish, dearest Jules, that you weren't such a nice guy, then I would not feel like such an ass when we quarrel, and you speak only sense."

I took another gulp of my ale and scratched the sand from my face. "The way I see it, there could be a Cambridge witch beside the Cambridge heir right now, telling her that life would be easier if they slipped into my bed chambers one night and slit my throat. Call me a fool for being hopeful that she would dismiss that attempt on my life, just as I have done. For we are merely pawns in our ancestors' war."

Toby's face darkened, and his lips curled up into a snarl. "Let them try."

"That was not the point I was making, though I certainly appreciate the eagerness to keep me alive." I sighed.

Toby drained his first glass, and then started on his second, as a young woman began to sing a song only to the strings of a guitar and the beat of a drum. In the song, she spoke of a soldier going off to war, leaving a wife and young son behind. The son grew into a young man, and yet, his father still did not return from war.

I listened intently, angling my body toward the singer, her eyes closed and a rapturous expression on her face. I imagined that was how it looked to be free to do as you pleased, like sing in taverns, or tend to a bar. The lyrics flowed from her lips. The young man started his own family, and he was soon called to bear arms and follow his father to war.

The sorrow of the song was not lost on me, as the singer brought the story to an end with the father and son reunited. Their bodies came back to their village to be laid to rest beside each other while their families mourned and cursed the war.

I felt such shame and sadness having listened to the song, and as the melody halted and the girl stopped singing, she opened her eyes and a tear slipped down her cheek. She blinked them away as I continued to stare, wondering if she was indeed a descendant of the people in her song.

"Stop staring at the girl. Unless you want me to see if she is free tonight?"

My head snapped back to face the bar, and Toby chuckled, slapping his knee as if my reaction was the funniest thing in the universe. The music slowly sparked to life again, but the girl did not sing again. Instead, she collected the glasses on the tables, humming along with the tune that played on.

She came to take away the empties. Having drained my glass out of embarrassment, I lifted my head and said, "You have a beautiful voice."

"Thank you, your highness," she replied with a bow of her head.

I ambled to try and give her a coin or two, yet the girl shook her head. "I do not want your money, prince. I sing because I was blessed by the gods, and it would be a sin not to use the gifts given to me. I mean no offence."

A blush heated my cheeks as I muttered. "No offence taken."

The girl hurried away, and I had the horrendous thought of how I was meant to charm the heir of my most hated enemy coven, when I couldn't even pay a singer a compliment without my face flushing the color of the richest tomato?

Mercy came into the bar then, and not unlike how the entire alehouse had halted at my presence, the crowd noted that something dangerous lurked in their midst, and the atmosphere changed. Patrons reached for their weapons, sobering suddenly while Mercy ignored them. It was inevitable that every single subject here knew who had walked into the alehouse; there was no one alive quite like Mercy, the king's shadow, his assassin.

I wondered what it would be like to be feared like Mercy, to walk into a room and put a halt to everything, not because of a title, but because I was the most powerful person in the room. My mind wandered back to the nightmare last night, to the king I had become who felt nothing and was feared by all. It brought a shudder to me. I stared at the glass behind the bar, and the eyes of an emotionless king stared back at me.

Mercy nodded to the barman, who slid a golden liquid toward him. He drank it down in one fluid movement. Inclining his head toward the door, Mercy left the alehouse, taking the tension with him as he went. Toby tossed a few gold coins on the table and stood.

He waited, and I realized he meant for me to walk out before him. I rolled my eyes at him, but strode out of the alehouse, Toby at my back. Once we had left, the music began to play again, and I grinned at Mercy.

"That's one way to stop a party, Mercy."

Mercy held up a single key. "A source of mine has indicated that a threat to Julian's life is evitable. They could not afford me a time, yet sooner rather than later was implied. We sleep in the same room, and in shifts. Tobias, you need to stay awake while I meet with my contact. When I return, you can sleep."

I blew out a breath and folded my arms across my chest. "And am I incapable of protecting myself?"

Mercy ignored my statement and I made for the stairs, shaking my head as I went. This threat happened to be nothing new, for there was always a threat against my life.

I settled onto the bed, resting my arms behind my head, and glared at the ceiling. I was still glaring at the ceiling when Mercy slipped from the room, and I turned to see Toby resting in a chair, his eyes closed but his body alert.

"You can sleep now, Toby. I will stay awake until Mercy comes back."

"Not happening. Sleep, Jules. You have a long day of princing facing you from tomorrow."

I did not tell Toby that I feared falling asleep for fear that I would dream. I did not explain to him that I happened to be terrified to dream of what I might become. I simply closed my eyes, willing myself not to slip into sleep, for the ache in my chest and the feeling in the pit of my stomach had me thinking that we had made a grave mistake going to the Samhain solstice.

chapter
six
rowan

THE REMAINDER OF OUR JOURNEY WAS UNEVENTFUL; after a blissful night of sleep despite Emilee's snoring, we were both up early and ready to leave. We contemplated leaving Paris to his own devices, but as we edged the horses away from the remote village, Paris and his stead came rushing up behind us. Having spoken to Emilee last night, even she appeared cold toward our companion, for which I was entirely grateful.

The owner of the inn had given us a warning that a snow storm was coming. The neutral territory we would soon descend upon would indeed be covered in snow by nightfall tomorrow. I had only seen snow once or twice in my life on rare visits to the Null regions with my mother. My rainforest home that barely saw a glimpse of sun, saw even less solstice inclined weather, and I could not wait to hear the crunch of sleet and snow beneath my boots.

We progressed quickly, our small party coming over the mountain and slowing as we came up to the wooden perimeter of the Null territory. The walls of the city climbed so high that they almost kissed the sky and wrapped around the city, stretching for miles. The structure was sturdy, but I couldn't help thinking that the walls would not be any sort of resistance if us magic wielders came knocking. All it would take would be someone with fire magic to reach out, caress the material, and engulf the city in flames.

The wall seemed to be thick as well, for guards walked atop the wooden structure, miniature dots in the distance as I arched my gaze upward. A contingent of soldiers came from huts at the base of the wall, just before massive wooden doors that no doubt had to be opened with sheer strength or brutal magic. They stood, hands on the hilt of their blades, and studied us carefully.

I tilted my head and assessed the soldiers. If they attacked, our best course of action would be to take out the older soldiers first, then focus on the younger, less battle-ready ones. While I was a tracker at heart, I was keeping a very big secret from my mother. I hid my talent for surveying possible outcomes and strategy. If my mother knew that I, like her, could predict the outcome of battle, see weakness in places and things, she would lock me inside the castle walls and use my other talents.

The last thing I wanted was to be a prisoner inside a tower and never see my beloved rainforest again.

One soldier, dressed in a khaki uniform and bearing the badge of captain on his chest, motioned for Paris to come forward, instantly dismissing me and Emilee as women. I snorted as Paris strode forward, jumped down from his horse, and held out his hand to the captain.

"Greetings, friend." Paris boomed in a voice that told everyone of his own self-importance. "I am Paris of House Cambridge. Before you is Rowan Cambridge, heir to House Cambridge. Please open the gates and allow the future sovereign entry into the city. Your High Lord is expecting us."

The captain turned his steely gaze toward me, and I rolled my eyes and spoke aloud. "Dear gods, Paris. You do like the sound of your own voice. Forgive him, Captain, I fear he might have been dropped on his head as a child."

A snicker rang out amongst the soldiers, and I could almost make out a faint flicker on the captain's lips.

"Welcome, Heir Apparent, welcome to the free state of Saor. We would ask that you refrain from using magic if at all possible and try to respect the customs within our walls. Acts of violence toward others, where unwarranted, will be treated as acts of war under the Peace Treaty and have serious outcomes. Do you understand?"

I bowed my head. "Understood, Captain."

The captain watched me under a narrow gaze before he beckoned with his hand. Soldiers moved in a flurry, grabbing hold of thick rope and pulling, their faces straining under the pressure. The gates to Saor groaned as they opened.

"Hurry along, Heir Cambridge, a storm is coming and the gates will soon be closed until it passes. Lord Ashbridge awaits your arrival at the keep. Please ask your herald to mount his horse so you can be on your way."

Paris' expression faltered and became a look of indignant horror at being described as a lowly herald, and I could not stop the laughter from slipping free. The soldiers looked surprised that I had the capacity in me to feel humor, and it was a sobering thought. I nodded at the captain as I steered Rhiannon forward, but let a stupid grin tilt up my lips.

"Come, Herald. Let's not dally any further."

I ignored the slew of insults Paris threw my way, guiding Rhiannon inside the walls of Saor, and waited until Emilee came up beside me before I took it all in. Inside the walled gates was a metropolis of a city. I could see the High Lord's keep in the distance, the highest point around the same height as the wooden gates.

A large clock nestled in between the tall tower rang out, striking fourteen times, a toll that rang out through the village. The entire city of Saor lay completely on flat land; there were no hills or vantage points. Apart from the High Lord's keep, there seemed to be no segregation of classes, no separation of rich or poor. The butcher shop sat in between the jeweler and the florist, and people milling about the streets saluted each other and wished them good day.

While our own little village was a haven, we still had different classes of people, those who served and those who reigned. The Dregs was our crime-ridden den of inequity where illegal deals were done, ill begotten gains occurred, and where a princess could melt in with the shadows.

Houses and shops all seemed to be placed next to each other, the masonry of stones and thatched roofing a brilliant contrast to the appearance of the wooden gates. People glanced in our direction, but seemingly took no notice, and I found myself slightly endeared with Saor.

Paris and his stallion pushed their way forward, getting in people's way and almost causing more than one incident like back at the village. I pulled the hood of my cloak further over my head, blocking my face from view, and gently slapped the rump of Emilee's horse.

We cantered along the cobbled streets. The

inhabitants of Saor went about their daily business, and as we happened by a school, I felt mesmerized by the children in the schoolyard, playing and laughing with joyful abandonment. I had never attended school like those children, for my lessons revolved around becoming a queen.

I dragged my gaze away from the school and continued to head toward the keep. I halted in surprise as we drew closer. Instead of being walled off, or caged in, the keep had an open steel gate, where people walked in and out freely. Deliveries for the ball were being brought in, and I angled my horse so that we would not be in anyone's way.

Paris, oblivious to the fact that we were not as important here as he would like, began to look flustered at the lack of welcoming committee awaiting us. A handsome man raced from the house, his body wearing the same uniform as the captain outside. His hair was dark, lips full and cheeks high. He smiled as he came up to us, and I could see Paris scowl as I continued to look at the handsome soldier.

"Forgive us, your Majesty. We had not expected you until after sunset. Our scouts did not alert us to your arrival in time for an appropriate welcome."

I slipped down from Rhiannon, shaking my head, and my hood fell down, revealing my face to the soldier. "I am merely an honored guest. I would prefer to remain under the radar as much as possible, sir. There is no need for any pomp or pageantry."

"I am not certain that anyone with such beauty could remain under the radar, as you put it, Your Highness."

I snorted, pretty sure that the soldier was not on

the front lines due to an affliction with his eyes. I heard Emilee sigh over my shoulder, and Paris mutter under his breath. Now, I was not one for formality or all that entailed becoming queen, so I extended my hand, ready to shake the soldier's own, when he caught my hand, turned it, and lifted the back of my hand to his lips.

Embarrassed, I pulled my hand away and glared at the soldier, yet he only deepened his smile, dimples pressing into his cheeks.

"It is a great honor to meet you, Lady Rowan. I welcome you into my home for the duration of your stay."

I arched a brow. "You are the High Lord of Saor?"

The man inclined his head. "I am indeed."

"But you're so young."

Rather than being offended by my bluntness, he simply said, "My father passed a few years ago due to a sickness of the marrow. I have been High Lord for almost three years. Tomorrow night, on my twentieth birthday, I shall celebrate four years as High Lord."

"I am sorry for your loss. I too lost my father, though I do not recall him at all." I had no idea why I told him that, but I felt inclined to tell him.

The handsome lord smiled again. "Thank you. Come now, Lady Rowan. Rest easy today, for tomorrow the festivities begin. There is a team of attendants ready and willing to assist you and your lovely companion in preparation for the ball."

The High Lord of Saor beckoned some stable hands forward, reassuring us that our horses would be treated like royalty. More people rushed up to us, reaching for our saddlebags, but a glare from me halted them.

"I am quite capable of carrying my own belongs, Lord

Ashb-"

"Augustus will do, Lady Rowan."

"Lord Augustus, I am not royalty within these walls. Please feel free to treat me as such. And it's simply Rowan."

I could almost hear the grind of Paris' teeth as Augustus chuckled. "Then you must call me Auggie. Everyone else does. I try to leave the titles for when it warrants it."

We were ushered to our rooms, far too quickly for me to get a lay of the land, delight blossoming inside me when Paris was pointedly told that he would reside in a room furthest away from the chamber where I would sleep with Emilee. When they said that we would have an entire wing to ourselves, they were not joking. Situated at the front of the house, the bedroom was so large that I felt the entire inhabitants of Saor could fit in here to sleep.

A large canopy bed sat farther off to the right, and the open plan room had a smaller bed just under the window. The bed was meant for Emilee, yet there was no way that my friend was going to be sleeping there. She would just have to climb into the oversized bed with me. Lush red carpet stretched across the sleeping area and into the spacious living area.

The living area consisted of two large chairs in front of a roaring fireplace with fruits and cheeses laid out for us to snack on. The walls, though bare, were painted a rich slate color that should not have worked, yet it was beautiful in its contrast with the red floor. What I liked very much about the room was that it lacked any overtly decorative items—no golden candles or silver chalices.

Once settled in our room and alone, Emilee flopped down on one of the large ornate chairs and all but swooned.

"Rowan, that handsome lord was so flirting with you."

"Emilee, please. He was flirting with my title." I tried to dissuade her from such thinking, because Emilee would try match making before we left for home.

Dropping a grape into her mouth, Emilee let loose a sigh of indignation. "You heard what he said, Row. He leaves titles alone until it warrants it. Why not have some fun while you are away from prying eyes."

I sank down into the chair opposite Emilee and almost groaned at how comfortable they were. "Prying eyes? You mean Paris, right? Or have you forgotten about my future husband? Unless Paris meets an untimely death, then there will be no fun for Rowan, not that I welcome any."

Emilee stretched out her legs and peered over at me. "I'm sure, Rowan, if you wanted to have some fun, Paris could be persuaded to find amusement away from you for the evening and then perhaps, drink so much that he does not remember a thing."

I narrowed my gaze, knowing how much Emilee hated using her powers for frivolous things like this. I gave her a tired smile and shook my head. Emilee's expression darkened.

"I can do it, Rowan. You know I can."

Sitting up straight, I ran a hand through the tangles of my hair. "I do not doubt that you can, Em. I simply do not want to be the reason you do. Perhaps, since Paris is rather annoying, I might get you to convince him that he has a rather unfortunate itch somewhere rather delicate. Now, that would be hilarious to watch."

Emilee giggled. "You are terrible."

I rose up and went to the giant bay window to gaze

out. "It would be the best entertainment I could ever behold."

It was an amazing view, overlooking the entire kingdom. Yes, Saor was a kingdom to me. Seeing an entire village working together to ready for the Solstice party and the incoming storm. Was this what it could be like if the Cambridges and the Montgomerys put aside our differences, forgave whatever slight was held against the other, and created a peaceful unification of people?

I laughed at myself for my foolish thoughts. Who was I to think that I, a mere girl, could hold any sway with the covens to try and forge a new world for all who walked this earth?

A knock sounded on the door, to which Emilee beckoned them in. Two young girls about our age wheeled in a rather long rail full of dresses of all shapes and colors. Emilee squealed and jumped to her feet, running her hands along the finery. She pulled a bright yellow monstrosity from the rail and made to hold it out in front of me.

"I will make you bleed if you come any closer with that."

Emilee grinned, but the two girls did not know where to look.

"Where did they all come from?" I asked the girls, my tone sharper than I meant it to be.

"Your mother sent a message that you and Lady Emilee would require attire for the ball. We assembled the finest Saor has to offer. Is it not to your liking, your Majesty?"

"None of them are pants." I remarked dryly, and Emilee laughed, rolling her eyes at me.

"Forgive the sovereign, girls, she has a dry sense of

humor that takes a bit of getting used to. Rowan, you are scaring these poor girls. What will you do when they send in someone to fix your hair?"

I lifted the strands of my hair out and asked. "What's wrong with my hair?"

The two women glanced at me, then at Emilee to see if I was jesting, which of course I was not. I rested a hip against the window sill as Emilee rambled on about the dresses with the girls. Another knock came at the door, and a row of high heeled shoes were wheeled in.

I'd had enough.

"Take those ankle breakers out of my sight and please bring me some warm water and dish soap. Oh, and some cloth. My boots will do just fine. If I am reduced to wearing a dress, I will not force my feet to endure torture like that."

The three girls scampered from the room, leaving all the rails behind them. Emilee frowned at me and shook her head, pulling a pair of flat dainty shoes from the rail. She pulled out a simple floor-length black dress with lace sleeves.

"This is perfect for you, Rowan. And if you hadn't of scared off the attendants, they could have shown you these. Let your hair loose, add a little bit of make-up, and not a sinner in this place would peg you as Rowan Cambridge, daughter of the forest."

I stared at the dress, and then at Emilee's grinning face. "I'll look like death in that dress."

"You will look regal and beautiful, and you will make every man in the room's eyes pop out of their heads."

I snorted and scratched my face. "I will look like a fool standing beside you. You must wear that yellow dress so as not to outshine me."

Emilee laughed, dismissing my words and continued to riffle through the dresses. I went back to gazing out of the window, suddenly wondering if the Montgomery heir had arrived and if we resided under the same roof. Was he looking out of a window like me, wondering what the hell he had signed up for?

I did not know what he looked like, this Montgomery heir. I only had a brief description, which I assume he had of me. As the only heirs, I assumed his parents had been as proactive of his appearance as my mother had been of mine.

Tomorrow night, we would step into the same room for the first time, and it would be the first time any Cambridge or Montgomery had set foot into a room without bloodshed. Perhaps, this time would be like every other time. I closed my eyes, trying to block out Emilee. I wondered if we should have stayed at home.

chapter
seven
julian

WHEN YOU LOOKED UPON A MAP OF VERNANTHIA, YOUR eyes went straight away to the largest parts of the country, Montgomery and Cambridge. Sprawling desert in one region, and plentiful rainforest in another; it was easy to see why Saor would be overlooked. The city might have more inhabitants than either Montgomery or Cambridge coven territories, but it held the tiniest amount of land between the two.

When the covens had fractured in two and claimed lands the furthest distance from each other, the Nulls, or nonmagical citizens of Vernanthia, were literally put right in the middle of the war. Over time, the little villages on the outskirts of the main city had pledged allegiance to one side or another. Nestled in the middle, the smaller portion of the country, its citizens almost always caught between the conflict in the neighboring magic territories. Some sided with us, others with the Cambridges, while the majority of the Nulls remained impartial, wishing for a resolution to a conflict that had been ongoing for centuries now.

The swelling storm had begun to rain down on us

as we came upon the gates of Soar, the city of the free people. While on the final leg of our journey, the sky had darkened to an angry shade of cerulean, and the droplets that hit our skin were icy cold. While Tobias grumbled and groaned, I could do nothing but immerse myself in the sensations. The almost freezing drops of water stung as they hit the bare flesh of my arms. To experience weather like this first hand, to really and truly feel cold, wet and almost numb, was far better than the manifestations of rain that I conjured in my quest for knowledge. For in the desert, even the infrequent bouts of rain were warm.

Soldiers were just about to close the gates when we came into view, and all three of us were quickly ushered inside, the large wooden gates closing with a thud that rang out through the city. While we awaited the soldiers to greet us and direct us toward our lodgings for the next few nights, I took in my surroundings.

Rows and rows of houses and businesses with candles lit in the windows to guide your way. It was a quaint little village, a homey kind of place, a place where I could see myself growing old and raising a family. With the incoming storm, the majority of people had already sought shelter in their homes, and the last remnants of people making their way to the bosom of their families strode with smiling faces, even stopping to chat with a friend or neighbor.

I had never stepped a foot over the edge of Montgomery territory, my one and only time venturing out of bounds ended in disaster. I remembered one such rebellion of my early years, where Toby and I sneaked away from training and ventured into the sands. All of seven years of age, we meandered the dunes, before quickly losing our way, for neither of us had thought to bring a compass. Night came in, and the sub-zero temperatures of the desert at night, and my fragile grasp on my elemental magic could only fashion the sand into a barrier to shield us from the wind. Had my father's soldiers not been able to find us, we would have no doubt frozen to death that night.

My father's obsession with the Montgomery coven continuing to rule their own lands, made him so paranoid that Cambridge assassins waited over the vast sand dunes in order to snuff out my life, halted any attempts, or any request I made to roam and visit the edges of our territory. Malcolm's response was that since I was the only heir to the throne, my life would not be jeopardized.

However, I had the distinct feeling, had my mother been able to conceive another child, then some accident might have befallen me, and less regard for my safety and wellbeing would have been considered. It lodged a notation of suspicion that Malcolm had been so eager to send me off on this mission.

Or perhaps he had more faith in his Shadow's abilities in keeping me alive, than his own son. That would not surprise me.

"Well if the weather doesn't kill me, then all this happiness and good cheer just might."

Toby's voice broke into my thoughts, and I frowned at my friend, shaking my head as I replied, "Behave, Toby. We are guests of this place and will treat it with respect. Just because it is not like the desert, does not mean it is not home to others. The sun and sand are not everyone's idea of heaven, you know."

Toby muttered under his breath, earning a slap at the back of his noggin from Mercy. Mercy seemed to know where he was going in this town, yet he happened to be a great keeper of secrets. It would take a greater man than me to pry those secrets from his lips.

As a soldier came up, dressed in a standard green uniform, and spoke to Mercy, his arms flailed about, pointing toward the town. Mercy nodded, and motioned us forward, the horse's breath showing in the rapidly chilled air. The sound of their hooves clattered through the empty streets, and as a gust of wind howled its way through the streets, I pulled my cloak around me tighter, my teeth beginning to chatter, and the wonder I had experienced slowly dissipated.

We rode up to a magnificent looking mansion, that seemed to stretch from one side of the sky-high wall to the other side. While Montgomery castle was surrounded by soldiers and sandstone walls, this property had little to no soldiers, and absolutely no security like my own home. While a steel railing surrounded the front of the mansion, which was a simple structure fashioned together by bricks and mortar, there was an open space leading up to the dwelling with no one manning the gate.

"This doesn't look like the most secure place in all of Vernanthia, does it?"

I nodded in agreement with Toby and wondered why Lord Ashbridge would allow his people to walk freely into his home. Saor might refer to itself as the free people—the small, dividing force between Cambridge and Montgomery land, but any one with the slightest tinge of ambition could sneak in and assassinate the high lord in his sleep with no magic precautions to save him.

As we entered the courtyard, stable hands dressed in the thickest of coats came racing up, beckoning us down from the horses. As soon as we dismounted and gathered our belongings, they hurriedly ushered the horses into the warmth of the stables. The doors to the keep opened and we ducked inside, thankful for the warmth as the door closed behind us.

Standing with a grin on his face was the person I could only assume to be Lord Ashbridge. He waited while we stripped off our cloaks and shook off the cold.

"A rather vast difference to the desert, I would say. Prince Julian, welcome to Saor and my home."

I grasped his outstretched hand, shook it firmly and replied, "Thank you for your hospitality, Lord Ashbridge. We are honored to be received as your guests."

"Call me Auggie, please."

"Julian. And this is Tobias, my second in command and Mercuree—""The Montgomery Shadow."

Mercy lifted his head, his silver eyes staring at our host. My hand slipped to grasp the hilt of my sword, readying to defend Mercy should the need arise. From the sudden stiffness in Toby's body, I could only assume he was poised to strike as well. Surprise flooded my body as Mercy gave a small smile. "Come now, Auggie. Let's not pretend to not know each other in front of the prince."

My gaze darted from Mercy to Auggie, as Auggie chuckled. "For someone who is a renowned spy, you lack any sense of fun, dearest Silver." To us, he grinned. "Come, let me show you to your rooms. My cooks have prepared some warm stew to heat your bones."

Auggie strode ahead of us and began to point out pieces of art adorning the walls. The hallway carried on for almost an eternity, and I have to admit to being pleasantly shocked by the lack of finery and appearance of wealth.

Despite being quite a large home, it seemed just that, a home. Rather a complete opposition to Montgomery castle, whose halls depicted the kings, now one with the sands of time.

When we crossed the halls, the house seemingly silent, I wondered if the Cambridge heir was already here. Had she stridden around the house and received a warm welcome from our host? Was she watching us now, studying us?

Auggie stopped at the end of a staircase and leaned against the banister that curved just before the bottom step. Mercy headed up the stairs without a second glance at our host, and for a split second, I thought I saw disappointment in his eyes.

"This is the only staircase that leads up to your rooms," Auggie said after clearing his throat. "I have left suits tailored to your specifications inside the largest bedroom. Three adjoining rooms that lead into a separate dinning or living area. Should you require anything, there is a chime that will bring an attendant to your rooms."

"I'm sure we will be quite alright, thank you."

Auggie bowed his head. "Of course. But I must remind you that while in my city, magic will be limited to needs be basis. I understand it is second nature to you, Julian, but within these walls, peace is paramount. Unless provoked, I ask you not to use magic." Our host looked pointedly at Toby. "Any violence upon another will be treated with the utmost seriousness. Sleep well, gentlemen. Tomorrow, the real fun begins."

Both Toby and I waited as Auggie walked away, and then we headed up the winding staircase.

"I wonder what they would do to restrain us, should we

break his silly little rules?" whispered Toby, not bothering to hide the glint of mischief in his eyes.

"I, for one, would rather not find out."

Toby chuckled and took the stairs two at a time, while I took my time climbing the vast staircase. Once I entered the room, my eyes widened. This entire suite of rooms was far bigger than our own little home, but if I had chosen to reside within the castle, then I would have a suite as fine as this.

Toby headed straight for the dining table, slipped off his boots, and having picked up a spoon, began to dive into the stew. Mercy had perched himself on the window ledge and began to devour his own bowl. My stomach rumbled, and I tossed my drenched cloak aside, hung my sword by the door, and joined them. As soon as the spoon was in my mouth, an abundance of taste greeted me, the most delicious meal I had tasted in a long while.

Once we had cleaned the bowls, we relaxed into our accommodations, but it wasn't long before Toby began to grill Mercy about our gracious host.

"So, *Silver*, how well do you know Auggie?"

Mercy stared out the window, the shadows hiding his face. "Auggie and I met a few years ago when I was on a mission. He had just become high lord, upon the death of his father, and we stumbled across each other. We struck up a conversation, and from then on, whenever I passed by Saor, I would stop in."

"And that's it?" Toby said with a wiggle of his brows.

"Yes."

"Are you quite certain? He is a rather attractive man."

"I'm sure he would be glad to hear you say that," Mercy retorted dryly.

Toby glanced at me with a wink. "Me thinks Mercy doth protest too much."

I kicked Toby under the table, causing him to yelp as I warned. "If Mercy says that's it, then that's it. He is entitled to his privacy."

My little act of violence did little dissuade Toby from grilling Mercy, and despite his stony silence, Mercy must have gotten tired of Toby's non-stop questioning, because one minute, our shadow was leaning against the window, the next he was gone. Toby searched behind the curtains, but Mercy had become one with the shadows.

"I hate when he does that," grumbled Toby, not meaning a single word.

I chuckled. "I'm just jealous that I cannot do that. It's so cool."

Toby didn't answer, just went around and checked all the rooms. He pointed to the furthest off one and grinned. "I take it you want the biggest room, Prince? Seems a shame to have such a gigantic bed when you'll be sleeping alone."

"Bugger off, will you!" I exclaimed as heat flushed my cheeks. Jumping up, I walked over to the washroom and twisted the handle. "I do not care where I sleep. Try not to summon a flurry of women to your bed while I'm gone."

"I cannot promise anything, Jules."

I shook my head as I closed the door behind me. Stripping off my clothes, I carefully folded my new uniform before I pulled the leaver to begin the shower. Sticking my hand under the flow of water, I grimaced at the coldness. Reaching out with my hand, I used my magic to heat the drops. Standing under the flow of water, I yanked the curtain over, and I washed away the desert and the journey, my skin started to heat once more.

After an eternity under the spray, I pushed down the leaver and stepped out. A fresh pair of workout pants and a short sleeves vest sat where I had left my uniform, and I prayed to the gods that Toby had slipped them in.

Drying and dressing quickly, I emerged from the washroom to the sound of Toby's snoring, and a smile tugged at my lips. Sprawled across the lounge chair, Toby had one hand over his face, the other tucked into his waistband. He looked at peace, well apart from the snoring that was loud enough to wake the dead.

Striding into the nearest bedroom, I pulled a blanket from atop the bed and covered Toby's slumbering body. I checked each bedroom and choose the smallest of the three to rest my head. Slipping under the covers, I closed my eyes and tried to will myself to sleep. I had to admit to myself that I was indeed rather nervous about tomorrow night's festivities.

But what I was terrified of, as the time came nearer, was returning to Montgomery lands without doing something that pleased my father. I wondered if I could slip away in the night and disappear? Mercy and Toby would come in search of me, but I could escape.

Stop thinking such silly thoughts. These are the cards you were dealt.

Even my mind mocked me. I heard a noise from outside my window and curiosity got the better of me. Sliding from the bed, I pulled back the heavy curtain to reveal the beginnings of a snowfall. Tiny flakes of snow danced from the sky, falling gracefully and slowly. There was not enough to stick to the ground, but I reached out with my magic and felt the snowflakes fall.

The small isolated garden, hidden at the back of the keep, seemed like a secret place, perhaps where one would go to think. A fountain sat in the middle of the frosty grass, and I imagined that on a less stormy, snowy day, water would flow from the spout at the top, and flow freely into the basin. Icicles formed on the curves of the fountain, glinting moonlight like diamonds in an almost starless sky. The grass had begun to soak up the snowflakes, and soon, if the snow continued to fall, I would be witness to my first ever snow storm.

A girlish bout of laughter caught my attention, and my eyes roamed over the garden. A cloaked figure whirled around in the center of the garden, her features hidden by the darkness of the night. Her cloak fluttered as she twirled, and I felt a pang in my chest that I wished I was down there, free to enjoy the snowfall.

I did not have to see her face to know that she was beautiful. I heard it in the joy of her laughter, the reckless abandon in which she danced amongst the snowflakes. I don't think that I had seen a more enticing sight before in my seventeen years than this girl twirling in the snow.

If Tobias could hear my thoughts now, oh how he would mock me so.

Another girl rushed into view, her hand gesturing in a frenzy, as the girl stopped twirling, her shoulders slumping in a sadness that had me wanting to shake her companion for disturbing the snow queen. And for a fleeting second, as they left the freedom of the winter garden behind them, I caught a glimpse of her smile, and it was warmer than the desert sun. The girl paused, as did her friend, and as if sensing eyes on her, she glanced up.

I stepped back out of view, leaving the curtain to fall

back into place. My heart hammered in my chest. It had only been a glimpse, but I knew that I had to find this girl. In those few seconds, I saw a freedom in her movements that I longed for myself. I did not care if she was a scullery maid, a peasant farmer, or anything else. I simply hoped that she would be at the ball and that I would recognize her smile.

Because hidden behind our masks, even for one night, I could be the man I longed to be, not the prince everyone saw. If only I had the courage to try.

chapter eight
rowan

I HAD AWOKEN THIS MORNING WITH AN ALMIGHTY SENSE of trepidation, that the unchartered waters I was about to submerge myself in would take me well out of my depth. Also, with the sneaking suspicion that someone had been watching me while I frolicked in the snow. When Emilee had come out to chastise me for slipping from the room unnoticed and going to explore, I thought I could feel eyes on me, but when I cast my eyes up at the window, I saw not a thing.

Laying in the bed, I refused to rise before it was afternoon, considering Emilee and Paris had spoken quite vocally outside the bedroom about my night time exploits, and when I had yelled that I would indeed be heading outside to traipse through the snow, Paris threatened to lock me in my room until the ball. And I knew he would do it.

So, I lounged in my bed while the winter sun shone through my window, the snow beckoning me to come out and play. As I heard the attendants arrive to ready us for the ball, I covered myself with the blanket and groaned. This happened to be my worst nightmare. I could see my mother's smile, as I smiled and curtsied, ever the princess. It would delight and amuse her all at once.

The bedroom door flung open, and I could almost taste the impatience in Emilee's voice as she spoke, "Get up, Rowan. Seriously. You cannot stay in bed all day."

I pushed down the blanket and glared at her. "If you'd have given me permission, oh great babysitter, to go outside for a little stroll, then perhaps I would have been up at the crack of dawn rather than avoiding the inevitable torture session."

Emilee sighed, giving me an exaggerated roll of her eyes. "You would swear, Rowan Cambridge, that I was about to stick needles in your eyes, rather than make you all pretty."

"I did not know facial reconstruction was part of your powers, Emilee. You could earn a castle full of gold with that."

Ignoring my sarcasm, which she was well accustomed to, Emilee rounded the bed and dragged me by the arm out into the sitting room, where I shrieked and tried to cover myself, my tunic barely touching my knees. Emilee ignored my pleas and shoved me into the bathroom, a steaming tub awaiting me.

I dragged the tunic over my head and flung it at Emilee, who snatched the garment and pointed at the bathtub. Huffing out a breath, I rid myself of my underclothes and climbed into the bath, sinking down into the blissful heat of the water. Emilee perched at the edge of the tub, handing me a salve before issuing instructions.

"Once you have rinsed your hair, lather a small amount into it. Count to 120 in your mind and then wash it off. It will rid you of those cursed knots that always manage to gather in your hair." Emilee then pointed to a bottle on the edge of the tub. "Do the same with that bottle, as it will give a shine to your hair. There is also a strawberry lotion for you to wash your skin in. They tell me it will leave the scent clinging to your skin. I have already requested a basket of all these goodies to take home."

Hearing her name being called from outside, Emilee slipped off the tub and fixed me with a glare. "Half an hour, Rowan. Then I come and get you."

I answered her by submerging my head under the water, breathing out through my nose. Only when I was certain that my taskmaster was gone, did I rise up from the water. I obliged Emilee and followed her instructions, growing quickly bored of this routine she had imposed on me. After completing the steps, I hugged my knees to my chest in the water and rested my chin on my knees.

Last night, shortly after Emilee had drifted off to sleep, I pulled my cloak around me and slipped soundlessly from my room. I could hear Paris' deep laugh and a very feminine sigh from his room, and I was content in knowing that he would at least be distracted for a time. At first, I contemplated trying to sneak around the keep. However, it seemed that preparations for the ball continued into the evening, with far too many bodies milling about for me to investigate unnoticed. I might be a tracker, and quite capable of evading my mother's henchmen, but even I could not walk into an open area unnoticed.

It was then I heard someone mention that it had begun to snow, and I managed to slip out an open door and step into the most tranquil of spaces. A secluded garden hidden from view of the outside world. The grass had begun to frost, the water in the fountain already frozen from the cold. I felt a cold drip on my nose and peered up into a sky that held a mere star or two.

Snowflakes fell from that sky and gathered on the grass beneath my feet. Here, alone in this paradise, I twirled as the snow fell heavier, more frequent. A faint memory had pricked at my senses, of a handsome man twirling me about in a snowy setting, taking me in his arms and spinning me round and round. Closing my eyes, I imagined that I was back in that memory and a laugh escaped my lips as I twisted and twirled in the snowfall.

Emilee had burst out the door then, a frightened expression on her features as she gave me a royal telling off for sneaking out. My joy had diminished in an instant, but I felt I was being watched. My suspicious glare up revealed nothing.

The memories of my father and of last night were quickly forgotten as Emilee came back in and scowled until I got out of the tub. She wrapped me in a fleece morning coat and not so gently nudged me into the craziness, urging me to take a seat in front of an attendant with a hairbrush and a scissors, a stern warning on her face to not make a scene.

I pressed my lips together and tried to ignore the snip of the scissors and the tug of hair as the attendant tried to detangle my locks. It would seem that the miracle salve was not so miraculous. By the time my body was stiffening from being seated for so long, the attendant called to Emilee, who nodded her approval. Holding out a mirror, I could see that my hair had been pulled back off my face, loose curls falling down to my shoulders.

When I merely lifted my eyes up, Emilee sighed before pulling me over to another station, where my lips were painted, powder was spread on my face, blush was contoured into my cheeks, and my eyes were streaked with whatever magic was used to make them all sultry.

This time, when Emilee showed me my reflection, the face staring back at me was not my own, but the queen they were trying to fashion me into. My friend must have seen the flare of panic in my eyes, because she shooed away the attendant, and taking hold of my hand, ushered me into the bedroom.

As I sank down on the edge of the bed, my eyes caught sight of an emerald colored gown that took my breath away.

"Is that dress for you?" I said, my voice merely a whisper.

Emilee grinned. "No silly. It is for you. The color reminded me of the rainforest and with your coloring, it's going to look fabulous on you. Plus, it is long enough that you can wear your boots underneath, if you wish."

I stood, grazing my fingers on the gown. Sleeveless, with pockets in the full skirt, it was floor-length with a bodice of diamantes etched into the waistband. It was an exquisite dress befitting a royal and would do no justice on me.

"It is rather poufy," I finally said, trying to deflect from the fact that I have fallen slightly in love with this dress.

Emilee opened a drawer and pulled out a thigh sheath containing a small little blade. "Easier to hide this if it is poufy."

I kissed her quickly on the cheek, ignoring her protests to not ruin my make-up, as she unzipped the dress and ordered me to dress. It amazed me how quickly the day went, all for one little event. Emilee sauntered off to get ready herself as I slipped into the dress, but not before fastening the sheath to my thigh. I reached around, trying to yank up the zipper when I heard a voice behind me and felt a hand on my hip.

"Allow me."

I let loose a hiss, slipping from his grasp and faced Paris, the fastening still undone. His eyes wandered over me, a cocky smile playing on his lips.

"My dearest Rowan. If the boys back home realized how well you scrub up, I assure you that it would not be so easy to be your consort. You look good enough to take a bite of."

"I warned you, Paris. Touch me again without my permission, and you will lose an appendage."

Dressed in his black on black tux, Paris looked quite handsome. But the most devilish of monsters could hide behind an angelic face. He continued to grin smugly, as if my threats were merely that, and I had little or no intention of acting upon them. Paris took a step toward me, and I poised myself to strike, saved when Emilee stormed into the room and ordered Paris from it. When he hesitated, Emilee braced her hands on her hips and smiled a very sadistic smile reserved for only certain people.

"I'm asking you to leave, Paris, under your own steam. Do not make me force you to leave; you will not like my magic when I'm done with you."

Paris sneered, showing his true colors, but sloped from the room as slippery as a snake. Emilee blew out a breath, indicating with her finger for me to turn, and fastened the dress up. I turned to face her again, grinning at the yellow dress that somehow seemed to radiate on her like the sun.

"Only you could make that dress stunning."

"I know," she replied with a grin before handing me a black mask. The eyes were wide enough on the mask not to hide whatever witchcraft the attendants had weaved on my eyes, while being curved up to not cover too much of my face.

I tried unsuccessfully to put on the mask and pull the elastic under my hair, until Emilee came and fixed it for me. Then, I slid my feet into my cozy boots with Emilee shaking her head in amusement. I let the dress fall down again and placed my hands in my pockets.

"These masks won't do much to mask who we are," I mused, rocked back and forth on my heels.

"Auggie said that won't be a problem. Come on. Let's go party."

"You sure you can do what needs to be done, Emilee?"

Brushing off my worry, she donned her own mask, linked arms with me and grinned. "Of course. I'm just going to ask someone very nicely to fetch what I need. There is absolutely no justifying breaking my nails or getting my makeup smudged."

I laughed, allowing Emilee to steer me from the room, ignoring the gasps as we strode by the attendants and out onto the balcony overlooking a grand staircase. The lights had been dimmed, and I strained to see or make out the faces of those who were filing down the hallway before disappearing inside a door. Maybe this was what Auggie had meant when he explained to Emilee that our identities would be still hidden, despite the flimsy mask.

We descended the stairs, the auras of the party goers tinging my vision, causing my steps to falter, cascading in an array of colors, like a rainbow on the edges of my vision.

I reached out and gripped the edge of the banister, cursing myself. It had been a long time since I had been in a room with this many people, and I had forgotten to ease myself into the sensations. I clamped down on my magic, trying to block out my instincts and smiled reassuringly when Emilee eyed me curiously.

Slipping into the steady stream of people, we inched closer and closer to the door where flutes of champagne were being handed out. Auggie stepped into view, looking ever the handsome host, his own mask covering his eyes as he grinned at us.

"Ladies, you both look ravishing tonight. May I escort you both down into the cellar." Auggie held out his arms, and when Emilee crooked her arm into his, I followed suit. The security at the door bowed as we passed, and I hoped it was due to the high lord, rather than my identity.

Castles danced against the shadows as we descended the stairs, with me praying that I did not trip over the elegant ballgown. The staircase was entirely black apart from the flicker from the candles. I could hear the melody of music, the sound of chatter as we paused in front of the doors leading into what I assumed would be the ballroom.

Auggie leaned in, his breath warm against my ear as he said, "Save me a dance, won't you, Rowan? I would like one day to tell my children that I danced with a beautiful queen under the cover of darkness."

"And then you can tell them how when the lights came on, you realized the queen was not as beautiful as she appeared in the dark."

Auggie left out a bellow of laughter, releasing us from his grasp as he pushed open the doors, and we stepped into pitch black. Like the stairway, candles flickered on the walls, the curtains drawn all along the windows, making it impossible to make out any distinct features. Small nightlights on tables illuminated the way. Every single guest in the room was dressed in elegant finery, masks of cat eyes and the likes hiding them from view.

The band struck up a chord, a haunting melody that had me tapping my feet. On one side of the ballroom, tables stretched with nibbles and drinks all laid out. Emilee snatched a flute of champagne from a passing waiter, and as he offered me one, I rolled my eyes and declined.

"How ladylike would it be to ask for a glass of ale?"

Emilee nudged my shoulder as she replied, "I assumed that you wanted to stay under the radar. A beauty such as yourself slugging ale from a glass would surely attract more attention than you are getting at this moment."

I took the opportunity to peer around, and a gaggle of guests watched us, the women with looks of contempt, the men with eyes of lust. I fixed them with a glare, most unladylike, and they turned away.

"It's that goddamn dress of yours. It's about the brightest thing in the room."

Eyes flashing with a sadness that had me thinking that I had offended her, she gave me a small smile. "I wish that you could see yourself as others do, Row. You are far from the ugly duckling you envision yourself to be. Now, let me go network. Please try not to break anything expensive."

I hissed at Emilee to come back, but my friend had already slipped into the void, vanishing into the bodies on the dance floor. My eyes wandered over the dancing bodies, those pressed up against one another, taking full advantage of the darkness. I wrinkled my nose when in the faint flicker of candlelight, I spied Paris clinging to a woman, his lips pressed against the nape of her neck. He must have sensed me watching him, for his eyes darted up to meet mine. He winked, and my stomach flooded with disgust.

I roamed the room, my eyes scanning the gathered crowd to try and find some sort of hint, or inclination, that the Montgomery heir was in the same room as me. But all I could see was a mass of bodies as the band kicked up a tune in a faster beat, and I noticed a suitor or two make their way in my direction.

Scowling, I backed away from the dance floor, until my back hit solid wall. Cursing Emilee for abandoning me to be my socially awkward self, I reached out, searching for Emilee's aura, and found it shining as bright as her dress, yellow against a burnt orange. She batted her eyes and smiled cordially at an elder gentleman, her fingers grazing his arm as laughter filled her eyes, the sound carrying across the room. Once I knew she was still within reach, I leaned against the comfort of the wall and began counting down the seconds until we could leave.

Had I been fooling myself? Thinking that I could act the princess for even an evening. A server strode past me, carrying a tray of ale. I snatched one from the tray and drank down a massive gulp, the bitter liquid refreshingly tasty. I took another large sip, and I hoped Emilee would stay safe in her endeavors, for despite the power my friend wielded in her veins, she lacked the instinct to defend herself. She could always command someone away from her, but Emilee would need the time to say the words. So, I would remain in the shadows and make sure she was safeguarded.

And while I kept a watchful eye on Emilee and nursed my ale, I wondered how in all that was holy was I to weed out the Montgomery prince in the vastness of the somber ballroom?

chapter
nine
julian

I SPENT MOST OF THE NIGHT TOSSING AND TURNING, then pacing the floor when Mercy failed to return to our suite of rooms throughout the day. Tobias chastised me for my fretting, considering the entire embodiment of Mercy's job meant that he tended to go off for days, sometimes weeks on end, without a word. Then, he would suddenly appear when we least expected him, as if he had not been on a dangerous spying mission for my father.

However, this time, Toby and I were with Mercy, and I could not help the unease curling in the pit of my stomach. As Toby reclined on one of the fireside chairs, his legs dangling over the side, I leaned back in my own seat as I closed my eyes, my mind drifting from Mercy to the mysterious girl dancing in the snow.

Her smile had been enough to make my heart leap, a feeling it was not accustomed to, and yet, despite my earlier reservations, I found myself eager to attend this masquerade ball, in the hopes I could catch the smile that seemed tattooed on my mind. Could I pluck up the bravery to ask her to dance or strike up a conversation, and perhaps forget that I had been sent here under murderous intentions?

"Do you think he spent the night with Ashbridge?" Tobias asked suddenly, his voice dragging me from my thoughts. Was I mistaken or was there a hint of something in Toby's voice?

I rubbed my forehead, wondering if I was imagining things. "I'm sure Mercy stayed where Mercy wanted to stay. Or with whoever he wanted to stay with. If he did at all."

Toby let loose a snort and folded his arms behind his head. "He could have at least sent word that he wasn't dead in a ditch somewhere. I mean he can literally pop in and leave a note, then poof out again. It's not that hard."

I made to answer, but a rough voice interrupted me.

"I assure you, I do not poof."

Toby darted upright, as did I, both our jaws hitting the floor as we took in Mercy's appearance.

Dressed head to toe in a black suit, dark shirt and shoes, the silver of his hair had been darkened to match the color of his outfit. He had pulled the long tresses back off his face into a plait. Most of the time, Mercy choose to hide behind his mane of silver hair, hiding eyes that were so unique, so uniquely Mercy that made him stand out. But now, those eyes of silver had been disguised somehow, and against the paleness of his skin, his almond colored eyes were remarkable.

"What the hell did you do to yourself?"

Toby's tone was dark, almost frightened, yet Mercy seemed oblivious to it, his mask of indifference not slipping. Yet, even across the room, I could see a slight tinge of pink staining his cheeks.

"I think it is rather brilliant," I interjected, trying to

understand why Toby would be so, so appalled by Mercy's transition. "Who would guess that the most talented spy in all the realm, one renowned for his silver coloring, could be such a chameleon and walk amongst the normal folk. It's like hiding a wolf in the guise of a sheep."

"That's the first time I have ever heard you speak like your father," Tobias spat, lurching from the chair with further mutterings of getting dressed. His shut his door with a loud bang, the fixtures on the wall shuddering under the force.

I glanced over at Mercy, who simply raised a shoulder. "Your guess is as good as mine."

Taking in the sight of one of my closest friends again, I smiled and told him once more that it was a brilliant disguise, all the while wondering if such a thing was possible for me. As if reading my thoughts, Mercy frowned, shaking his head.

"The chemicals used to change the color in my eyes burn like the midday desert sun. The coloring in my hair is mixture concocted from pig's blood and some plant roots. It will wash out as soon as a drop of rain touches it. I do these things because it is necessary sometimes to be someone else. Do you hate yourself that much that you would hide from the world?"

Clasping my hands behind my back, I rock back and forth on the heels of my feet. I consider my words carefully, aware that Mercy would do anything to protect me, no matter the personal cost to himself. If I asked him to help me run from the future I did not want, then Mercy would do it, as would Tobias. They would give up everything they knew, if I asked them too.

I forced a smile on my face, dragged a laugh from

inside me, trying to sound flippant, yet it came out sounding strangled. "Never mind me, I had far too little sleep last night. Let me go get ready, and we shall continue on our quest. I won't be long."

Striding across the room, I passed by Mercy, who snarled at me with an iron stare and a grip on my arm to match it. "Say the word, Jules. Say it and there would not be a person on the earth that would find you. And if they did, they would not live to tell the tale."

I heard the solemn vow in his words, heard the absolute certainty. I rested my hand over the one that held my arm in a vice grip and said, "I know, and I am grateful you are on my side. There will be no running today."

Mercy let me go, and I hurried off to get ready. We had all decided to dress in non-descriptive suits, all black so that we would blend in with the shadows, for not all of us had Mercy's talents. When I emerged fully clothed from my room, I felt rather insignificant in comparison to my two friends. It was like looking at light and dark, yin and yang.

Mercy had always been so unique in appearance that it was hard not to see why he would attract attention, and Toby was what you would expect from a prince, handsome, smart, a little smug. His dark hair, long lashes, and devilish smile fluttered many a maiden's heart. I shifted uncomfortably, aware that out of the three of us, not a single sinner would think that I was indeed a prince. And it was surprisingly freeing all the same.

We made our way toward the ball, slipping down the winding steps, before crossing through what must be Auggie's personal dining room. Mercy led the way, leading us through many a room before he came to a stop in front of a set of double oak doors.

"We know what it is we were sent here to do. I will slip out after a while and do what I need to do. Toby, you must never talk your eyes off Jules. If someone figures out who he is, then they may use the cover of darkness to attack."

I shook my head. "There will be too many people inside."

"It's what I would do."

Brushing off that statement, I simply said, "Plus, I'm not some defenseless princess. I can look after myself."

Mercy rolled his eyes and pinned Toby with a glare. "Can you keep it in your pants for a night?"

A snarl curled Toby's lips, an inhuman sound I had not heard before from my friend. "Don't insult me, Mercuree. I would not be Julian's first choice to watch his back if I was not capable. Now give me my bloody mask so I do not have to listen to you anymore."

Mercy handed him his mask, then handed me mine also, less disturbed by the sound of Mercy's full name on Tobias' lips than I, a thing that rarely happened. Whatever was happening between these two, it unsettled me, as much as it was beginning to unsettle our friendship.

I slipped the mask on over my eyes, and though simple, it covered most of my features. Mercy shoved open the oak doors and ushered us inside. When the doors shut behind us, for a moment, darkness engulfed us, plunging me into a panic. I could not see a thing apart from the flickering of flames. I cursed myself for my unease, until a voice in my ear instantly calmed my nerves.

"It can be a little frightening, at first, to face your first experience of sheer darkness. But the shadows are not your enemy, Jules."

I remembered then, that as a child, with the power he wielded, how terrifying it must have been for a small boy to be engulfed by the shadows. And I was not a young child, simply a prince who lived in a place where even in the darkness of night, there was an abundance of light.

Quashing down my unease, I waited until my vision acclimatized with the darkness, and I began to see the outlines of men and women who were already enjoying the festivities. Toby immediately snatched two glasses of ale from a waitress, leaning in close until she giggled and went in search of another. Handing one drink to me, another to Mercy, Toby's eyes roamed around the room, gauging from our possible target.

When the waitress came back with Toby's drink, she tried to rouse him into some more flirting, yet with a sideways glance at Mercy, he willed her away, his stance all rigid. By the time this trip was over, I would have to knock their heads together. I turned in Mercy's direction, readying myself to ask what in the name of the gods was going on, but Mercy had already vanished, this darkened abyss a playhouse for someone like him. The entire room was awash with shadows, the candles and torches strategically placed to create a mirage of shadows dancing against the walls.

I took time to take in the sight before me. Mask clad revelers dancing in the center of the room, their bodies clung to one another. Some drank from expensive flutes of bubbly champagne, others conversed in huddled corners. There was laughter and song, the band high on the dais behind us striking up slow melodies and fast paced reels. All of these people were enjoying the spoils of merriment in the safety of the high lord's domain.

I heard a familiar sound, the laughter from the hooded woman dancing in the snow. My gaze wandered over to where, not far from we were, two young women stood with Augustus. One of the girls, the one who had come rushing out to stop the winter girl and her laughter, was dressed in a bright yellow gown that seemed ridiculous in the scheme of things, considering it was an event that had been all about hiding one's identity. I met Augustus' gaze over the top of her head, and he nodded once.

My attention however was transfixed by the beauty that stood with them. Dressed in an emerald green dress, that bloody mask shielded her full features from me. Her companion said something to her, and she laughed, easily and with a light-heartedness that felt like an explosion in my chest. Her smile, it was brighter than the torches burning around her. I allowed my eyes to roam over her. She was around my height with her dark hair clipped back, flowing down to kiss her shoulders in a way that had my fingers itching to touch them. Her bare arms were muscular and strong and as I reached out with my magic, I felt the swirl of power in her.

As if sensing my eyes on her, the girl twisted in my direction, her eyes held mine for a flicker of time before my cheeks reddened, and I looked away. When I dared to look once more, she had cast her attention back to her friends.

"Go talk to her already."

I jumped at the sound of Toby's voice, who was grinning at me so much, I could see the white of his teeth.

"Go talk to her already," he repeated, inclining his head toward the person I'd been staring at. "You've been standing there staring at her for quite a while. It's starting to get weird."

"I haven't been staring," I said with not much conviction as I took a large gulp of my ale.

"Yes, you have. Now is the perfect opportunity to go and ask her to dance. Considering she's been eyeballing you when she thinks no one is looking, I do not think she will refuse you. Besides, I'm pretty certain the gorgeous creature beside her is the future queen of the Cambridge coven. You go romance her attack dog. Leave the princess to me."

There was a hint of menace in his tone, a wolfish smile on his face. I put a hand on Toby's arm. "We will not insult Ashbridge's invitation by waging war here. It is horrid enough that we are stealing under his nose. Promise me, Toby. No bloodshed here."

"Unless provoked, my Prince, there will be no bloodshed."

I lift my arm from Toby's as the seriousness fled his features. "Now, go get the girl."

He pushed me forward and I almost stumbled in the dim light, causing me to glare at him for a moment before I rolled my shoulders and prayed that I don't make an absolute fool of myself. My heart thundered like a drum as I made my way toward the girl, noticing that her eyes were the same color as her dress. My palms were sweating, and I licked my lips to try and rid myself of the dryness.

I stood a mere breath away from her when she turned in my direction, and I could not find the words to speak. Her companion, the girl Toby thought to be the Cambridge heir, giggled, even as Auggie chuckled, a dash of mischief in his eyes. But I blocked them out, my steely focus on the girl with the green eyes and a smile made of sunshine.

"I was wondering, M'lady, if you would dance with me?" I held out my hand, trying to ignore the tremble.

She blinked in surprise and took a step back, looking at the Cambridge heir for direction, confusion dousing the spark in her eyes. Her companion grinned, and I could see why Tobias thought her beautiful, yet she could not hold a candle to a girl who found joy in dancing in winter snow.

"Of course, she will, won't you, Ro?"

"I certainly will not. I do not dance."

Her voice, it rang in my mind like a caress. I made to pull back my hand, but her hand was forced into mine, as the Cambridge heir replied, "Then be glad that the music playing is a slow one. There is not much to it but swaying. Go, have fun."

Ro, the girl, glanced at me and gave me a weary smile. "Looks like I have my orders."

"One dance. Then if you wish, we will say our goodbyes, and you can forget you were ever forced to dance with me," I tried for humor, and it worked, as she erupted into a bark of laughter.

Hand in mine, we walked toward the dance floor. That was where it got awkward. It was like she had not been asked to dance before and knew little of how to act with a partner. I lifted her arms and placed them on my shoulders, before I tentatively placed my hands on her hips, a ghost of a touch. When she did not flinch, I stepped in closer and allowed my lips to curl up.

We began to move, the only parts of our bodies touching were where our arms were linked, yet my entire being felt as if it was on fire. The world slipped away, I was dancing with the most beautiful girl in the room, and I felt as if I could take on the world.

Her gaze had been focused on the spot in front of her, her eyes turned to the floor so that she would not have to meet my eyes. I squeezed her hip, and she peered up at me, a vulnerability in her eyes that had not been there before.

"I'm not that terrible a dancer, am I?" I questioned as I spun her, silently thanking my mother for the dance lessons she forced upon me as I child.

"I would not say terrible, however since it has been quite a while since I danced with someone like this, I haven't much to compare to."

I laughed; I couldn't help it. "You are utterly charming." The music came to an end, but I was reluctant to let her leave my arms. Another soft tune kicked up, and when she did not step out of my embrace, I steered us into a far corner and swayed with the music.

"I thought you said one dance."

Any confidence that I had built up within the bars of the previous song seemed to deflate, and I made to step back when she frowned.

"I'm sorry. Here you are being all nice and handsome, and I'm being prickly."

She thinks I'm handsome?

A blush reddened my cheek. "I must admit, was it not for the shield of darkness, I would not have found the courage to ask such a striking girl like yourself to dance. I am, as my friends would say, ravaged by a terrible affliction called shyness."

She studied me for a moment, her nose twitching in quite an adorable way, and I reminded myself not to speak those words to my friends, for I would incur an unmerciful amount of teasing.

"You don't seem so shy to me."

A strand of hair escaped from behind her ear, and without thinking, I reached out to tuck it behind her ear once more, my fingers grazing her cheek, just under the curl of her mask, her intake of breath sent a jolt throughout my body. She chewed on her bottom lip, and my eyes focused on her lips. They looked so soft, so kissable, that I felt inclined to let myself indulge in a kiss that might or might not have ended with a smack to my face.

I leaned in, my fingers still on her cheek as I said, "Tell me, M'Lady. What would you wish for in this world, if you only had one wish?"

Her eyes contained a sense of relentless certainty as she held my gaze, the entire universe standing still as I waited for her answer, an answer I felt myself rather eager to grant. A smile curled over her lips, and my heart seemed to skip a beat as she said the words that sent me down the path contemplating that I had found the person I was meant to fall in love with.

"Freedom," she whispered as if she daren't say the words out loud. "I wish that I was free."

chapter
ten
rowan

THE MOMENT THE WORDS LEFT MY LIPS, I CURSED MYSELF for being compelled to answer the handsome stranger's question. His eyes, glacier blue against ice white, widened for a moment in surprise, and I felt my cheeks heat. His lips curved into a smile as he leaned closer to me.

"Freedom for oneself is always an admirable wish."

"It's stupid."

"Not at all," he replied, a sense of sadness in his tone. "We are all shackled by some obligation or another. Freedom sounds like a nice adventure."

I lifted my gaze up, and magic thrummed in the air. For a moment, I could see nothing but him, the entire room vanishing as I longed for nothing more than to press my lips against his and see what is was like for a boy to kiss me because he wanted to kiss *me*, not Rowan Cambridge, the future monarch of the Cambridge coven.

Just as the boy with the ice in his eyes leaned in, as if he meant to kiss me, my breath caught. If it was possible for my heart to burst out of my chest, then at that exact second, I felt it would do just that. Then, a voice sounded to my right that made bile creep up my throat.

"I think it's about time the lady dances with her betrothed."

My lips curled into a snarl, and disappointment coiled in my stomach. My blue-eyed stranger glanced from me to Paris, the same disappointment all over his face. I moved to give him some excuse, to tell him that this was why I longed so much to be free, but I could see understanding in his eyes.

Instead of answering Paris, my dance partner took a step back, grasped my hand, and raised it to his lips. A tinge raced through me as the warmth of his lips pressed against my skin. His eyes held mine for a moment more before he gave me a smile that had a muscle in Paris' jaw ticking in annoyance.

"Perhaps we will have the chance to dance again before the party ends."

"Perhaps." I returned his smile, hoping that I would get the chance to see him again, our dance cut tragically short by Paris.

I stood watching as the stranger nodded briefly to Paris, turned on his heel and was lost to the crowd a bare heartbeat later. Spinning on Paris, I hissed as he grabbed my wrists and yanked me closer into him.

"How dare you dance with another like that. You are mine, Rowan, and I do not share what is mine."

I tried to pull my hands free of him, aware that we were attracting attention from the revelers. When that didn't work, I inched closer, and when I was a mere inch from his face, I said, "Take your hands off me, Paris, or so help me gods, you will not awaken in the morning."

Grinning smugly, Paris said, "You won't kill me, Rowan. If you had that killer instinct, then your mother would have chosen someone softer for you than me."

I snicker, finally yanking my now sore wrists from Paris' grasp. "I don't have to get my hands dirty, Paris. How much ale have you been slugging back tonight? A gold coin or two to some poor serving girl, and a vial of poison ends up in your drink. Or there's one of the scorned lovers who are sick of seeing girls coming from your room. It would not take much for Emilee to convince them that a garrote to the throat is what's best for you."

Leaning in as if I meant to press a kiss to his cheek, I whisper into his ear, "Or maybe I just haven't unleashed that killer instinct in me, Paris. You've seen me hunt. You know what I can do with a blade. It would give me some real satisfaction to gut you like I'd gut a boar."

As he made to grab for me again, Auggie stepped up to Paris. My hand itched to smack the brute across his face. Auggie glared at Paris, a look that said he had better not start anything he wasn't willing to finish. The two men continued to stare at each other until Paris swore and gave us his back, retreating from view.

I let loose a sigh of relief and thanked Auggie for his assistance. He held out his hand, and the next thing I knew, I was being whirled around the dance floor, laughter rumbling from my throat, and my altercation with Paris all but forgotten.

After a dance or two, Auggie pulled me off to the side. His face was littered with concern, and I gave him a small smile.

"Will your mother really make you marry that clown?"

"Unless I can kill him before my twentieth birthday. I have three years to plan it."

Auggie dropped a hand to my shoulder. "You need

any help with that, you come ask me. I know some people."

With a chuckle at the seriousness in his tone, I knew he meant it, but I tried to persuade him otherwise. If Auggie helped me in any way, Mother would lay waste to Saor, and despite being here for only a short while, I was becoming enamored with the place.

Placing my hand over Auggie's on my shoulder, I nodded and said, "I don't plan on marrying Paris, but it is my task to complete. I would not risk your home for anything. Mother needs me alive; you all, not so much."

Auggie's face darkened, a steely resolve in his features. "You get into trouble, you come to me. If you wanted to run, sweet Rowan, then I would do everything in my power to aid you. I promise you that."

I knew he meant it, felt the magic in his vow even if he had none of his own. A vow made was magic in itself and not easily broken. My throat thickened as I felt pressure build up, my eyes watered slightly, and I cursed myself for my weakness. I was so tempted to take him up on his offer, gods be damned of the consequences.

Then, an image of Saor filled my mind, laid to waste by mother's wrath, bodies splayed out and the snow-covered streets stained in the blood of innocent bystanders. As the only heir, mother would move heaven and earth to locate me, and then lock me inside until I ascended the throne. I could not stand being held captive, whether by my crown or by my mother.

A crushing amount of anxiety flooded my brain, and I struggled to catch my breath.

"I need some air," I managed to grunt out, ignoring Auggie's expression of concern as I all but bolted across the dance floor, bypassing Emilee when I caught sight of an open door and slipped out through it, stepping into a winter wonderland trapped on a balcony.

Snow blanketed the ground, continuing to fall in a steady pace. The chill crept up my spine, reminding me that I was indeed alive. Glancing at the wonderous view before me of Saor, the frosted houses of those living within this small, but vast village glistening in the moonlight, like light reflecting off glass. From city boundary to city boundary, white clung to the ground, to house, to this balcony for dear life. I held out my hands, gathering the snowflakes in my palm, relishing the iciness that burnt my skin. My breath blew out, and it almost iced in front of my face. I shivered, wishing I had a coat to shield me from the elements, but I loathed to step back inside and away from this quiet beauty.

"It is quite a sight to behold, is it not?"

I jumped as the voice sounded behind me, my small snowball ready to take aim as my heart pounded. My gorgeous dance partner held up his hands in apology. His back was to the wall of the house, one leg resting on the leg of rail curving around the balcony, the other dangling off the ledge. Against the backdrop of snow, his eyes seemed so much bluer, more striking, his hair dampened by snowflakes.

"I'm sorry I startled you."

"That's ok. I just was not expecting anyone to be as mad as me and brave the snow."

I shivered under the intensity of his gaze, and he darted up out of his sitting position, stripped off his suit jacket, and walked over to drape it over my shoulders. When I tried to reassure him that I wasn't entirely cold, and that I did not want to be accountable if he froze to death, he simply grinned and draped his warm jacket over my shoulders.

"My blood runs unusually hot. I barely even feel it."

I had to believe him, for the jacket was toasty warm and I snuggled into it, his scent swirling around me, like the ocean on a cold day. I leaned on the edge of the balcony railing, peering out at the vastness of snow, my companion doing the same. Our elbows grazed each other's, the touch almost scalding.

"It's so …" he muttered, hesitating as if trying to find the right word to say, "white."

A giggle slipped out, and I clasped a hand over my mouth. I was not the type of girl who giggled at strange men, even if they were devastatingly handsome.

"It's snow," I stated, laughter evident in my voice as I teased him. "It's supposed to be white."

With his eyes full of wonder, he inclined his head to look at me. "I grew up in the desert. I don't know much of weather, let alone snow."

My heart sank as I considered he might be part of the rival coven, living on the outskirts of the infamous Montgomery fortress. Closing my eyes, I summoned my own magic, felt it waken as it thrummed through my veins. Opening my eyes, I latched onto his aura, a bright burst of sunshine with hints of peaceful turquoise. This boy did not have a bad bone in his body, according to his aura. He pulsed with life, with goodness. And I wanted to soak myself in it.

"Ro?"

I blinked, forcing my magic down, gulping in a breath of ice-cold air that burnt my lungs.

"I'm sorry. Did you say something?"

His smile made my insides flip as a faint blush crept from his neck to his cheeks. It was adorable. He fidgeted with the collar of his shirt as he said for the second time.

"What brings you out here for some quiet reflection?"

Running my fingers through my curls, I blow out a breath. "Parties are not my kind of thing."

"Mine either," he replied with a grin. Talking a clump of snow from the rail, he held it in the palm of his left hand and placed his right hand over it. While his hand hovered, I felt his magic pulse, strong and confident, as the snow in his palm began to move, the flakes gliding until they formed into the shape of a horse. He held onto it for a moment, then handed it to me.

"I can't stop it from melting, but it is rather pretty, if I do say so myself."

Not even bothering to laugh at him, I studied the snow horse, grazing it with my finger, touching cold snow. I set it down on the railing and said, "It's beautiful."

"But not as beautiful as you."

I laughed, and the boy looked at me like I'm daft. I shake my head. "I am far from beautiful but thank you."

He frowned, staring at me with intent. "Why would you say that?"

Running my finger down the snow horse, I considered my answer before I replied, "I grew up surrounded by beautiful people. My best friend, my mother, even that ass who thinks I'm going to marry him. Compared to them, I am quite ordinary."

"My two best friends, I have always felt that I walked in their shadow. Two extraordinary people that I would happily take a sword for. I've always believed that having beauty on the outside counts for nothing, if you are not beautiful on the inside also. A kind heart, a relentless spirit, a longing for more from life. Some of the most striking people I have met have been so ugly on the inside, it is hard for them to be considered beautiful. If you are ugly inside, for whatever reason, then you cannot be beautiful on the outside."

My heart melted at his words, and I believed he meant everything he said. I fully comprehended that he saw past a person's face and saw the beauty in their souls. And the way he was looking at me had me feeling like I was the most beautiful girl in his world.

"I am not that type of girl, the one that boys fall in love with," I said, my voice hushed, but he heard me.

"I doubt that very much."

I brushed off my sudden sadness with a forced laugh and nudged him with my shoulder. "I bet, in whatever village you come from, with words spoken like silk, you have left a slew of broken hearts in your wake."

"I am not the type of boy that girls fall in love with."

He gave me back my words, and I heard the sadness in his tone. From his aura, this boy was so full of life and love that it seemed a shame he did not have someone to return that love. I was starting to get a clearer picture of who this boy, the one whose name I had yet to learn, really was.

A boy who voiced his opinion, thought little of himself and more of those he held within his heart. Fiercely loyal, willing to put others before himself. He longed for someone to call his, someone who wanted him for him. And wasn't that what I secretly hoped for also? Nobody, not even Emilee, knew that when I closed my eyes, I pictured a future where I roamed the forest, came home to my cabin in the woods, a warm fire, and a man who loved me, not my crown.

And while I might have been considering Emilee's idea of fun while I was here and away from mother's scrutiny, this handsome stranger was not a one-night stand kind of person. He was someone who, when he did find someone worthy of his love, would love so fiercely it would shatter the world.

I had prided myself for keeping my heart walled for years, afraid that I or someone

else would get hurt if I let myself love. My destiny was not my own. And here I was falling for someone who thought girls would not fall in love with him.

"I don't even know your name, and I've made you all melancholy."

He held out his hand, which I took, his touch a brand against my flesh.

"Hi, I'm Jules. Nice to meet you, Ro."

I made to correct him, but revealing my full name would also reveal my true identity. So, I returned his smile and said, "It's nice to meet you too, Jules."

The music struck up rather loudly, the melody flowing out through the crack in the open door. Jules, with my hand still in his, pulled me upright, as snow began to drift down from the navy skyline in earnest. His hands drifted down to my waist, and I instinctively wrapped my arms around his neck, my head resting against his chest. I could hear the thrum of his heartbeat against my ear.

Without another word, we swayed in time with the music, lost in our own little snow-covered world, and I knew, deep in the fibers of my being, that after tonight, after meeting Jules, I would not be the same again. It was silly, to feel like I had met someone I would not forget, considering I barely knew him. But sometimes, our hearts simply need someone to see us for who we are really are to ignite into flames.

"I could stay like this, with you, for an eternity."

His words echoed my own thoughts, and my heart almost burst, this invisible thread that seemed to be weaving its way from my heart to his, tightening even as we danced. At sixteen years old, this was the first time, besides Emilee, that someone had made me feel like I was worthy of love, of belonging.

I shuddered at the fickle thought, that I was falling in love with someone I barely knew, because he has showered me with compliments and insights. We, this, could never be, and I could not love Jules, no matter how much my entire being was screaming at me that I could.

And yet, I would leave in the next two days, and I would probably never see him again, for he lived in the territory belonging to my mortal enemy, the person who wanted my head on a silver platter and my kingdom for his own. I wanted to believe that we could have something, secret meetings maybe with Auggie's help. Nothing could compare to the way that I felt, in this moment, wrapped in Jules' arms, safe and wanted.

Or so I thought.

Just as I was under the assumption that I could not feel any more emotion inside me than in that moment, Jules lifted a hand from my hip, placed one finger so that it rested just under my chin, and angled my head so that I looked straight into his glacier eyes. I held my breath, anticipation flooding me.

And then Jules did the simplest thing in the world.

He leaned in and kissed me.
    And the world cracked open.

chapter eleven
julian

HER LIPS WERE PETALS OF FLAME AGAINST THE ICY fingers of her touch, her fingertips digging into my neck as she pulled me closer. My hand snaked up and gripped the sides of her face, terrified that she would see sense and pull away from me. We kissed under the stars until neither of us could breathe. She kissed like she was drowning, and I was her air. When we broke apart, my hands still firmly on the sides of her face, we both gasped for air.

I pressed my lips quickly to hers again, wondering where in all that was holy had I plucked the courage to kiss this amazing girl. I felt like I was weightless, as if the power in a single kiss could grant me the ability to fly. In all of my years, this was why I had never felt the slightest thing for anyone else. Because sometimes, it took a soul deep connection to make you realize what you wanted in life.

When she lowered her lashes, then opened them again slowly, I could see the vulnerability in her eyes. I opened my mouth, my fingers still holding her face, prepared to tell her just how special I thought she was, when the door to the balcony swung open.

We both jumped apart and immediately I missed touching her. I glanced at Ro, snowflakes tangled in her black curls, her lips kiss swollen, and an expression on her face that said she felt exactly the same way as I did. She pressed two of her fingers to her lips and looked at me with a hunger that made my heart stop.

"I've been looking for you everywhere! What are you doing all alone in the sno-"

The Cambridge heir burst our little bubble with a pop, and Ro almost instantly stiffened in a manner that had me bite back a snarl at the interruption. Although she had just spotted me standing there, her mouth formed an o and she peered at Ro in surprise, a gigantic grin spreading across her face.

"Oh, I didn't mean to interrupt. I was beginning to worry."

I was growing to hate this girl, this person who I may have to wage war against, yet I never detested her more than in that moment, when Ro, the girl who thought boys could not fall in love with her, had begun to creep inside my heart and warm it more than the midday sun ever could. A blush colored her pale cheeks as she glanced at me once more and made to leave.

"Wait," I begged, absolutely terrified that I would never see her again. "Will I see you again?"

The Cambridge heir looked from me to Ro, and Ro grabbed her hand and headed for the door. As she shoved my mortal enemy through the door, Ro paused, shrugging my jacket from her shoulders, the saddest smile toying with her lips. I took a step forward, and she held up a hand to stop me, folding my jacket and placing it on the stone rail beside the door.

"Thank you for tonight. I do hope we bump into each other again. Goodbye, Jules."

And then she was gone, the air sucking from my lungs as she disappeared from sight. I stumbled over to the door and grabbed my jacket. As I crossed the threshold, my eyes scanned the darkness until I caught a glimpse of her snow drenched hair. I was not ready to say goodbye to her. It was as if, with the kiss we had shared and our identities hidden by our masks, some ancient magic had bound us together. I mourned the loss of her, like I had known her a lifetime, and had lost my only tether to this world.

It was as if I had found my soulmate in a single moment, when we first said hello, and a familiar feeling that we had said hello before. It was as though, in our first and possible our last kiss, our lips met and our souls had whispered welcome home.

I made to follow her, beg of her to see me again, when Toby stepped into my path, blocking my view. When I moved him out of my way, Ro was gone. There was a pain in my chest that I couldn't explain. Toby stared at me, wondering what had me in such a state.

"Jules, you okay?"

"I think I've just fallen in love."

My friend chortled, halting suddenly when he took in my serious expression. I touched my finger to my lips, ignoring the alarm darkening Toby's eyes. Every single instinct in my body was pleading with me to go after my winter girl. It was like I could feel her moving further and further away from me, and I didn't like it one bit.

"Jules, don't be stupid. One kiss does not make you fall in love with someone. Believe me."

Even though I was curious to delve deeper into

Toby's statement, I couldn't rest right now. Suddenly, the party lost all appeal, and I needed to get out of there. I made a beeline for the doors we had come through, when Ashbridge happened to walk by.

"Leaving so soon, gents?"

"I think the journey has tired out our prince."

I glared at Toby but was taken aback when Ashbridge spoke again.

"Or is it that the party has lost interest for him, considering his beautiful dance partner has also fled the party?"

"What can you tell me about her?"

Toby blinked at the almost pleading tone in my voice, but Ashbridge was possibly the only hope of seeing Ro again, and I was not proud enough to not beg.

Ashbridge sighed, pity in his eyes as he clasped me on the shoulder. "It would be in your best interest to forget about the girl, Julian. I may not be able to see into the future, but all I can see is heartache and misery there. This is not the girl you are destined to be with."

Unwilling to listen to the man's words, I brushed off his hand, feeling my magic stirring. "Don't patronize me, Ashbridge. You do not know me well enough to give me unwanted advice."

I strode past him, bumping him slightly as I went with Toby on my heels. We made our way in silence back the way we had come, and I took the steps two at a time until we were in our rooms. I ripped off my mask and tossed it aside, along with my jacket, wishing that I had been able to see all of Ro, traced the ridges of her features without the blasted mask impeding me. I headed straight for the window, in the hope my winter girl would be in the garden again, but all that I could see was a blanket of snow.

"Jules, what's with you? I know it's been a long time since you've had a kiss, but this is bordering on obsession. It's rather creepy."

I clasp my hands behind my back and continue to stare out at the snow-covered city. "I can't explain it Toby, but this girl is different. It was as if she were magic herself, and she's caught me in her spell. The thought of never seeing her again, it's enough to bring me to my knees. Have you ever felt that someone knows you better than yourself, even if you hardly know each other at all?"

Toby didn't answer my question, simply stated facts that I did not want to hear. "Does it really matter, Jules? I mean, I'm all for losing yourself in a woman or two, but this girl, she's part of the Cambridge coven. There cannot be a future for you and her."

By gods, I knew he was right, but I did not want him to be.

"And besides, while you were kissing a pretty girl in the snow, I was doing my job and getting information. This magic you felt from the girl, it's quite possible that you were feeling her specific magic. The rumor circulating was that the Cambridge heir, whose magic no one seemed to know about, had brought her maiden of persuasion with her. With the very words spoken from her lips, she could make you drive your own sword into your chest with a smile on your face."

I shook my head, reluctant to believe that what we had shared, what I had felt, was a trick of the mind. The girl who told me she longed to be free would not shackle someone else's free will. The girl who kissed me until we were breathless and clung to my neck was not a girl who would inflict that type of violation on me.

"Jules, she might just have put the whammy on you, just a little."

"Stop."

"Be reasonable, Jules." Toby demanded, his voice a growl. "This is not a fairy-tale. The prince doesn't always get the girl. The girl isn't always wholesome and pure. The girl might just be a little vicious bitch who is trying to mess with your head. You do not fall in love with someone you've known for barely an hour."

At his defamation of Ro's character, I whirled around and lashed out with my hand and my magic, holding Toby to the nearest wall using the air in the room. My friend's eyes widened in surprise as I rescinded my magic and he dropped to the ground.

I glanced at my hands, horrified, for I had never used my magic against Toby in anger before. Perhaps his statement held some weight. Had the siren gotten into my head and convinced me that I could love her? Could she use magic like that to incite such anger when someone spoke against her?

"I'm sorry, Toby."

Toby got to his feet, shaking his head. "If you were not my brother in every way but blood, I would punch you in your handsome face for that. Maybe it would knock some sense into you, because at this moment, Jules, you are acting like you are out of your mind."

I slumped down into the nearest chair, scrubbing my face with my hands, feeling utterly exhausted all of a sudden. Closing my eyes, I tried to calm my racing mind. I heard Toby fumble with a bottle and the clink of glasses.

A few minutes later, there was a tap to my shoulder, and I opened my eyes to Toby holding a tumbler out to me.

I muttered my thanks and grasped the cup without drinking. Toby flopped down on the loveseat by the fire. He motioned with his head as the fire had begun to dwindle. I sighed, holding out my hand and focusing on the embers that still sparked, urging them to ignite. Flames burst into the fireplace, and Toby sighed.

"Now, that's a valid use of your magical prowess."

I took a gulp of my drink, relishing the burn in the back of my throat. I kicked off my shoes and rolled up the sleeves of my shirt. We sat in a comfortable silence for an age with only the crackling of the fire to be heard. It was surprising, also, not to hear anything from the party going on several floors below us. Bloody murder could be taking place, and we would be oblivious.

It was then I realized that we had not seen sight nor sound of Mercy since we initially arrived at the party. The clock struck midnight, and I looked at Tobias. He was staring at the shadows around the room, as if he expected Mercy to pop into existence at any second.

"Mercy will be fine. He always is."

My words did little to reassure him, but as I tried and failed to push thoughts of Ro to the back of my mind, I wondered what it was that had Toby in such a tizzy. I found it hard to grasp that his actions might be some sort of romantic jealousy, because I would have seen it before, right? I would have noticed if my womanizing best friend had feelings for my other best friend surely.

I almost laughed at the thought of Toby having feelings for Mercy. My mind was awash with romantic notions tonight, and I wished I could banish them from my mind. I gulped down the rest of my drink, closing my eyes as I rested the tumbler on my knee.

I was assaulted by images of my dead coven members at my feet, my sword drenched in the blood of my enemies. I tried to open my eyes, but I forced myself to watch.

Blood dripped from my sword as I yelled another order to fight through the resistance. I could see the silver of Mercy's hair as he slashed and struck, blood spraying into the snow. Innocent bystanders screamed and raced through the city trying to escape the bloodshed. I watched as Toby lashed out with twin blades, ripping intestines from long gashes, the victims clutching their stomachs in an attempt to prevent their deaths.

My eyes wandered across the battlefield. She was as beautiful now as she had been the first time I had seen her dancing in the snow. Now she danced a different dance, one with blood and death. Our eyes clashed against the swelling storm, her face aged about a decade, but still the winter girl who had taken my heart and ripped out my capacity to love.

"Kill the king!" she roared, and the Cambridge soldiers obeyed her. I wanted to be the one to kill her, I wanted her to feel what I felt, to realize that she had marked herself for death when she had made me believe that I could love her.

She came at me, but not before she ran her sword through Toby from behind, as he battled two of her men. Toby hit the snow with a thud, his eyes wide in shock. But I had little time to mourn my friend. Mercy screamed, his blade causing havoc on the battlefield. I stepped over the array of bodies until we stood the closest we had stood in each other's presence in years. It seemed appropriate that it was here in Saor, where we had first met, where we shared our first kiss, on winter solstice, surrounded by snow, where she would meet her demise.

And it was only fitting that her death came at my hands.

Her raven hair was braided off to the side, her face pale, her rose colored lips as enticing now as they were back when we were teens. Her nose was red from the cold, her face streaked with blood. Standing in the snow, she looked every bit the warrior princess and as beautiful as I remembered.

"It's a good day to die." She grinned, wiping my friend's blood into the snow.

I dug my blade into the frozen ground and let my magic surge to the forefront. I had spent years, decades, dreaming of exacting my revenge, and honing my magic. Summoning the snow under my control, I formed a wall of ice around us. It was impenetrable, and the soldiers would watch as I crushed her with the air already in her lungs.

She lunged for me, but I was stronger than she was. With a smile on my face, I struck out, grasping hold of the air in her lungs and commanding it from her. She clutched her chest, and I delighted in her terror.

"Please, Julian. I love you. Don't you love me too?"

"The boy you loved is dead. The girl he loved will soon join him."

She held my gaze for a moment, and for a brief heartbeat, in those eyes of oak, I saw the girl I had once loved. And with a wave of my hand, I snapped her neck.

I darted from my chair with a yelp, the glass that had been resting on my knee smashing as it hit the ground. I could taste the copper of blood on my tongue, could smell it in the air. I glanced at my hands, relief flooding me at their lack of bloodstain. What the hell had just happened to me? For I believed that it was no mere dream that I had envisioned.

"Bad dream?"

I turned to see Tobias watching me, the flames of the

fire having almost died out.

"I dreamed that you died, and I couldn't stop it."

"Well that's rather cheerful, isn't it? Did I die well?"

"It was a warrior's death."

Lifting his empty tumbler in a toast, my friend grinned. "Then I died happy. They will tell tales of my bravery and my handsomeness."

"And perhaps your humility."

"That too, but mostly of my handsomeness."

It felt wrong to laugh after the horrors I had dreamt. I never wanted to turn into the man who could snap someone's neck in cold resolution without any resemblance of emotion. That man was not someone I ever wanted to see staring back at me in the mirror.

"Mercy still hasn't come back."

"He will. He probably already has. Have you checked his room?"

Toby nodded and rolled the tumbler between his hands. "Yeah, he hasn't been back. And it's almost morning."

I glanced out, and sure enough, the sun had crept into the sky whilst I had been dreaming of death and blood. I wanted to reassure Toby that our friend would be more than okay, but with the uneasy dread in my stomach, I wasn't certain I could be sure of anything in that moment.

"The snow fell harder overnight. One of the servants came by a while ago and said that the doors to the city had been wedged shut by the storm. We will have to wait until the snow melts or can be cleared away from the gates before we can leave. We'll want to make sure the horses will be able to travel anyway. So, it looks like we are stuck here for another day or two."

I hid my smile from Toby, because to me, being

snowed in for another few days did not sound like the worst thing in the world.

chapter twelve
rowan

I DREAMT OF BLOOD AND WAR LAST NIGHT. I IMAGINED A battlefield where the mysterious boy with the bottomless blue eyes stood across the way from me, those blue eyes behind the mask that had once twinkled, now deep and lifeless. I saw myself as a warrior queen, willing to strike down those who opposed her, who valued her people and the lives of her coven. But deep inside, my heart was torn in two. Love for the boy I remembered and hatred for the king who stood against me.

Divided by a blanket of snow, the remembrance of any sentimentality was washed away by the blood that stained the frosted battlefield. I touched my cheek, felt the scar tissue, and knew for certain that Jules had been the one to do it. He regarded me with a cold indifference, and any warmth we had shared had long since vanished. With the wave of his hand, he snapped my neck.

I came awake clutching my throat, gasping for air as if I could feel the caress of death upon my soul. Pulling my knees to my chest, I wrapped my arms around my legs and closed my eyes. But all I could see was the unrepentant smile of the man who murdered me.

It did not come as a surprise that I would dream such horrid dreams when I met a boy who made me feel alive for the first time ever. When Jules had kissed me, it felt as if my entire being had been woken up, as if until that moment when our lips met, I had been living in a stasis and not surely living until that moment. When he had asked if he would see me again, I wanted so very much to tell him yes, allowing the words to slip from my mouth and telling him how much I yearned to see him again.

I was not that girl; the girl who swooned over a boy and forgot herself.

A knock sounded twice on my door, and Emilee strode in, her eyes worried and her features strained. She flopped down on the bed on her stomach beside me, and I waited for her to speak.

"Your mother is going to kill me!"

"Perhaps. But for what reason this time?"

Clicking her tongue at my sarcasm, Emilee rested her chin in her hands as she looked at me. "I failed to get the item she asked of me. When I finally located it, the scroll was already gone."

Running my fingers through my hair, I wondered what scroll would be so important that my mother would send us on this mission. Although I was extremely curious, I hesitated in asking Emilee to tell me more, for she would have to be the one to divulge any information to me. I would not please my mother by being any way interested in her political games.

In a couple of hours, we would leave this place, and my chest ached at the very thought. I rubbed my hand over my heart and glanced down at my friend.

"Why do I feel there is more to that scowl than a lost

scroll."

Blowing a hair from her face, Emilee replied, "The snowstorm grew worse while you were snoring all day. We cannot leave Saor until the snow stops falling, and they can clear the gate. Could be a day or two, at least that's what Auggie said this morning when he knocked."

I leapt from the bed and threw the heavy curtains open. Sure enough, a crisp, clean blanket of white stood before me. The town was eerily quiet, not a soul wandered around as dusk began to creep in. I couldn't believe that I had slept all day and missed the beauty before me.

Against the backdrop of a navy sky, stars began to blink into view, flakes of snow still journeying to the already snow laden ground. Oh, I longed to cast open the window and dive right into the snow. One of my only memories of my father was when he would tell me tales of heroes and monsters and how, after one rather eventful snowfall, both the hero and the monster halted their war to play amongst snow.

Laughing at my father's tale, a cynical soul even back then, my mother's warnings of blood and death much more vivid to a child. But my father had claimed that his story was true, as he kissed my forehead and told me that mother nature could put a stop to any war, any disease, any bloodshed. Then he told me that I was like mother nature, wild and uncontainable, and he believed I had within me the ability to be a hero, to halt a war.

My mind wandered back to my dream, and I shivered. Eager to cast aside thoughts of death, I peered over my shoulder at Emilee who groaned.

"When you look at me like that, I know trouble is afoot."

"You are under no obligation to join me in trouble. Maybe, you are better off pretending that you know nothing of my plans. Plausible deniability, as they say."

Emilee sat up as she sighed. "What are you planning, Rowan? Are you going to pop off to see the desert boy who kissed you under the stars?"

I faced away from Emilee, hiding my smile. If we were to be stuck here for another day or two, what was the harm in seeing him again. An invisible thread was pushing me to see him again, all of him, the boy without the mask. In the light of day, or dusk, would his blue eyes twinkle like the stars?

Brushing off Emilee's exaggerated sighs, I pulled my hair into a braid, before dressing in my usual black pants and a long-sleeved top. I was slipping my feet into my boots when Emilee said, "I'm not going to be able to stop you, am I?"

Pausing as I laced up my boots, I lifted my gaze to meet hers. "Would you try and stop me? I cannot explain what is going on, but for the first time in my life, I feel like someone chose me for me, not for a silly title. If I am to face life married to a man I despise, in a role I want no part of, would you, my dearest and only friend, deny me the chance to experience life?"

Emilee shook her head. "I just do not wish to see you hurt."

Having finished lacing up my boots, I sheathed a dagger into a slot in the boot. "I can look after myself."

"There are other ways to be hurt that are not physical."

I paused, hating the sound of sadness etched in her tone, battling with the urge to protect Emilee, and my need to see Jules again, even if it was for one last time.

"Please be careful, Rowan. If we cannot leave, that means the Montgomery heir is stuck here too. I do not wish to see your blood staining the snow."

"Neither do I. Now, if Paris comes a wandering, please tell him that I am asleep."

Grabbing my cloak, I tossed it over my shoulders before settling the hood in place. I opened the hinge on the window and swung it open, my foot already braced to hoist myself up.

"By the gods, Rowan. Use the front door at least!"

I wink over my shoulder at my best friend. "Where would be the fun in that?"

Launching myself up, I grip the sides of the window, the frigid air slapping across my face, my breath almost freezing in front of me as I glance at the distance for me to drop. It was only two floors down. Considering I had dropped from higher heights, the drop did not frighten me in the slightest. I heard Emilee slide from the bed behind me, and I stepped out into nothing.

As I freefell from the window, adrenaline rushed through me, my body light. I felt as if I could soar. It was over too quickly, and I bent my knees ready to hit the snow. I landed with a soft thud, the snow surprisingly solid under my feet. I braced a hand out in front of me to prevent from tipping over. The sharp artic bite of cold instantly chilled my fingers, and I brushed the snow off my pants.

Peering upward, I saw Emilee shake her head as she closed the window with a quiet snick. A smile crept across my face as I began to traipse through the snow, my movements silent in this winter wonderland. I rounded a corner, ducking into the shadows as two Saor soldiers came into view, their teeth chattering with the cold. Suppressing a chuckle, I wondered how the inhabitants of Saor coped with the variable weather. It was as if they experienced all the seasons in one day, yet did not know how to deal with a sudden change in the weather.

Once the soldiers ambled out of view, their complaining carrying across the wind, I remained in the shadows and began to wonder if I had made the right decision. Would my boy of mystery still want to see me again? How would he react to me just showing up at his window?

A little voice in the back of my mind urged me on, so I closed my eyes and thought of the boy with the blue eyes and sunny aura. I concentrated on his aura and his aura alone. When I opened my eyes, the pull became almost painful, my stomach clenching at the need to track down the object of my magic.

I followed the pull, clinging to the shadows and avoiding being seen until I was standing in the garden I had danced in on my first night in Saor. The fountain was still frozen over, icicles glinting against the moonlight. The evidence of my previous visit had vanished under a blanket of snow. The feeling that someone had watched me that night made sense now, for I was almost certain that Jules had been watching me.

My eyes wandered up the wall, until I could see Jules' aura inside the building. Bright, and yellow, it called out to me like no other, my magic almost screaming at me to finish the hunt. The pull would not stop until I laid hands on my target, the longer I left it, the worse the pain would be.

Underneath the window, a trellis crept up the wall,

vines of ivy weaving in and out of the wood. I cupped my hands over my mouth and breathed out to try and put some heat into them. My heart began to beat a steady rhythm against my chest as I placed a booted foot on the end of the trellis, my cold hands less painful than the pit of magic in my stomach.

Creeping up the wall, I managed a quick incline, resting my butt on the window ledge as I considered that I might just be mad enough to knock on his window and beckon him to open it up. The wind whipped my braid against my face as I lifted my head and gave a gentle tap.

Nothing happened, so I tapped again, this time hearing a heavy footfall come toward the window. For a split second, I feared that the Montgomery heir would open the window, pushing me to my death before I could even blink, but as I perched myself on the window ledge, I rolled my shoulders and braced myself for whatever reaction I received.

The window opened, and my breath hitched in my chest. Behind the mask, Jules had been handsome, but now, getting the full view of his features almost made me loosen my grasp and fall. Eyes of molten blue, sun-kissed skin, and hair the color of sand, his lips were pressed together in a frown until his eyes landed on me, and the wind almost got knocked out of me again.

Jules looked at me like I was beautiful, like he saw nothing but me, as if he had been searching for me, and a smile crept over his lips. My heart skipped a beat. I dropped my hood and gave a small smile.

"Hi." As soon as the word left my mouth, I blushed, suddenly unsure of myself.

"Bloody hell, you could have fallen."

I shrugged in response, and he rolled his eyes, holding out his hand. The moment my palm touched his, the pain receded, and I was tugged inside. My feet met solid ground, strong arms pulling me into a warm embrace that I wasn't expecting, but it felt like coming home.

"Not that I am not glad to see you again, but what are you doing here?"

Suddenly feeling foolish, I pulled away from him, glancing at the window. Here I was, thinking that I was living my life, and I had never felt so self-conscious in my life.

As if sensing the change in my personality, Jules cupped my cheek, his thumb caressing it as he said, "I have not stopped thinking about you since I last saw you."

"Me either." I heard myself reply, my words nothing more than a whisper. We stared at each other for what felt like forever until he pressed his lips to my forehead. Heat flushed my face as I rested my hands on the warmth of his skin.

"This is crazy," Jules murmured, but I wasn't sure if he spoke to me or himself.

"Do you want me to go?"

A growl sounded in his throat and I grinned. "I'll take that as a no."

His lips met mine, and the world fell away, until it was just Jules kissing me. Groaning as he pulled away, he traced the outline of my face as if he was seeing me for the very first time, and he was, I guess. We no longer had any masks, we could see each other clearly.

"I never thought I'd see you again."

Stepping back, I smiled. "Thank the gods for the snow."

He chuckled, the sound sending my magic into a spin. "Thank the gods for the snow." He repeated my words back to me and then he said, "You are the most beautiful girl I have ever laid eyes on."

"I bet you say that to all the girls." I laughed, trying to shake off my sudden awkwardness.

He shook his head, stepping in front of me again. "No, believe me, I do not. You have caught me in some sort of spell, and I find myself saying and doing things I wouldn't normally do."

"Is that a good or a bad thing?" I asked, chewing on my bottom lip as his eyes watched my action with hunger in them.

"It's a very good thing."

He kissed me again, and I couldn't help but think this feeling, surely it could not last. All of my doubts were lost in the touch of his lips, the feel of his hands on my skin, and I wanted more, I wanted more with him.

A knock came at his door, and I had unsheathed the dagger before Jules could even blink. He held a finger to his lips as a knock sounded again.

"Jules, you okay in there? I thought I heard something?"

My heart began to race as Jules chuckled and said, "Just me stumbling in the dark, Toby. I'll be out in a moment."

"You sure?"

"Quite certain. Just let me die of embarrassment in private a moment, eh?"

The voice outside boomed with laughter, and we listened as he walked away. I sheathed my blade, Jules arching a brow. "You are full of surprises, aren't you?"

I snorted. "You have no idea."

Jules glanced at the door again, his face torn.

"Go, it's okay."

He took my face in his hands again and kissed me with a quick press of lips. "Tell me you will see me again. Please don't let this be the last time. We owe it to ourselves to find out whatever this thing is between us. Tell me you'll see me again."

The urgency in his voice, the desperate words, made me feel powerful, and just as desperate as he was to see me, I was desperate to cling to this feeling for as long as possible.

"I'll see you again."

The promise in my words seemed to hit us both, magic swirling around us like fireflies. I pressed my lips to the curve of his jaw and made for the window. Once I had clambered up to pause in the frame of the window, I felt the weight of his eyes on me.

"Meet me tomorrow night, just after dusk, in the stables. We won't be interrupted, I promise."

I let a smile tug on my lips, as I began to climb down the trellis, not wanting to give Jules a heart attack by jumping out of the window. When I hit the ground once more, I lifted my eyes to see him staring right back at me.

The world was tilting on its axis, and I feared that after the last few days in Saor, I could never go back to being Rowan Cambridge ever again. And that thought exhilarated me as much as the feel of Jules' lips on mine.

A drop of snow landed on my nose, and I heard the sound of soldiers coming from over my shoulder. Heart full to the brim, I darted across the snow, not caring if anyone saw me. I passed a couple of soldiers, who beckoned for me to stop, but I cast up my hood and raced through the snow. Coming to a stop under the trellis that would take me back to my room, I gulped in breaths of icy air, my lungs constricting under the harsh burn.

There were times in your life when you were glad to be alive, that even the burn of cold breath in your lungs reminded you that you were indeed very much present, and the joy of a boy's kiss could ignite a spark within you that could burn for days. If I went to my death tomorrow, then I would die with a smile on my face, for up until this moment, I wasn't truly alive.

chapter thirteen
julian

As I closed the window and watched my winter girl race through the snow, I fought hard against the niggling voice in the back of my mind. It was screaming at me that whatever divine force had forged this tether between us would crumple it to ruins in a short space of time.

This girl who scaled a wall in the midst of a storm in order to simply pass the time of day, she was a rare diamond that I wanted to keep with me. When Ro disappeared from my field of view, I leaned against the wall, my fingers drifting up to press against my lips. It was almost as if I could feel her lips lingering on mine.

I knew she belonged to a rival coven, but there had been times before where alliances had switched, when those with unique magics were persuaded to join the other side. However, that had never happened when it came to a member of the royal family. Could I explain to my father that I felt braver, stronger, and more myself when I was with her?

Malcolm Montgomery would most likely laugh in my face, mock me over my foolishness, and disparage any sort of relationship that could blossom between us. And I, for one, did not have the luxury of abandoning my title for the faint hope of love.

I would go to my meeting with Ro and drown myself in the sensations of being with her, kissing her, holding her close, and then I would walk away, left with only the ghost of my memories. It did not fail to cross my mind that a spell might have been woven to make me feel as if not seeing her would be worse than not taking my next breath. If there was magic, if this was a spell, Ro could just be a victim of her matriarch's orders as well.

Stretching the muscles in my neck, I reluctantly leave the confines of my bedroom, spotting Toby as I exited. His back was to me, his shadow flickering in unison with the flames. His hands were clasped behind his back as he stared into the fire, as if the flames would reveal answers to which he sought.

"It is unusual for you to brood, my friend. That job is solely reserved for me."

Toby turned his head in my direction. "Since it has been so hard to remove that goofy grin from your kisser the last few days, I felt as if the roles needed to be reversed. It is the only way our friendship works."

I chuckled in response, taking in his appearance, dressed in workout pants and top. When I quirked an eyebrow and motioned to his clothing, Toby grinned and said, "Ashbridge has invited us to train with his unit. He wants to show those with, how did he put it? An unfair magical advantage that even mere Nulls could be fierce warriors."

The idea was ridiculous, but I could fathom why Toby was amused by it. No one within these walls knew that

Toby had no magic and could take down each and every one of Ashbridge's regiment without so much as breaking a sweat.

"Then we must go and show them exactly why the Montgomery witches have the best not-so-secret weapon at their disposal. Failure is not an option, Tobias." I schooled my features and tried to keep a straight face. "The general of my future army cannot lose to mere mortals."

Toby spun to face me, his features brightening as his smile widened. "Then let us give these fools a show. I promise to try and not knock you on your ass, your Highness."

We readied ourselves, dressing in comfortable clothing and waiting patiently for the call to come to lead us down to where we would engage in some sparring. Neither of us mentioned the missing Mercy, but I half expected him to show up when we least expected him to. It always seemed that Mercy, after a particularly tough mission, retreated into himself until he found his way back to us.

Ashbridge himself came to escort us to the training space, not far from the ballroom where I had first encountered Ro. In a way, I was grateful for the distraction, as nervous energy seemed to build up and up until my knee bounced. The small space, where a couple of Ashbridge's unit were already running drills, lacked the intensity of the sun-drenched desert, the solid flooring vastly different from sparring in the sand.

The temperature in the room was rather chilly, since the windows were open with the lick of frost from the outside seeping in. The smell of sweat and steel permeated the air. Surrounding the main floor was an array of seats for viewing. When I took the chair offered to me by Ashbridge, he leaned in and whispered, "I think my soldiers are quite nervous about-facing Tobias. His ruthlessness and accuracy have spread even to Soar. They say that he moves like water."

My lips kicked up as I simply smiled, storing that little titbit for Toby to amuse himself with on our long journey home. But it was Ashbridge's next sentence that caught me by surprise.

"They also say that the future king is no slouch. They say that even when he does not control the entire atmosphere around him, he is a skilled fighter, not one who would linger off the battlefield and allow his soldiers to fight for him."

Resting my hands in my lap, I tilted my head slightly to get a better look at Ashbridge. His words seemed as if he was fishing for something, as if testing me with a single statement. I considered my response, asking myself if his statement was true. Would I lead instead of order?

"It is one thing to order men and women into battle for you, but striding into battle beside them forges a loyalty that cannot be broken. To die beside your soldiers is a worthy death. To watch as your soldiers die all around you and then toast their sacrifice, that does not make someone a king."

My answer seemed to surprise Ashbridge, for he blinked, then nodded, as if my words had assured him that I was not a monster… considering who my father was.

"Jules!"

My head snapped up as I heard Toby calling my name, heard the sing of a blade coming toward me. There was a collective gasp among those who had gathered in the training space. The blade came right at me, but I was prepared for it. Reaching out with my magic, I curved an invisible hand around the hilt of the weapon, slowed the motion in which it travelled toward me, and stood up slowly, controlling the movement until the hilt was firmly grasped in my hand.

I grinned, nodding to Ashbridge as I strode over to Toby, rotating my wrist so the blade would twist and twirl. Toby had picked up two smaller swords and winked at me. Just like back in the sands, Toby and I would put on a show fit for a royal banquet.

Without warning, Toby struck out with one of the blades, which I quickly blocked. Tucking one arm behind my back, I grinned at Toby. "You want fair and square, or does anything go?"

"Let's go fair and square. No need to use magic when we can impress them without it."

We smirked at each other, backing into the center of the room, aware that the entire room had focused on us and watched with bated breath. We must have looked a sight, the boy who would be king and his general, grinning at each other as we tipped our blades together. Then, we moved.

We did not hold back, our swords clashing like thunder in the small room. With every strike that Toby aimed at me, I blocked and struck out with my own blade, barely giving him a moment before I reacted. Toby did indeed move like water, flowing and swaying against my attacks. Toby kicked out with his right foot and caught me in the stomach. I stumbled back, digging the sword into the ground to steady myself, but I looked at Toby with mischief in my eyes.

Those who watched us seemed utterly confused at how

I could let Toby strike me, and despite them supposedly not knowing who I was, I had an idea that rumors began to circle about our identities.

As I rested my hand on the hilt of the blade, Toby held my gaze and rolled his eyes, as if the crowd watching was already boring him. We circled each other, neither of us relenting to the other. We knew each other's tells, we knew every bluff, ever fake inclination, every weakness. As Toby feigned with his right, I caught his left with my sword, causing him to drop his second blade.

Kicking the sword up, I clutched the twin blades, swirling as Toby came at me. We struck, we dodged, we had near misses that had people gasping, but in the end, Toby was always going to beat me at one-to-one combat. Without my magic, I was no match for a relentless Toby. He managed to distract me for a second by uttering that there was a girl watching me.

When I turned to look at the empty space, Toby kicked out, much like he did a couple of days ago in the sand, and I hit the ground hard, hard enough that it knocked the wind from me. My sword clattered to the ground, and I chuckled.

The entire room applauded, soldiers standing at the sides now even more wary of us than they had been. Ashbridge clapped as he came across the floor, before extending his hand. I clasped it and rose, gingerly rubbing my aching back as Ashbridge shook Tobias' hand.

"That, gentlemen, was nothing short of impressive. You two put my soldiers to shame."

Toby ran his fingers through his hair, as he handed his swords to a young soldier. "We have been training since we were children. Your soldiers have skills, Ashbridge, but they cannot compete with those of us bred to fight."

Ashbridge ferried his brow, turning his attention to me. "Why did you not use magic to defend yourself? I'm certain that you both using magic could have turned the fight on its head."

I glanced at Toby, who shrugged, as if he cared not for his secret to be exposed. Stepping into Ashbridge, I lowered my voice, my words nothing more than a murmur on the wind. "Using magic against someone who has none does not make you a better fighter. It simply makes you a lesser man."

Ashbridge glanced from me to Tobias, before he nodded, an expression of respect lightening his features. With a clap of his hands, Ashbridge motioned for normal training to resume. I picked up my own sword, stopping as a small hand reached for it at the same time. I hesitated, peering down at the small red-haired boy that watched me with rounded eyes. His hand trembled like the very close proximity of me scared him to no end.

Trying my best to smile, I lifted the sword and handed it to the young fella. All of my life, I had never wanted to see fear in someone's eyes as they regarded me, as I had seen many a time in my father's presence. There was this one time, when young witches were being tested to see if their powers were worthy of surviving their coven. A young girl was presented to Malcolm, and the girl was absolutely terrified and began to cry. When Malcolm started to weep, a mirror image to the small child, he banished her from his sight because she had the ability to make people feel what she was feeling and toy with their emotions.

The fear in the mother's eyes had stuck with me, even more so when the child disappeared from court, never to be seen again. I was under no illusion that had my powers not been as strong or as effective as Malcolm wanted, I would have met my end in a similar fashion.

That was not the kind of king I ever wanted to be.

The moment the thought popped into my mind, I flinched. When had I begun to think of myself as a king? When had the decisions I made, or how I appeared to the outside world, clashed with becoming king?

The boy took hold of the sword and scurried away, and I became aware of someone watching me from the corner of the room. Mercy lingered by the darkened corner, his head inclining as he motioned me over.

Clasping Toby on the shoulder, I pointed to where Mercy had been standing, and walked away, unease clenching my stomach. Mercy slipped out the door, and I followed him.

The next thing I knew, Mercy had me shoved up against the wall, a snarl on his lips. On instinct, I summoned the air in the room and grasped his throat. What the hell was going on? In all of our years as friends, Mercy had never laid a hand on me with the intention of harm. I had to believe that one of my dearest friends was not about to try and kill me.

Toby burst into the room and growled as he pushed at Mercy.

"What the hell are you doing, Mercy?"

But Mercy did not budge as I swiped with my hand, trying to get free of his grasp. And then I realized really how dangerous my friend was. There was little emotion in those silver eyes of his, the tattoos that crept along his shoulders and ensnared his neck seemed to have come alive as they twitched and moved under the strain of his grasp.

"Have you any idea what you have done?" Mercy snarled as Toby yelled at him to let me be free. Toby grabbed Mercy's elbow, and it seemed to break the spell. Mercy released me, and I stayed against the wall, my breathing ragged.

"Have you lost your mind, Mercy? What you just did is treason!"

I held up my hand to stop Toby from chastising Mercy, for I longed to hear exactly what had inclined him to wish me harm.

"I'm waiting." I managed to scrape out, shocked at how steady my voice sounded, even as my heart thundered in my chest.

Mercy threw his hands up in the air, stalking away as if he needed to calm down before he explained. Hands in his pockets, he turned back to us.

"After I located the scroll and secured it, I've been doing some covert spying, trying to locate the Cambridge heir. I wanted to see if there was a way for us to kill her before we left. I found her, but found something else as well."

I rubbed my arms for something to do as I said not a word, hoping Mercy would continue on, holding up my hand when Tobias made to speak. When Mercy ducked his head, before lifting his liquid gaze to meet mine, I saw fear in his eyes.

"I tracked her, her little siren friend, and their escort down. I watched in the shadows for a chance to get her on her own. I rejoiced when she slipped free of her friends, and I stalked her, my chances to rid the world of the Cambridge heir within my grasp."

Mercy stalked back toward me, and the only thing preventing him from getting in my face was a wall made of Toby. Head shaking, Mercy went on.

"I had my blade poised as I emerged from the shadows, her throat mere inches from my strike. Imagine my surprise when the Cambridge heir scaled a wall to knock on your bedroom window. Imagine my even greater surprise when you greeted her like she were an old friend, and then kissed her like you needed her to breathe!"

Icy filled my veins. What was he trying to say? No, Mercy was wrong. The girl I had kissed and craved was not the Cambridge heir. The fates would not be so cruel.

"You've got it wrong," I protested, knowing the truth even as I said the words, my mind whirling. "She's the friend. The other girl in the yellow dress is the Cambridge heir."

Mercy shrugged off Toby, and stood in front of me, his hands falling to my shoulders. "The girl that crept into your room is none other than Rowan Cambridge, heir to the Cambridge coven, and your sworn enemy. I wish it wasn't true, Jules. But by the gods, Rowan Cambridge."

Slowly, I placed my fists to my temple and pieced together the shards of my heart, Ro was Rowan, my despised enemy. When she had spoken of being free, she meant that she wanted to be free of the chains that bound her; her queendom. The girl that I had kissed, the girl that I wanted still with every ounce of my being, was the daughter of my rival.

I thought of Rowan, smiling at me, her eyes as eager as mine, as she kissed me back with as much passion as possible. I remembered her dancing in the snow, the joy in her movements and how I had started to see a future in her eyes. Dancing in the dark, with her in my arms, had been the happiest moment of my life. And now, even the sliver of hope that we could be together had been quenched.

Suddenly, my dream made sense, as if some mystic force had been trying to lead me down this path, and a strangled cry escaped my lips. In a fit of rage, I pushed my magic outward, the windows shattering as I let loose a scream. Mercy and Toby ducked, panic flaring in their eyes as glass splintered through the air. I could smell the copper tang of blood as glass pricked my skin, but I did not feel any pain. I felt entirely numb.

I had been wrong. So utterly wrong.

The fates could be so cruel.

chapter fourteen
rowan

TIME TICKED BY EVER SO SLOWLY, THE NERVOUS ENERGY in me irritating Emilee so much that she fled from the confines of our rooms and did not return for several hours. I could not sleep, I could not concentrate, all I could do was stand idle and count down the hours until I laid eyes on Jules again.

My lips tingled, as if I could still feel the brand of his kiss on them. It was as if with each kiss, I became more addicted to him, felt myself dreaming of a life with him, like I had stumbled upon the other half of my soul and realized I had not been whole my entire life.

I felt rather stupid, thinking that I had fallen so fast in love with a boy I barely knew, one that happened to belong to a rival coven. Yet, when I thought about having to mount my horse and leave this winter wonderland, nausea pooled in my stomach, and an odd sensation fluttered in my chest.

Emilee had questioned me about my meeting with Jules, trying to pry some information from me, but I could not tell her that I was falling for a boy from a rival coven, for she would believe some spell had been woven over me and would move heaven and earth to drag me from this place, this place that had seen me not be quite myself.

It was midafternoon when Emilee arrived back, her cheeks flushed and a scowl marring her pretty face. Removing her coat, Emilee tossed it aside and flopped down on the fireside chair, snow clinging to her boots. She let loose an exaggerated sigh and cast her arm over her eyes. Emilee was nothing if not dramatic.

"Are you just going to sigh, or are you going to tell me what has put you in a foul mood?"

Removing her arm from her eyes, Emilee peered out at me under her full lashes. "I went in search of the item your mother wanted me to find, but one of the kitchen boys told me that Auggie was livid since the item had been stolen on the night of the ball. No one knows who got to it before me, and no one has any clue where I might find it."

I folded my arms across my chest. "Perhaps if you told me what it is that you search for, I could help you?"

Emilee snorted. "Nice try."

I shrug, glancing out the window, my eyes watching as the sun began to descend, but in agonizing slowness. I had already washed and dressed, and then changed before going back to my original outfit. My hair had been left loose, then pulled back, before I settled on the braid I usually wore. I'd even snuck in and sprayed myself with some of Emilee's perfume, something I never usually bothered with myself.

"It's not that I don't want to tell you, Rowan. Your mother put a geas on me to prevent me from telling anyone directly about what I search. You know I would tell you if I could. But then again, we all have our own secrets."

I knew she was referring to my infatuation with the Montgomery witch, but I do not think she understood that for once, I had something that was mine, and mine alone, and I was loathe to share it with anyone just yet.

"There is nothing for me to tell. And it is not a secret. I told you that I met with him and plan to meet him once more. We danced and talked. And when the snow clears, we will all go our separate ways and never lay eyes on each other again. Life will go back to normal, and we will all forget that Rowan had a little fun for once."

Stomping her boots on the floor, Emilee glared at me, her steely gaze making me wish I could look away, for one look into my best friend's eyes could make me spill even the biggest of secrets.

"Keep your secrets, Rowan. You are entitled to them. I just do not want to see you hurt. But that does not mean you can't have a little fun. Rowan, make sure you are safe in every way though. I have a medicine that will prevent any unwanted heirs, if you understand my meaning."

My cheeks heated rapidly, as I flinched, my heart pounding in my chest. I thought Emilee was jesting, yet her eyes were heavy and serious. I felt the need to explain myself.

"I have not slept with him, Emilee. I do not plan to. The thought had not even crossed my mind until you mentioned it. As to unwanted heirs, I never, ever plan on having children. And look who I am being forced to marry. I will never lay with Paris. If that means I never have sex, I'm okay with that."

I had hours yet before I had to meet Jules, yet the room suddenly became impossibly hot and suffocating.

I walked over to where my cloak hung, slinging it over my shoulders, and slipped my feet into my boots. As I crouched down to lace them, Emilee muttered a curse, then let loose a sigh.

"I did not mean to offend you, Rowan. But you seem different here. You usually walk around with the weight of the world on your shoulders. Here, you laugh easily, you *smile*. You were reckless before, but here you are more so. I just did not want you saddled with a babe, something else for our sovereign to use against you."

Having finished lacing up my boots, I walked to where Emilee sat and pressed my lips to both her cheeks. She grasped my hands and smiled.

"Thank you for worrying about me," I said, trying to reel in my emotions. "Kendra despises me because I am her only heir. Perhaps she will find some poor sap to give her another child, and then I can run away and become one with the forest. I go to see my mystery boy, because if that can never happen, when I am seated on that throne, the crown on my head and a husband I despise by my side, I want a fond memory of a boy who kissed me without knowing who I really am."

"I understand, Ro. I really do."

Rising, I headed for the door, escaping early because I did not wish to linger any longer and discuss uncomfortable things. I loved Emilee, I really did. But Emilee had always wanted to be within the royal circle, and I was the future sovereign.

The Friar would tell me that I am far too young to be so cynical.

Mayhap he is right.

Cracking the door open just a peep, I peered outside

to make sure the hallway was empty before I slipped out, and quickly descended the stairs. Popping the hood of my cloak up, my fingers grazed over the small blade on my hip, knowing it was already there, but seeking the comfort of the metal even so.

At the end of the stairs, servants rushed about, dinner almost upon them. They bowed their heads to me in passing, but I assumed this was what they did for all of Auggie's guests, not just myself. Under the cover of the cloak, it would be impossible to see my features. I passed by the array of paintings of previous high lords of Saor, and trudged down the hall. I heard my name behind me, but I keep moving forward. It was only when a hand landed on my shoulder that I reacted.

The blade was out of its sheath and pressed against flesh before I took my next breath, my eyes clashing with the current high lord as my lips curled. A smile played on his lips, and I snarled, my hands steady and unwavering.

The few around us gasped in surprise, but Auggie reassured them that he was quite fine, ushering them away. When we were alone, I removed my blade from his throat and slid it back into place.

"Who has hurt you in the past that the slightest touch tips you to violence?"

There was understanding in his voice, and I hated it, as a tirade of memories flashed through my mind. The trips, the tricks, the bruises, the humiliation; a childhood filled with bullies. If it had not been for my willingness to learn to protect myself, then things might have been so much worse.

"Those who would not so much as dare to put hands on me now. It is not easy, having one hand on the crown when so many others desire it."

"Indeed." That was all Augustus said, though I could see a new respect for me in his eyes. He no longer saw me as just a princess, but as more. If he had questions for me, Auggie did not ask them, his reason for stopping me seemed forgotten.

I spun on my heels, leaving Auggie standing in the foyer of his home, watching me as I stepped out into the fresh air. I gulped in some cool breaths, feeling the temperature had risen since last night, the air not as frigid. Snow had stopped falling, and the road leading down to the gate was in the process of being cleared away. By morning, we would be able to depart and travel south, heading back to Cambridge land.

Darkness was not yet full, a sliver of light guiding my way as my feet moved, crunching under the melting snow as I slipped into the stable. I walked past the stalls, inhaling the scent of horses and hay, smiling as I came to a stop outside where Rhiannon was housed.

"Hey, girl." I say with a smile. "Have they been treating you well?"

A snort was all I got in reply, as if my horse was scolding me for bringing her to the frozen place and away from the grassy plains of our homestead. I chuckled as her dark eyes watched me, her head coming out over the door of her stable, my hand automatically going to the bridge of her nose. I gently rubbed it and patted her neck.

"Tomorrow we will go home, tomorrow we will leave." Talking to her, I was unable to hide the sadness in my tone or mask the lump that formed in my throat. As if sensing my sadness, Rhiannon nudged me with her nose and whined.

"I'm okay, girl. I promise."

"If the horse does not believe you, then why should others."

I jumped at the sound of Jules' voice, and jerked back from Rhiannon. His tone was clipped and hard, his body stiff. He stood a few feet away from me, and even as I gave him a warm smile, for some reason, Jules did not return it.

The stables were empty, the only sound at the moment was the sound of our breathing and the occasionally whine of a horse. Jules stood with his hands clenched into fists, his face a blank mask. I stepped toward him, and he backed up a little.

"What's wrong?"

My voice cracked, and I cursed myself. A flicker of emotion flashed in his eyes before they darkened. Eyes that once twinkled with mischief and vitality suddenly went cold and lifeless as he stared at me.

"Did you know all along, or did you decide to play me when you figured it out?"

"Figure what out?" I could not hide my confusion. "Jules, I do not understand. What has happened to put that look in your eyes?"

With a growl, he scrubbed a hand down his face so hard I was sure that he would leave an impression. He glared at me for a solid five minutes, then blinked in surprise.

"You have no idea who I am, do you?"

I shook my head, then stopped. Maybe he figured out that I knew he belonged to the Montgomery coven; maybe that was what had angered him so.

"I know that you belong to the Montgomery witches, but I thought there would be no harm in what we are doing. It is only for a moment of time."

He laughed, and the sound sent chills down my spine; it was the same indifferent sound from my dreams. Jules shook his head, and I could feel the magic swirling inside him, feel the wind kick up again as he tried to control whatever storm raged inside himself.

This time, when he took a step in my direction, it was I who retreated.

"If it is true, and you have no idea of my identity, tell me who you think I am."

For a moment, the words caught in my throat, and I searched my mind for the words he might want to hear, because I wished not to hurt him. But I realized that I was only hurting myself, forcing pretty words and bowing to a man I would not see ever again after this night.

"Does it matter?" I cried. "You have already decided I have deceived you. From the look in your eyes, nothing I can say or do could convince you otherwise. I will leave you to your anger. Goodbye, Jules."

As I moved to go around him, he blocked my path. We glared at each other for a moment before we moved like magnets pulled together, and Jules was kissing me, angerly, like he did not want his lips on mine. He backed me up against a stable door, his body hard against mine, the breath gone from my lungs, my mind all foggy.

When Jules pulled his lips away from me, he rested his head against my forehead and muttered, "What spell have you woven over me, Rowan Cambridge?"

I pushed away from him, stunned. He knew my identity, that was why he was so enraged. I placed one hand on the hilt of my blade, the other momentarily clasped over my mouth as I tried to quell the sickness in my stomach.

"How long have you known?"

"Not long I was not going to come tonight. But like a siren, you called me to you and I was sunk. I wrestled with the decision all day, whether to simply leave you here waiting and wondering why I never showed. Perhaps inflict some of the hurt that I was feeling on you. Yet, I couldn't do it to you. And I wanted to see your face when you explained things to me. I needed to see if you lied or not. I had to see if the girl I danced with and told me she longed for freedom was not a witch who had put a spell on me."

I shook my head vigorously, as if I could dispel his words from my mind. I had tainted our time with my lies, and now, now it had come back to haunt me. I felt as if a knife had been shoved into my chest.

"I did not mean to deceive you, Jules. But I knew, I knew deep in my heart that even as I found myself … wanting to spend time with you, that I could never have more than a few stolen movements with you. I mean, you are one of the Montgomery heir's closest companions. There is no future for us."

Jules barked out a laugh and closed his eyes. After several heartbeats, he opened those glacier blue eyes again and our eyes met. I could see he still wanted me. I felt in in his kiss, in his body, but something bitter had taken hold inside Jules and for the life of me, I could not figure out what.

"You really do speak the truth, Rowan. *Rowan.*" He said my name like I was poison, and my blood ran cold. "How could I have been so stupid? How did I not figure it out? How could we all have been fooled? Oh, I know, because the girl who was the actual princess acted like she was a mere foot soldier."

So, like most people, Jules thought Emilee had been the Cambridge Heir, the one with the poise and grace and desire to be royal. There was no fault in that.

Jules came closer, so that my back hit the stable door again, his hands on either side barring my exit, the saddest smile on his face. My hand moved of its own accord, and I had to stop myself from reaching out to touch him. I knew this would all end, but I could not have predicted it to end quite like this.

"I have always prided myself on my control. But I lose it around you. I suddenly saw a future, one I had never seen before, but the fates are cruel and spiteful. I saw you dancing in the snow, and I wanted you, wanted something for myself for the first time in my life." Jules reached up a hand and cupped my cheek before he continued. "Then you walked into the room, and my heart was stolen. I never believed in love at first sight until you crashed into my life. But my heart is full of love, and I despise it."

A tear slipped down my cheek, and I knew not what to do to make this right, how to make his pain go away. I wanted to take him in my arms and press my cheek against his chest. I longed to kiss him, even it was for the last time.

"And you still haven't figured it out, have you?" he demanded, making me feel stupid. "You are staring at me like I have lost my goddamn mind, and perhaps I have. You think we cannot be together because I am close with the future king of the Montgomery coven? Let me put the final pieces together for you, Rowan Cambridge. Let me introduce myself properly."

Jules leaned in so close that I thought he was about to

kiss me once again. As the wind crashed against the doors of the stable, banging loud enough to sound like thunder, I shuddered as Jules looked at me like I was nothing. And maybe I was.

"I would say it is a pleasure to meet you, Rowan Cambridge, but it would be a lie. My name is Julian Montgomery, and I am heir to the Montgomery crown. It would appear that we have fallen in love with the enemy. Still want me to kiss you?"

chapter fifteen

julian

My words hit her with the same impact a blow might have, her eyes widening, her jaw dropping, and tears welling in her eyes. I felt like a bastard for inflicting pain on her. I longed to reach out and brush her tears away, to hold her in my arms and tell her that it was alright, that neither of us had any idea and that we could both go our separate ways in the morning and forget this whole sorry affair.

However, I could not lie to her, even now, even when I suspected that this was all a plot devised by her to lure me here to kill me. I took a step back to allow her space to comprehend my words, remembering my violent outburst and the shards of glass I had to pluck from Toby's skin after I shattered an entire room full of windows.

I did not lie when I told Rowan I had fallen in love with her. I had. And the way I was feeling now, I did not think I would ever fall for someone like I had for her. I would return to Cambridge, knowing all along that one day, my nightmare might become a reality. I possessed in me the power to snap her neck, having known what it felt to love her.

"How could this have happened?" Rowan whispered, as she wiped the tears from her eyes. I saw her hand slide to her hip, had felt the blade on her hip, yet if she drove that blade into my heart, I would consider it to hurt less than the constant ache that lingered.

"We screwed up."

Rowan looked at me, her features beautiful and alluring as my gaze dropped to her lips. I wanted to kiss her. I yearned to lose myself in the sensation of kissing her and forget that one day, maybe sooner than either of us believed, we would stand on opposing sides and wage war.

We stood there, in the stable, amid the horses, two royal regents, and neither of us knew what to say. Rowan brushed the tears from her eyes, moved her head from side to side, and shrugged.

"So, have you come to kill me then?"

"It's what I was sent to do, but no. I wish you no ill harm, Rowan."

"Stop that," she snarled.

Unable to mask my own confusion, I looked at her bewildered. "Stop what?" I asked.

Rowan clenched the edge of her cloak as she replied, "Stop saying my name like that."

"Like what?"

"Like you want to kiss me."

"I do. Goddamn it, Rowan, I want to kiss you so bad it hurts. I know what's at stake. I understand the implications of us, but I feel like if I don't kiss you now, I won't be able to breathe."

"Then kiss me, Julian. Kiss me and make me forget that I am supposed to hate you with every fiber of my being. Kiss me one last time before we leave this city and embark on our journey home. Does it feel different? Kissing me as someone you should hate, or does it feel the same as all the other girls you have kissed? Kiss me one more time so that I will remember the first time I was truly kissed by Julian Montgom—

I did not let her finish before I captured her face in my hands, my mouth slanted over hers, hungrily and almost feverishly kissing her. This kiss, this kiss was an explosion, like we understood that if we came apart, it would be for the very last time, and by the gods, I did not want that.

When Rowan wrapped her arms around my neck, dragging me down into a deeper kiss, her lips parting, I forgot that we were mortal enemies, I forgot that I was supposed to hate her. I neglected to think about the fact I was sent here to kill her. I lost myself in the sensation of her; it was as if when our lips met, like fire and powder, brought together hastily, we could explode.

We came apart at the same time, both of us panting, neither of us willing to step from the other's embrace. I reached out and brushed a hair from her face before she could even lift her head to look at me.

"What are we going to do, Jules?"

Rowan was looking to me for reassurance, but I had none. I waited a little longer before I answered, the scars on my heart already beginning to form.

"I don't think there is much we can do, Rowan. What would you have us do? Runaway together? Ask Ashbridge for room in Saor and spend the rest of our days fending off our parents' attempts to knock sense into us and drag us home?"

Her voice was small when she whispered. "I'm quite good at evading capture. And no, I'm not standing that. I cannot fathom leaving here and never seeing you again. You asked before if I had woven a spell over you, and to that I say, if I have woven a spell on you then it has returned threefold, because it has made me fall in love with you too."

I kissed her again, a quick press of lips as she trembled at my touch, and I had to stop myself from pushing further, from taking more than I deserved.

"Hold me, Jules. I'm falling apart."

I pulled her to me, releasing a breath as her head rested on my chest, her hand placed where my heart was beating rapidly against my chest. We stayed like that for a while even as Rowan said to me, "Hearts are not supposed to hurt like this. They are not meant to fall in love so quickly, and certainly they are not supposed to break so fast. Time will heal all wounds, that's what they say, but I doubt that. I fear our hearts will not heal from this, Jules, no matter what happens after tonight."

I feared she was right. I felt different, I certainly did not feel the same as I had a week ago. I pressed my lips to the top of her head, and with every ounce of willpower I had, I stepped out of her embrace and away from her.

Beautiful brown eyes watched me, wondering if I suddenly would strike out and leave her dead here in the stables. I wouldn't, I couldn't. I did not know who I was without her. I remembered the king, the future me in my dream, and wondered if this was the moment in which I closed off my heart and became cruel. There were moments in life that shaped you, that forged you into the person you would be for the rest of your life, and I, without a shadow of a doubt, believed that this would haunt me for many years to come.

"I wish we could be, Rowan. More than I can try and persuade you. I have fallen in love with you, and it breaks me that I have to leave. That we cannot be. If we had been borne unto another life then perhaps. But, we cannot be. We have to accept that."

I knew I was trying to convince myself, not Rowan, because I knew if I kissed her again that I would not leave. I would stay within the walls of this city and await the war that would certainly rage in order for our respective covens to get us back. There would be bloodshed, innocent lives lost, and all because two people who should never have met, did so and fell in love.

Drinking her in one last time, I grasped her hand, my entire body coming alive with just the barest touch of her skin, and lifted it to my lips. "Goodbye, Rowan Cambridge. It has been an honor to know you. May we meet again, in another life."

"In another life. That sounds like fun, Julian Montgomery. Safe travels."

I turned before I could do anything stupid, like get on my knees and beg her to stay, to spend the night with me, or by the gods, tell her that I would gladly run away with her, forsake my life for her. I would burn the world for the chance to be hers, and that could never be.

I stormed down toward the exit when I heard a scuffle behind me, and the sound of my name of Rowan's lips. I spun round. To my absolute horror and dread, Mercy had an arm around Rowan's waist, another poised at her throat, a dagger glinting in the moonlight.

Holding up my hands, my eyes focused on the dagger at Rowan's throat, I consider my words before I addressed my father's shadow, appealing to my boyhood friend.

"Mercy, no harm has befallen me. Let Rowan go. We will go our separate ways, and no blood needs to be shed this night."

Eyes of silver met mine as I came a little closer, silently begging Rowan to not do anything reckless for now. Mercy did not loosen his grip, the shadows around him swirling angrily as he glared at me.

"Have you forgotten that she is the enemy. I could slit her throat right now and we would unite a kingdom. We would remove Kendra Cambridge from power and the Montgomery witches would rule all of Vernanthia. Is that not the goal here, Julian? To rule and snuff out all those who oppose your father?"

"I love her."

Mercy shook his head. "Then you are a fool, overcome with hormones. You barely know her and she you. You would throw away your crown for her?"

"In a heartbeat."

The stable door was wrenched open with a creak and Toby strode in, whistling a tune as he came to stand beside me. He nudged my shoulder and grinned, before turning his attention to the girl captured in Mercy's arms.

"So, this is the infamous Rowan Cambridge? It's a pleasure to meet you."

"Likewise," Rowan gritted out. "I'd shake your hand, but I'm a bit caught up right now."

Toby chuckled, glancing at me. "I can see why you like her. I'd like her too if she wasn't on the wrong side of things."

I spotted Rowan inching her hand toward the dagger on her hip and blurted out. "Rowan, don't!"

Mercy has the blade pressed against her abdomen a

second later, a grunt leaving Rowan's lips as she scowled.

"Kill me then, Shadow. Oh, I know who you are, assassin. You are kind of hard to miss. I once wanted to be like you, one who could blend in with the shadows, disappear and not be found. I used to believe if I asked the gods enough then they would grant me the ability to hide. But they never answered me. I just made myself better."

Toby inched closer to Mercy, and fear seized hold of me, rendering me unable to move. Toby's stance was all quiet confidence, relaxed and unthreatening, but both Mercy and I know, this was all for show.

"Come on now, Mercy. Let the pretty girl go. I'm sure, just like me, you heard that entire conversation, and Rowan here means our Jules no harm. They were leaving on good terms, as good as can be expected. Let her go, Merce. Haven't they both suffered enough."

Mercy blinked, his eyes darting from Toby to me and then glancing down at Rowan. His grip loosened, but the door to the barn opened again, and the girl we all thought was the Cambridge heir strode in, the biggest grin on her face.

"Seems like I missed the entire party."

"Get out of here, Emilee. Please just go." Rowan begged of her friend, but the girl simply walked past me and Toby and grinned at Mercy.

"Hold that thought," Emilee said to Mercy and he froze, panic flooding his eyes. Rowan rolled her eyes and sighed. The girl, Emilee, turned her attention to us. Studying us for a few minutes, her gaze finally settled on me, and she smiled.

"This must be the boy who has you jumping out of windows and breaking all the rules. Handsome."

"Julian Montgomery." I said as an introduction and Emilee giggled, leaving me to wonder how I ever thought this girl was the future queen of Cambridge.

"Oh, Rowan. You've been breaking all the rules. Now, Julian, I think it is time your friend releases my friend of his own accord. Or I will break each and every bone in his body when I order him to do so."

The siren. Rowan was never the one who could make you do things with her voice. It was this girl standing between me and the girl I loved, held captive by my best friend.

I tried to scrounge as much authority as I could into my voice. "Mercy, let her go."

"You are not my king yet."

"No, but I am your friend. Please do as I ask. I wish to see neither of you hurt."

Emilee turned back to look at Mercy, her head tilting to the side. "Mercy," she began, her voice like a song. "Please let go of Rowan and drop the daggers."

I could see Mercy try and fight the compulsion, but even the strongest of us could not fight against the siren. Mercy growled as he released Rowan, the daggers falling to the floor with a clang. Rowan quickly snatched up her blade and kicked away Mercy's.

"Now sit down like a good little boy while we all have a chat."

Mercy dropped to the ground, his long legs crossed in front of him, his hands balled into fists. If he did not hate the Cambridge coven before today, he surely did now.

Emilee turned to us, and I could see the whites of her eyes, her magic evident as she smiled sweetly at us. "Now, will you let us leave or must I ask nicely?"

Rowan set her hand on Emilee's arm. "That's enough, Em. You've done your job. I'm safe. Thank you."

"I would never have let him hurt you." I stated but I knew that if Mercy had taken her with him into the shadows, I would be powerless to stop him. We stood facing each other, myself and Toby, Rowan and Emilee.

"Despite the fact that you just made my friend, the continent's most feared assassin, look like a puppy, that was actually pretty cool. What does it feel like?" Toby asked. Curiosity could get him killed.

Emilee tilted her head to the side and opened her mouth. "You think that I am so beautiful that you want to get on your knees and worship me."

Toby stared blankly at her but did nothing. I glanced at him and he shrugged. Emilee frowned and ground out another order.

"Take hold of Rowan's dagger and stab yourself with it. Somewhere that won't kill you."

"I'd rather not." Toby retorted dryly, and Emilee glared at him confused. She glanced at me, and I shook my head.

"I have no desire to feel what it's like."

Turning back to Mercy, she ordered him to get up and he immediately did. Glowering as she roamed her eyes over Toby, I saw the moment something clicked in her mind.

"Ha, Ha. Very funny. Bring with you a shield and ask the siren to dance."

"What the hell is a shield?" Toby demanded.

"A shield," Rowan began, "Is a combat witch whose main power stems from the ability to withstand mental manipulation. Meaning any witch who is a siren or has any telepathic abilities cannot penetrate your mind. It is exceedingly rare and very much sought after."

Toby threw his hands in the air in frustration. "I've wanted magic my entire life, and you tell me that I have it, and it's a stupid mental shield? I'd prefer to continue thinking I'm a Null."

I tried to process the fact that Toby has had magic all along when Emilee said, "You have within you the capacity to shield an entire battlefield of soldiers from mind control. It is hardly a stupid power."

"Let's debate the stupidity of Toby later on. What happens now?" I folded my arms across my chest and casted my gaze in Rowan's direction, desire racing through me when I saw that she had been watching me.

"We go our separate ways." Rowan stated. "We call a truce until we are both in our respective territories and then we see what the future holds. But I can't trust the shadow. Not after everything. Emilee?"

Emilee turned her attention back to Mercy. She was like a viper, titling her head, her words dripping like poison as she uttered an order. "Mercy, you will let us leave and not come after us for one whole night and one whole day. You will leave with your prince and not follow us. If you do, you will experience pain like you have never felt before. Only when you have gone far enough, and my compulsion is broken, can you come for us."

An animalistic growl rumbled in Mercy's throat as he lurched forward, only to sink to his knees and bellow in pain, clutching at his head. Toby raced over to aid him. Emilee walked over to the stable door, leaving just myself and Rowan to stand and stare at each other.

I never knew that love could feel this way. It was like agony and ecstasy. It was pain, and it was joy. In her eyes,

I could see she felt it too.

Striding after Emilee, she paused, going up on her toes to press her lips to my cheek.

"Goodbye, Jules."

And then she was gone, sweeping from the stables and taking my heart with her.

chapter sixteen
rowan

WE LEFT SAOR BEFORE THE SUN HAD RISEN THE
following morning. Having said our goodbyes to Augustus
last night after our encounter with Jules, we had little
reason to linger longer. The roads had been cleared, the
snow having melted overnight as the storm relinquished
its hold over the city. The captivating winter wonderland
had disappeared along with any hope left inside me.

I never imagined that I had the capacity to feel so
hopeless. However, each time I remembered that Jules
was the son of my sworn enemy, I lost hope all over again.
My black mood was commented on frequently by Paris
throughout our journey home, and my veiled threats of
mutilation did nothing to cease his incessant remarks.
Even a warning from Emilee did not thwart his ramblings.

Despite the others pleading with me to stop, I
refused to spend another night away from home and kept
Rhiannon moving until her hooves stepped over the Null
border, and we were home. The outbound journey to Saor
took us three days, but traveling both day and night had
us home in just over two days.

Once I handed the Rhiannon's reigns over to a stable

hand, I spun on my heels and headed for The Dredge and the only person who might not judge me for falling in love with the one man in the entire continent that I could not be with. Emilee called after me, yet I ignored her. I had embarrassed myself enough by bursting into tears and spending the last night in Saor trying to stop them. I had rested my head in Emilee's lap, her fingers combing my hair in soothing motions.

Not long after, I had fallen asleep, exhausted and weary, waking in the morning and shutting down my emotions before we left. But as the gates to Saor closed behind us, I could not prevent myself from glancing over my shoulder, as if I expected Jules to race after me and beg me not to leave.

A moment of madness, that was all.

The Dredge was alive and heaving, the rowdiness comforting as I stomped through the puddled streets. Ignoring the bow of heads, I meandered down to where The Friar did his dealings. I slipped through the familiar cobbled streets, ones that I had graced even as a young child after having escaped from a nursemaid or two, eventually to be found hiding in one of The Friar's weapons trucks in the evening.

Over the years, I was a regular visitor to the Dredge and not many took much notice of the princess wandering down the grubby streets. While I couldn't forge lasting friendships, there wasn't many a folk who did not greet me or offer up something sweet to eat or drink.

This close to evening, he should be just about to close up shop, but when I arrived at his stall, his apprentice was in the process of closing shop.

"Where is the Friar this evening?"

The apprentice fumbled when he saw me, almost dropping the magnificent blade in his hand. I cringed, softening my tone so as not to scare the boy. It would be such a shame for him to drop those works of art and damage them before they could be sold.

"Please, I'm just looking to have a word with him. Is he here?"

The boy shook his head. "He had something personal to attend to, your Highness. Where I do not know."

I nodded my head. "No worries, friend. I can find him by myself."

Standing in the middle of the murky market, I closed my eyes and focused on The Friar and his aura, trying to block out the fact the last time I had used my magic as such, it had been to track down Jules.

Jules.

A stab to my chest almost had me crying out. I tried not to think about *him* and focused on the string of amber aura with outlines of black that belonged to my friend. The pull in my gut sprang me forward and I went with it, relishing in the power flooding my veins. I stormed down the streets, ignoring anyone who tried to stop me.

Soon, I was venturing out of the Dredge and into the rainforest. Normally, I would stop and enjoy the peace and quiet of the forest, inhaling the scent of the rain on the grass, of moss and of bark, of deer and of earth, but today, I was on the hunt and nothing could stop me.

The pain in my stomach began to grow, leading me into a part of the forest I had not explored before. I hesitated, noticing as a hooded figure pulled back a curtain of leaves and ducked into a hidden cavern. Amazing. When the leaves fell back into place, not a sinner would have been able to see the hidden cave behind it.

I could sense the Friar inside the cavern and, pulling my own cloak over my head, followed the man, lifting the veil and slipping inside soundlessly. I backed up against the wall as my eyes adjusted to the dark, taking careful steps until a wall of torches illuminated my way. As I neared the end of the passageway, I could hear the rumble of voices, could feel the pull of the aura I had come in search of.

The passageway came to an abrupt halt, and I found myself standing in the mouth of an alcove where a meeting was taking place. The Friar stood at the top of this makeshift room, and once my eyes landed on him, the ache in my stomach lessened. It would not go away completely until I laid hands on the man who knew my father the best.

Rows of benches lined the small room, torches lighting up the area. I sat on the furthest bench from where The Friar stood and folded my hands in my lap. I recognized some of the men and women from Cambridge, and some I did not know at all. I ducked my head as The Friar's eyes roamed the room, the assembly falling into silence when he lifted a hand.

"Friends, welcome to our meeting here tonight. I know some of you risk much by gathering here, so you have my thanks."

Grumbled replies, then silence once more as the Friar continued. "War, my friends, it is upon us. I have been informed that the Montgomery witches are in possession of the scroll and will know now what is to come. We must insure that our cities and our people are not victims of ancient bloodshed."

Treason... all of this was treason... meeting in secret... if they realized that I was here, then my life would most certainly be forfeit. I would have laughed, considering that this was the second time in a couple of days my life was under threat.

"The kings and queens will stand by as we, their subjects, face off against each other and lay our lives on the line for them. We did not ask for this war; we do not want it. We have to consolidate our power and remind them that without subjects, they rule over empty kingdoms. Our cache of weapons has grown twofold in the last month, despite any weather that might have hampered our efforts. But our comrades in arms bring news to us this day. Augustus?"

Shock and fear washed over me as Augustus Ashbridge, the high lord of Saor, stood beside the Friar with a somber smile on his face.

"Friends," he began, and everyone turned their attention to him. "I have born witness to the animosity between the covens. Only days ago, did Prince Julian of Montgomery stop the shadow from slitting the throat of Princess Rowan of Cambridge. If not for the siren, or the prince, Malcolm Montgomery would be ruling the continent today. We all know the shadow is not known for showing mercy."

Even as my heart raced, I could have laughed at Auggie's play on words. Mercy had no mercy. It was almost poetic, the revelation Auggie had been spying on us all, and we were oblivious. What else had he born witness to?

"I spoke with both the prince and the princess separately, and I think they would be amicable to hear us out. The Friar will speak with Rowan about the possibility of a ceasefire, and I might have the opportunity to speak with Prince Julian. But if any of the Cambridge witches have any ideas on how to approach the prince, please feel free to come forward. Discreetly, if needs be."

Before I could stop myself, I had risen to my feet. Considering everyone had been seated, my standing in a room full of traitorous fools stood out. Both Augustus and The Friar glanced my way. Augustus, who seemed oblivious to my identity, smiled encouragingly at me.

"My dear, have you something to offer?" Augustus asked, even as the Friar let loose a curse. It only stood that he recognized me; my cloak would stand out. Steeling my resolve, I prayed my voice held steady as I regarded the men at the top of the room.

"I would assume the princess would be less amicable to treason when she found out that she had been spied on," I said, my voice low and powerful. I allowed myself a moment or two and then continued speaking in a regular tone. "Perhaps, her feelings would be hurt to realize her one confidant had been playing her for a fool her entire life. Perhaps, for a brief ceasefire, she would call upon Prince Julian herself and track down every single traitorous peasant who dared consider the prince and princess pawns in their rebellion."

The Cambridge witches had realized who I was and were struck motionless as I lowered my hood. I held the gaze of the one person I thought would never betray me and smirked.

"And mayhap I will unleash my wrath upon you all and take you heads back to throw at my mother's feet? That is the punishment for treason, is it not? Should I seek out your innocent family members and string them up in front of the castle that will one day be mine to remind you what happens to those and their kin who want to orchestrate a coup?"

The people sitting nearest to me scampered away, and I pulled the dagger from my hip, the one given to me by the man whose gaze was locked on mine. I scanned the room for potential threats. There was always one person stupid enough who had something to prove.

A young boy of maybe fifteen lashed out, his fist coming into my field of vision. I ducked his fist and kicked his knee with my heavy boots—boots enforced with steel, thanks to the Friar—and heard the bone in his knee crack. When he went to the ground, howling in pain, I braced my booted foot on the curve of his neck, trying not to flinch when someone who was more than likely his mother cried out.

"Anyone else want to have a go?"

The room remained silent as Auggie came down toward me. When he was within striking distance, I pressed a little harder on the boy's windpipe and Auggie froze.

"Rowan, come now. You don't wish to harm anyone."

"You do not know me, Augustus Ashbridge. You only get to fool me once, the next time, you will be the fool."

"Rowan." I heard the voice of my mentor, and I froze, a snarl tugging at my lips. Everyone had backed away as far as possible. I could see the twitch of fingers and growled. "If I so much as smell magic or see the flicker of fingers, you will see why I am exactly my mother's daughter."

"Rowan," he said my name again with a sigh. "You are not your mother's daughter; you are your father's child, and he is the reason why all of us are standing in this room right now. Kendra killed him because we were working on dethroning her. Your father held you in his arms and did not want this life for you. She found out his plans and had him killed."

"How the hell am I supposed to believe anything you say now? You lied to me. You made me trust you. I came to you when I needed a confidant, and you probably came here and told them all how weak and pathetic I am."

As the Friar came closer, I was surprised to see how much his hair had greyed. I hadn't noticed before. Nor had I noticed the slight limp in his right leg or the shake of his hand. My friend had become old, and I had not noticed. Or perhaps my mother's magic now came to the forefront, where I assessed the situation and sought out weaknesses. As he stopped beside Auggie, I had already worked out how to take them both out and make my escape.

My mother would have been so proud.

"I know how your mind works, Rowan. You could kill the both of us in the blink of an eye if you wanted to, but I know you won't."

"Shut up!" I yell, shaking my head, pressing down harder on the boy's throat.

Auggie and the Friar shared a look, and I growled. "Did you train me all these years in the hopes that I would be the perfect little puppet on the throne for you all to manipulate? I'm sorry to disappoint you, because I would rather die than be someone's puppet."

The Friar runs his fingers through the stubble on his chin. "I want to give you your freedom. Is that not what you have always wanted, Rowan? Freedom."

It was then Jules' voice came back to haunt me. I shuddered as I remembered how it felt in his arms, and how I had divulged my darkest wish to him.

"Tell me, M'Lady. What would you wish for in this world, if you only had one wish?"

"Freedom. I wish that I was free."

I removed my boot from the boy's throat and kicked him away. I braced myself for a fight when Augustus ordered everyone from the room. I memorized faces and auras as they scampered down other passageways. I would hunt them all down.

When there was no one left but the three of us, The Friar moved away and poured himself a drink. He poured one for Augustus and raised a brow at me, silently asking if I wanted one.

I rolled my eyes in response and edged to a wall where I could see all the exits and entrances, just in case someone decided to be brave, or foolish, whichever way you wanted to think about it.

"I had not wanted you to discover us like this. I had planned on telling you before you married Paris. I might have done it sooner, especially since Augustus here tells me you and Julian Montgomery have forged some sort of friendship."

My cheeks heated and Augustus smiled, even as the Friar said, "Ah, so more than a friendship."

"I would say, Lawrence. She scaled a wall to knock on his bedroom window."

My cheeks flushed hotter. "I did not know who he was when we met. I only learned who he was on my last night in Soar. And we are straying from the point. You are planning on killing my mother, are you not?"

"Your mother is not a good person. Nor is she a good queen," The Friar countered, scowling as I replied.

"But she is still my mother."

The Friar took his drink and sat down on one of the benches. "Will you not come sit and listen to me just for a while? If you decide that it is of need to take my head to your mother, then I will not stop you. Have I not cared for you for many a year, Rowan, much as I promised your father I would? Come sit with me for a moment, and we will tell you our story."

He continued as I flinched at the pain building in my stomach. He reached out his hand and despite my reluctance to touch him, I knew I must in order to complete my hunt. But I hesitated.

"Rowan take my hand. There is no need to be in unnecessary pain."

I clasped his hand in mine, the relief instant. The pleasure of completing my hunt washed over me, and I couldn't help but groan, snatching my hand away the instant I felt the urge to hunt dissipate.

Cautiously, I took a seat a considerable distance away from the two, resting my hands, with my blade firmly in their grasp, on my lap and glared at the two men. When neither of them spoke, I cleared my throat and said, "Come on, then. Tell me the tale of how you became a traitor."

Augustus laughed, and I wanted to smack the smirk from his face. Ignoring me, he winked at The Friar and stated, "I can see why you chose her, Lawrence. She has spark and fire. We need her."

The Friar smiled, and I held his gaze, wanting him to see the anger seething inside me. I loved my mother, I really did. Yet, there was a part of me that did not like her. I knew there was a chance she had been responsible for my father's death, a father I could only recall in small darts of memory. If it was true, then she had to pay, but I would be the one to mete out justice. Not these would be rebels.

As if reading my thoughts, The Friar's smile deepened, and the man who cared for me for years was in his eyes. "Sit with me a while, Rowan Cambridge, and I will tell you our story. Yours, mine, your parents and even young Augustus here."

I motioned for him to hurry up, and he chuckled, watching me play with the dagger in my hand.

"This, Rowan Cambridge…is a tale of two houses."

chapter
seventeen
julian

To say the journey home was unbearable would be an understatement. With Mercy not so much as uttering a word, and me being moody and distant, it felt as if we had been traveling for weeks, not days. Even our brief stop at the tavern did nothing to brighten our moods. We ate, then retired to our beds to sleep, waking early to get on the road again.

I imagined how my father would react, if he knew that I had the Cambridge Heir within my grasp, and not only had I prevented his assassin from taking her life, but I had also found myself unable to banish her from my thoughts. He might have forgiven me, dispelled my romantic notions as the foolishness of youth, probably blaming my mother's influence.

However, Malcolm Montgomery would never forgive me for leaving the Cambridge heir alive and well. If he discovered what I had done, he would be livid, and heads rolled when Malcolm Montgomery lost his temper.

But what I feared most about my actions was who would bear the brunt of the fury that was bound to come. As his only heir, my father could not inflict his wrath on me, and that spelled disaster for the two people I cared most about. Since Mercy was considered too high of a commodity to lose, there was this deep-rooted sense that Toby would be the one to suffer for my indiscretion.

Then again, what I felt for Rowan could not be described as an indiscretion. Since the moment I laid eyes on her, it was as if I could not breathe without thinking of her, could not sleep without dreaming of her, and even now, as my mind drifted to thoughts of her, I ached to be near her. She was half a continent away, and it felt like an ocean.

We arrived back on the outskirts of the village shortly after sunset and dismounted our horses. A servant girl came up to the stables as we were sorting the horses, advising us that our presence had been requested.

When asked if we had time to bathe and change, to make ourselves presentable for the king, the girl shook her head and advised us that he was already waiting in his throne room for us and had been for an hour or so.

So, we left our horses in the care of the stable boys and dragged our tired selves into the castle, none of us speaking as we opened the doors and walked up to bow before our king.

I had wanted to ask my friends a million times on our return journey if they would tell my father about Rowan and what had occurred, but I had not felt brave enough to ask. My father had not so much as glanced in my direction upon our arrival, and questioned Mercy and Tobias only.

Standing in my father's throne room, they gave him a rundown of our misadventures in Soar, minus my liaison with Rowan, thankfully. I would never be more grateful to them than I was in that instance. I let Mercy and Toby speak, standing off to the side, pretending to be indifferent to their recounting of our days in Soar. Mercy, who I had barely spoken a word to on the journey home, handed a paper parchment to my father. Then, he was dismissed.

My friend glanced at me before he vanished into the shadows, leaving me and Toby alone in the room with my father. I waited for Toby to delight in telling his king that he was not a Null, that he had a valued resource at their disposal.

"Have you anything else to report, Tobias?"

"Afraid not, your highness. Our stay in Saor was regretfully uneventful."

My gaze snapped in Tobias' direction, but he was smiling at my father and paying no attention to me. My father dismissed him with the wave of his hand, and Tobias dropped to one knee, hand fisted over his chest, before rising and striding from the room.

As soon as the door closed behind Tobias with a thud, Malcolm Montgomery turned his attention to me. I allowed a mask to befall my face.

"Anything that you would like to add, Julian?"

"Nothing of note, Sir. Tobias spoke true. Our visit to Soar was uneventful."

"And the Cambridge heir?"

I dug my nails into my palms as I tried to remain composed. "We saw neither sight nor sound of her. When we went in search of her, apparently, she had left as soon as morning broke. Or rather, slept outside the Ashbridge compound. Forgive me my failure, Father."

"It is late; you are dismissed. Your mother would like to see you in the morning."

My father rose from his throne, as I dropped to my

knees and fisted my hand over my chest, dropping my head. When I lifted my head, my father was gone. I rose slowly, rubbing my temples. I had expected Mercy to tell Malcolm all about my stupidity and was surprised that he hadn't. Both of my friends had taken me by surprise tonight.

I dragged my feet across the floor, and my mind wondered what Rowan might be up to right at this moment. She had not been far from my thoughts over the last few days. When I closed my eyes, she was there, and when I slept, I dreamt of her. I had thought that learning who she was would douse any flames of passion or affection that I felt for her, but it hadn't.

Pushing open the door, I was surprised to see Toby leaning against the wall, his eyes closed. I waited for a second before I opened my mouth to speak, however Toby cut me off.

"No questions, not here."

I understood what he meant, the walls had ears inside the castle, and our words might not be private in these corridors. The only reason we knew that our dwelling was not under scrutiny was Mercy's ability to root out a spy.

Toby and I walked in silence down the long corridor of kings until we were out in the warm evening air. We had crossed halfway over the training sands before Toby said a thing.

"I never thought I would miss the sun so much or rejoice in it. But after witnessing the ice of Soar, I am grateful to call the desert my home."

I chuckled in spite of my dark mood, and Toby grinned. He shoved open the door to our home, paused for a second and then sighed, stepping aside so I could walk through the doorway. Mercy sat at our dining table, three glasses and a bottle of desert spirits in front of him.

Indicating for us to sit, Mercy dared me to defy him with his eyes. I stripped off my coat and kicked off my boots before I obeyed, motioning for him to pour into my glass. I knocked back the liquid, coughing as it burned my throat, causing Tobias to laugh loudly.

After I composed myself, I scrubbed a hand down my face. "Can we not leave this until morning? I am too tired to be lectured by you tonight, Mercy."

"No lectures. You have my word."

Toby took the glass handed to him by Mercy and joined us at the table. He watched us cautiously, but he was Tobias and it wasn't long before the quiet was too much for him, and he said, "What was it like, to have to do what she told you to do?"

"Infuriating."

Toby chuckled and drained his glass, reaching out to grab the bottle and pour himself another round. I leaned back in my chair and listened as they barbed with each other. It was not long before my mind drifted off far from the desert and to the girl I shouldn't have been thinking of.

I wondered if she was thinking of me, as much as I found myself thinking of her. I know we did not leave things on the best of terms, but would she welcome me with a kiss of her lips or the kiss of a blade?

"Earth to Jules, come in Jules?"

I sighed and focused on my friend again. "Sorry, I was miles away."

"With a certain raven-haired temptress?"

I rubbed my temples for the millionth time that night. "She's not a temptress, Toby. Just a girl. Did she seem so evil to you?"

Toby shrugged his shoulders. "Nope. I found myself liking her. But Jules, once the crown is on her head, the world tilts, and she becomes ever more the enemy."

I rested my elbows on the table, my chin on my hands. "But what if there was no need for her to be our enemy. If we could enforce the peace treaty so that there was no threat of war? What if, every single person on the continent of Vernanthia could move freely between territories without fear of death?"

They both looked at me like I grew an extra limb. Then, Toby shook his head in dismay. "That would happen in an ideal world, Jules. But not our world. This war between the houses has gone on for generations. Some fleeting romance with a rival isn't enough to stop a century of fighting. Think reasonably, my friend."

I sipped my drink, and sighed. "I am thinking reasonably, Toby. Imagine what it would be like if we spent more time living life and not preparing for a war that might not come. If we were free to choose what we wanted to do with our lives, and not forced to be something that we are not. If there was no war, if this ancient grudge was not ours to carry, how much happier would we be?"

"That's the thing about you. Jules. You see the sunshine where there is none. You want to play peacemaker, not king. But I have seen many things as your father's shadow, and this ancient grudge as you call it, runs far deeper than you can imagine."

Toby cleared his throat and gave us a grin. "While you both have valid points, what I want to know is… how the hell did I end up with such a stupid magical power?"

I chuckled, as this was what Tobias had been

griping about all the journey home. Not that it was hard, considering that Mercy and I had barely uttered a word. He spent the long and arduous journey home bleating on about the rubbishness of finding out that he was never a Null.

"Why did you not mention this to my father? I thought you'd be shouting from the rooftops."

Toby shot me a glare, drumming his fingers on the table. "And what would I say. Oh, by the way, Malcolm old pal, when Mercy had a knife to the Cambridge heir's throat, and her siren friend brought Mercy to his knees, we discovered that I have the mental magic of a bloody shield. How the hell is that useful?"

"At least you were not stripped of your will and forced to act like a marionet," Mercy muttered as he poured himself another drink.

We laughed at the seriousness in his tone and the look of scandalization on his face. Soon we were all laughing uncontrollably and as quickly as that, the tension evaporated from the room. We continued to laugh for a few more minutes, and then once we had regained our composure, we drank another round.

"I want to see her again. I need to see her again. There has to be more to our story than this. This cannot be the way it ends."

An idea popped into my head, the plan formulating in my mind even as I glanced at Mercy. "Maybe you could deliver a note for me, Mercy. One note delivered to Rowan where I can tell her how remorseful I am about what has transpired. Would you do that, Mercy? Would you deliver her a message for me?"

The room quieted, and I waited for a response from

Mercy holding my breath. He was watching me, assessing me, and I wondered what he saw when he looked at me so. After what felt like an era, Mercy reclined in his chair and folded his arms over his chest.

"You are asking me to go into enemy territory just to leave a love note?"

"Are you telling me that you haven't been in the Cambridge stronghold before?"

His slow smile told me all I needed to know, but he kept me waiting for a few more minutes before he asked, "And sending her this letter, will this lessen this insane obsession you have? Will this be enough for you to put this behind you and move on?"

"Yes," I replied, tasting the lie in my words. "I just want her to know that I mean her no harm or ill will."

Mercy nodded, believing my lies, and I swallowed hard as he told me to go write my letter and he would deliver it. I rushed to my room, sitting at my desk with a quill and some ink, trying to put down on paper what it is I wish to say. But everything seemed so small and paled in comparison to what I wanted to say.

And then I realized what I had to say could not be said on paper, it must be said in person. So, I wrote my note, asking Rowan to meet me in the rainforest. I considered asking her to meet me in Saor, but in the grand scheme of sweeping gestures, I would embark on a journey into enemy territory to tell her what I wanted her to know.

I finished my note asking Rowan to meet me in five days' time at dusk and sealed the letter shut so that Mercy would not sneak a peek. When I came back down the stairs and handed Mercy the letter, I felt such guilt as I had never felt before.

"And this will be the end of it. The chapter is closed, and you will make every attempt to move on?"

"I promise." The words almost stuck in my throat as Mercy took the note and vanished into the shadows. I did not expect him back before dawn, nor did I know how quickly he could jump the shadows. All I knew was that I needed Mercy out of the house so that I could escape the desert and make my way undetected across the continent.

Perhaps Mercy was right; I had become obsessed with Rowan. But not seeing her would only make me obsess about her more. Some expression must have crossed over my features, because I turned to see Toby watching me.

"Why are you making that face?"

"What face?"

"The face you make when you are thinking of doing something really, really stupid."

I brushed off his questions with a laugh and mulled about in the kitchen area for a while before Toby muttered that he was off to bed and ambled up the stairs. Perching on top of the counter, I listened until sleep claimed Toby, his snoring so loud he might have woken the dead.

Quietly rushing upstairs, I shoved some clothing into my bag, and quickly redressed myself, removing my Montgomery uniform and dressing in non-descriptive clothing. I grabbed a scarf to shield my face from the desert and also to prevent myself from being spotted. I left behind anything that might have given away who I was or where I came from.

I came down the stairs, trying to figure out how I would get someone else's horse from the stables, considering Blitz had just returned from such a long journey. Gathering some bread and cheese from the cupboard, I shoved them into my bag, slinging it over my shoulder as I head for the door.

I had almost managed to get out of the house when I felt someone watching me, the hairs on the back of my neck standing to attention. I knew who it was even before he appeared out of the shadows. Mercy appeared and I almost leap out of my skin, even though I had half expected him to show up. His face was grim, and I could tell he knew all along that I had been untruthful.

Opening my mouth to apologize, I glanced down at his hands, rejoicing when I saw they were empty. Although there was nothing to stop him from disposing of the letter and telling me that he had delivered it.

Silver eyes watched me as I set down my bag, my shoulders hunched. I open my mouth, knowing I should apologize. Mercy stopped that.

"If you wanted to go see her, truly wanted to see her, then I would have taken you. All you had to do was ask."

I blinked for a second, having not expected that. Maybe he was testing me to see if I would have followed through. But then I saw his expression and the worry in his eyes.

"I overreacted." Mercy stated. "When I put the blade to Rowan's throat. I saw how you looked at her, I knew that she was important to you. But you are important to me, Jules. And any relationship that you and Rowan would have would be tainted by your family names."

"I know all of this, but I cannot stop myself from thinking about her. If she meets me, then there is something there. If not, I will return here with my heart broken and never speak of her again. But where we left it, how we left it, it does not sit well with me."

I leaned against the counter and sighed. "As long as there is still this niggling feeling in the pit of my stomach, I won't be able to move on. Will you help me to go and see Rowan one last time?"

"Planning a vacation without me?" A sleepy voice said from the stairwell as Toby came into the room. "We all go, or we don't."

The question in my eyes, I glanced back at Mercy and waited an agonizing minute before he answered.

"If we must die in enemy territory, we go together."

chapter eighteen
rowan

I LISTENED FOR ALMOST AN HOUR IN SILENT contemplation as the Friar told me the story that we all learned growing up. Once upon a time, there was only one witch coven throughout the continent, living in harmony with their non-magical neighbors. There was no war, no grievance, no hatred. The world was a peaceful place.

Then, some slight happened. It was unclear which side caused the fracture within the coven, but the Cambridge witches blamed the Montgomerys; and they blamed us. Power became all consuming, and kings and queens ruled their respective sides. The war raged for decades, spilling blood. The soil of our continent was tainted by the fallen.

When a ceasefire was called, for almost a century after, both covens tethered on the edge, waiting for the chance to spill blood once more. I had heard the story many times before, and nothing had changed since the first time my tutor had explained the history of how the royal lines were formed.

"I know this is not unfamiliar to you, Rowan, but it does feed into how we, the rebels, came to be. Please bear with me."

I rolled my eyes, clutching my dagger as I waited impatiently for him to continue. All the while, Auggie grinned at me, and I wanted to punch the smirk from his lips.

"Your mother wasn't always so hard. It was only when the crown was placed on her head that she began to change. She became obsessed with her legacy, and the legacy of her kin. Before, when she was just a princess, she married your father, who was the head of Cambridge army."

"Can we get to the point?" I sighed, my eagerness to be out of here evident. "I know all of this. I know how my father died. I know all of that. What I want to know is why you would tarnish my father's name by suggesting that he was responsible for this act of treason."

Auggie chuckled. "Is she always this impatient?"

The Friar gave me a smile, but my expression did not so much as twitch. "No, as a child, she was much worse."

I stand, unwilling to listen to him speak of me with such familiarity. This man was a traitor, and I had a responsibility to report him. My eyes darting to the exit, I take a step toward it.

"Wait, Rowan. Before you condemn this old man to death, hear me out one final time. Thomas would have wanted this of you."

"But my father is dead and cannot ask anything of me," I snarled, trying to blink back the tears in my eyes.

"Then let me tell you the truth of how he died."

I freeze where I stand, wondering if I could trust the man standing in front of me. For years, I had been the subject of gossip, listening to hushed whispers from those who thought I could not hear them as they called my mother the black widow who devoured her husband in a jealous rage. They spoke of her like a viper who had poisoned my father. And when he had died, once the mourning week had concluded, Kendra Cambridge went about her duties like my father had never mattered to her in the slightest.

We were never allowed to speak his name in her presence, and every single year that passed when I continued to look more and more like him, my mother hated me a little more.

"Are you going to tell me something that I don't already know? Are you going to blame my mother for his death, like all the rest of them? Even if it is true, what can be done of it. My father has been dead for over a decade. Unless you can raise him from the ashes on the wind, there is little that can be done about his death."

The Friar rested his hands in his lap, and I continued to stare at him, wondering how I could have been so stupid. How, in all my many years visiting the man who was gifted with metals, did I not know that he had been planning to dethrone my mother?

"When Thomas came to me and told me that Kendra had given birth to a beautiful baby girl, where I should have seen excitement, I saw only fear. All along when Kendra had spoken of her dream to unite the covens under her rule, Thomas had been behind her. But as he stared into his baby girl's eyes, Thomas decided that he did not want this life for you. And he decided to bargain a way out."

"There is no way out for a royal. We become queens or we die."

The Friar gave me a sad smile, and my heart began to pound. Was there a chance that I could be free, and

I couldn't believe that I was even contemplating it, but could I have a chance of happiness with Julian?

"I see it in your eyes, Rowan. Eyes so like your father. You do not want to be sovereign. Believe me if you want, but Thomas made an agreement with another, someone within our circle, who had agreed to help you both. Thomas was to steal you away from Kendra until you were old enough to be free of her influence.

"However, on the night that you both were supposed to leave, Thomas was called to a breach on the edge of the territory. And he never came back. I had raced to the scuffle, yet when I arrived, my best friend was already dead, his blood staining the grass."

Swallowing hard, I wiped a tear from my eye as anger boiled inside me. I knew all this, I had heard the tale of how my father died defending his territory. What I found hard to believe was that he would try and steal me away from here and away from my mother.

"Kendra," the Friar continued, his lips pulled into a twisted snarl, "told the kingdom that a Montgomery spy had crept in under the cover of darkness and murdered her husband. She saw it as an act of war, but the army disputed that, and little by little, we were all relieved of our posts."

Auggie glanced at me, and I hated the sympathy in his eyes. Mortified as tears began to creep down my cheeks, I wiped at them furiously, not wanting these men to see me show any weaknesses.

"What your mother did not know was that my father was in the woods that night to meet with Thomas." Auggie said, and my attention snapped to him. "It was my father who had agreed to hide you, Rowan, and they were meeting one last time to make final arrangements. My father watched from behind a tree as one of Thomas' soldiers, under the order of his queen, ran his sword through the heart of the queen consort."

I could taste the truth in his words, though I did not want to believe him. My hands trembled so much that I almost dropped my dagger. A chill caressed my spine, and I shuddered. I wanted to scream and rage at them for lying, for weaving words in the hope that I would not inform my mother of their treachery.

Rubbing my temple, I allowed myself a moment to breathe before I responded. "Say I believe you, say that I take you at your word, what is it that you want from me? I heard you say that you were going to come to me, tell me what was going on. Now is your time, Friar. Tell me why I should let you live."

"Because this group is made up of witches and nulls, from both sides, who wish to see an end to this hatred. Thomas convinced us all that we could change the future for *everyone*. No kings, no queens, just citizens of Vernanthia. A council with equal voices. No more bloodshed, Rowan. People would be free to be anything that they might aspire to be."

The Friar looked at me, his eyes so full of hope that I wanted to believe in the words that he spoke. "Imagine it, Rowan. You would not be forced to marry Paris. You could live the life you wanted, the one Thomas wanted for you. You would be free."

I snorted and brushed a stray hair from my face. "Freedom is such a pretty word. Especially when it comes as a consequence of what, my mother's death? Blood will stain all our hands, Friar. Where is your religion in all of this? Can you justify murder? If that is the case, what makes you any better than my mother?"

The Friar made to speak, but Auggie rested his hand on his shoulder and spoke instead. "There are more of us involved in this movement than you think, Rowan. On both sides. I know that you and Jules formed some sort of bond while in Soar. As the two future rulers of your covens, would you not like to have a civil accord with him? Rather than be forced to kill each other on the battlefield?"

My mind flashed with images of my dreams, the ones where Jules killed me, no love or lust in his eyes as he snaps my neck, only indifference. My mind was a whirlwind of confusion, and I could not think straight. My chest tightened, and I felt a wave of panic swirling around me.

"I need time to think. I will not say a word for this night and a day. Nor will I spill the secret of where you hold your little rebellious meetings. If I do not come back tomorrow night, then you know that I want no part of this. And, I will have nothing more to do with either of you."

"I understand." There was a sadness in the Friar's tone that I could not stand to hear, yet I pulled my cloak over my head, sheathed my dagger, and headed for the exit. I paused, just as I reached the mouth of the cavern, turning back to face the man I thought was my friend.

"Will you try and kill me if I do not come to your way of thinking?"

"You are Thomas' daughter, Rowan. I would hope that there is more of him in you than Kendra. I would hope things would not come to that conclusion."

That was a yes then. I shook my head and rushed up

the passageway, stepping out into the crisp fresh air as I gulped in breaths. I could not believe that I had stumbled upon the rebellion, and that members from each part of Vernanthia had chosen to be part of it.

I walked back to the castle in a daze, ignoring those who tried to stop me as I traipsed up the long steps to my bedroom, which was situated in the highest tower in the castle. I loved to sit on the window ledge and gaze out over the continent. I pushed open the door, closing it and standing there in the darkness for a minute before I stripped off my cloak and kicked off my muddy boots.

"And where have you been until now?"

Jumping with my hand on my dagger, I whirled round at the sound of my mother's voice, trying to pick out her location in the dark. I heard the sound of a match being struck and suddenly a flame sparked to cast a terrifying shadow against my mother's grim expression. I relaxed my stance and gave my heart a second to calm its rapid beating.

"I have been away from the rainforest for too long," I said, trying not to allow fear to sound in my voice. "I just had to allow myself a moment or two to feel at home again."

"I expected a report the moment you arrived back. I waited for you all evening. Instead, I had to find out from Emilee how your adventure went. Even Paris was more forthcoming than you."

I bowed my head, pretending to show some remorse, although I had none. My mother rose from the chair that sat next to my small collection of books I had inherited from my father. Kendra had little or no time for reading.

"I'm sorry, Mother. What is it that you wish to know?"

The smirk tugging at my mother's lips made my blood run cold, I could not help but wonder if she knew about my encounter with the rebels, her spies everywhere.

"I had thought that I had gotten rid of all those who would move to betray me, especially within my own house. It saddens me to learn that I had not."

"Mother, I-"

"Silence!" Kendra's yell rebounded off the stone walls, and I swore her voice must have been heard throughout the castle. I clamped my mouth shut, my heart trying to free itself from my chest as I ran over possible ways to escape inside my mind. As if she read my expression, Kendra shook her head.

"I remember that expression, it's one I have seen many a time in my reflection. Another secret my only child has kept from me. Not only have you much of Thomas' magic, but you also carry some of mine in you."

It was the first time my mother had spoken my father's name in a decade, and it sounded foreign on her tongue. She circled me, her elaborate gown swishing against the floor. The crown atop her head glinted in the flicker of the flames.

"This makes you valuable, Rowan. Much more than you were before. But, you have hidden things from me, and I cannot allow it to continue."

Waving a piece of paper in my face, she grabbed my hand, ordering me to read it. As I did, I felt all kinds of emotions—fear, hope, love, remorse. Written in an elegant handwriting, I read the words and committed them to memory.

Rowan,

I have not been able to stop myself from thinking of you since we last met. I regret how things ended and need to see you, if only for one more time. I will come to your rainforest, in five nights time, and I hope that you will meet me.

If you decide not to, then I wish you well. Maybe, in time, we can be in each other's company without the weight of our names.

Five nights, Rowan… I hope to see you then.

~Jules

MY BREATH CAUGHT AS I CLUTCHED THE NOTE TO MY chest. My heart sped up as I lifted my eyes to my mother's. She watched me with disgust, and I hoped and prayed that she did not know who Jules really was.

"And who is this boy who manages to slip a note under your pillow in the dead of night?"

"Just some boy I met in Saor. He is no one really." My words came out in a rush, and I knew by her expression that Mother did not believe me, especially as she made to snatch the note away from me. I snarled.

"Emilee, come here please."

My heart sank as my best friend came into the room, tears staining her face. I knew, knew that I was lost. Emilee could barely spare me a glance as she sidled up next to my mother.

"Emilee neglected to tell me about this boy when we first chatted." Kendra began, her fingers twirling into Emilee's hair as my friend flinched. "Considering she failed to locate the item I sent you in search of, it seems she has failed me twice."

"Leave her be." I squeaked out, but I was ignored as Emilee gulped back a sob.

"When I showed her the letter, and after a little persuasion, Emilee told me about your little dalliance with Jules." She spat out his name like it was poison. "You have the most handsome man vying for your hand, and you choose to have relations with a Montgomery mongrel. How could you?"

My excuses formed behind my mouth, readying to tell Kendra that I had not known Jules was a Montgomery when I had met him, when I had kissed him, when I had felt my heart reach out for his. But the words that tumbled from my lips enraged her.

"I love him."

Kendra chortled, a rough sound as she rolled her eyes at me. "Love him? Love him? You do not know him. What a stupid, naive little girl you are. I did not raise you to be full of romantic notions. You are to be sovereign, Rowan."

I balled my hands into fists by my side. "I do not want it. I do not want this life that you want for me. I wish I was not your daughter. I wish I was anyone but me!"

I slapped my hand over my mouth, and Kendra sneered. I cursed myself for my outburst. Her fingers grabbed hold of Emilee's scalp, and she yanked Emilee up on her toes. My friend shrieked, but I was powerless to help her.

"Do it," Kendra ordered, and I glanced at the window for a chance to escape.

Suddenly, I was ensnared from behind, Paris' warm breath on my neck. "I will make you regret that you choose a Montgomery scum over me."

I jerked, trying to get free of him, bile in my throat, but hands gripped my chin, and I was forced to look into Emilee's tear-heavy eyes.

"Rowan," she began, her voice choked with emotion. "You will not leave this room of your own accord. You will stay here until I release you from this order. You will only leave if your life is in peril, or you have no other choice."

Emilee's compulsion ensnarled me like a whip against my flesh, and I screamed, the sound like a feral animal. Once the compulsion set in, I could not bring myself to leave. I pushed free of Paris' hold and sank down to my knees, ignoring Emilee's sobbed apologies.

Kendra shoved Emilee away, and the girl fled from the room. My mother looked at Paris and said, "Go greet the Montgomery heir when he is due to arrive. And bring me his head."

"With pleasure," Paris replied with a sickening grin. I lunged for him, but he was already over the threshold before I could lay my hands on him.

I turned to my mother, ready to beg for Julian's life. One look at her expression, and I knew that anything I could say in his defense would be wasted. She had issued his death sentence.

Kendra swept from the room, pausing in the doorway to say, "I do this for you, Rowan. You brought this on yourself. When the boy is dead, you might see sense."

She closed the door behind her, and I tried my hardest to get free of the room to no avail. I sank down on my knees, Jules' letter still in my grasp, and screamed until my throat burned.

chapter
nineteen
julian

WE DEBATED OVER THE EXACT PLANNING OF OUR TRIP into enemy territory for the next few days. And when I say debated, what I really meant was that we fought tirelessly about who would be first to go with Mercy. Considering Mercy could only take one of us through the shadows with him at a time, Toby argued that leaving me alone to my own devices might not be the wisest thing to do.

I countered Toby's argument by stating that should anything untoward befall me whilst I waited for Mercy and Toby to join me, then Toby was my best chance at survival. I also stated that Rowan would run at the sight of Mercy, and that I needed to be there when she arrived in the forest.

Mercy was silent as ever while Toby and I continued to argue about the best course of action. Mercy waited until we had exhausted all our theories and planning before he made his offering.

"Since I am the one who will have to transport you both through the shadows, in the end, it is my decision to make. Jules will go with me first and obey every instruction that I give before I leave him alone in enemy territory. Then, I will go back and get Toby. If Rowan arrives before we do, then Jules will not move an inch without us."

His last statement was punctuated with a stern glare in my direction. I promised with a nod of my head, forgoing the words that would bind me to comply with Mercy's request. Toby frowned and grumbled a slew of words that almost turned the air blue.

With all the discussions and organizing, I had little time to worry over my nerves about seeing Rowan again. My nights had been plagued by the same dream, over and over again, repeated in vivid color, waking me with a start, covered in sweat and my breathing ragged. On more than one occasion, I scanned my hands, as if I could feel Rowan's blood staining my palms.

We had been sequestered inside our home for the last couple of days with only a brief trip out in search of supplies. If our presence around the castle was missed, there was no indication of such. I had, however, paid a short visit to my mother after my father's request and chatted idly about my impression of Saor and the wintery weather we had encountered.

Growing up, I had always been amazed at how, when my mother walked by, all eyes went instantly to her. Others had said that it was her beauty that had attracted my father's gaze and I could see why. Her hair was a sandy color like my own, but it seemed to sparkle against the desert sun. Her skin was kissed by the sun also, almost golden in color. When she smiled, it was as if the sun itself smiled upon you and instantly warmed you. Our eyes were identical, but I always imagined that the great oceans of old, the ones we read stories about, were the color of Amelia Montgomery's eyes.

I asked my father once why he had chosen my mother as his queen, and his answer did not surprise me.

"It was a shame, boy," he stated, as if it was the only conclusion anyone could have come to. "It was a shame that a woman so beautiful be left to wither and grey without being queen. Someone as beautiful as your mother deserved only to become my queen."

When my mother asked me a question, for perhaps the tenth time with no response from me, she asked if there was something troubling me. The little boy in me wanted to spill my secrets to my mother, but I feared, deep down, that no matter that I was her only child, her loyalty to my father and the kingdom of Montgomery outweighed any fondness she might have toward me.

I brushed off my distracted state and played it off that I had had a disagreement with Toby over something insignificant. My mother smiled and patted my cheek, much like she had done whenever I came to her crying over something that was said in passing by boys within my regiment, or, whenever I had said or done something to displease Malcolm.

Now, as my mother studied me with those eyes, I felt the weight of my lies against my chest. I did not want to lie to her, but it saddened me that I could not trust my own mother with my secrets.

After chatting some more about the latest bit of literature she had recommended to me, I bid her farewell with a kiss to cheek. I had almost made it to the door of her suite when my name on her lips halted me. I turned back to face her, watched as she rose and came to rest her hands on my shoulders.

Our eyes met, and for a moment, I thought my mother could read my thoughts as she said. "I wish only happiness for you, Julian. You believe that, don't you?"

"Of course." I had replied, because that was what was expected of me. My mother gave me a sad smile, before she ensnared me into an embrace, something she had stopped doing during my teen years under Malcolm's orders, as if a hug from my mother would make me soft.

"The stars will align for you, Julian. And when they do, I can see great things and so much happiness for you. Do not be afraid to carve a path for yourself."

And with that, she dropped her arms, turning from me and disappearing into her bedroom before I could utter a syllable. I stood there, mouth agape for an age before I could move my legs and head back home.

I never fully understood my mother's magic. I had assumed that her magic was contained within her beauty. That was what had lured my father to take her as his wife and queen. I considered how my mother used to advise me to bring something to shield my eyes during drills in the sand dunes, and a sandstorm had raged so suddenly, we could not find any shelter from the brute strength of it.

Another time, many years ago, as Toby and I hid behind one of the stone pillars in the throne room, my mother had issued a warning to my father against sending Mercy on some mission. Malcolm, of course, dismissed my mother's warning, and Mercy had come home with a wound so deep, it took three healers and all of their magic to remedy him.

What if my mother really had premonitions? Would that account for the dreams of blood and death that I was having? Were the dreams harbingers of a path that I was torpedoing toward?

Shortly after lunch on the fifth day, we gathered in the kitchen and hashed out the finer details. I tried to tamper down the excitement and anticipation building up inside me, but I could not wipe the grin from my face.

"Jules, I will drop you off in the rainforest, and you will wait for us in the exact spot that I leave you. If any danger comes lurking, you hide. You do not engage any enemy combatant. Do you understand?"

"Perfectly."

All three of us had dressed in non-descriptive black clothing, down to the black boots on our feet. I wondered how Mercy would take us from one side of the country to another but thought against questioning him. I would surely know soon enough, as I travelled the shadows with him.

Mercy sheathed his twin blades in a crisscross on his back. Toby snapped on his belt, an array of daggers and blades attached to it, before he fixed the strap over his shoulder and looped his own sword across his back. I followed suit, strapping on my blade and belt, before sheathing a small dagger in the sheath on my ankle.

Mercy studied us for a moment, his silver eyes roaming over us. When he seemed content that we were sufficiently armed, he nodded and backed himself into the corner where the shadows clung to the walls.

"When I first rode the shadows, I felt ill after every jump. If you feel queasy, close your eyes until I tell you to open them."

Mercy beckoned me forward, speaking to Toby as I moved to stand in front of him. "I will need a few minutes after such a long jump to collect myself before we ride the shadows. If I do not appear in one hour, something has gone wrong, and you will need to tell the king. It would be in your best interest to pretend that you know nothing of our plans."

As Toby made to protest, Mercy looked away from him and at me. "Are you ready?"

I gave a slight incline of my head in answer, and Mercy motioned for me to come closer. As I stepped close enough that our bodies almost touched, Mercy embraced me by wrapping his arms around me. I was vaguely aware of Toby muttering under his breath before Mercy pulled us back, and we pitched into darkness.

Until my dying day, I would recall the very moment the shadows engulfed us, the feeling of weightlessness as for a bare instant, I was nothing but shadow. My senses dulled until there was nothing but the darkness, a stark and dangerous beauty. Even in the vast nothingness, I felt freer than I had ever felt before, and I understood what lured Mercy in every time he became one with the shadows.

It was as if I was standing in the ocean of the night sky, and no stars dared shine and disturb the silent beauty of it. I felt a longing, a longing to stay here among the nothing and enjoy the peace that had washed over me.

And although it felt like an eternity and an instant, all in one, I felt the moment Mercy pulled us from the shadows All my senses returned with a jolt, and my feet reached solid ground again. Mercy released me from his grasp.

My stomach threatened to revolt as the feigning sun burned my eyes, and the rain falling around us sounded like thunder in my ears. Reaching out I steadied myself against the coarse trunk of a tree, bending over with eyes closed and tried to stop myself from emptying the contents to my stomach on the forest floor.

"Are you alright?"

"I am," I answered Mercy as I rose. "But please stop yelling at me."

Mercy chuckled and shook his head, looking none the worse after our journey. He cracked the muscles in his neck, peering out into the forest as he said, "It is as green as I remember it."

It was my turn to laugh as I glanced up at the sun, hidden behind somber clouds filled with rain. We made it, and just in time by the looks of it. I saw Mercy run scenarios in his mind, sensed his reluctance to leave me here without any backup, but I grinned at him, trying to reassure him with my easy tone.

"Go and get Toby, or he will have worried a hole in the ground with his pacing. I promise not to move unless forced to do so."

"I could wait."

I sighed, yet understood his dilemma. "Mercy, I haven't come this far to be foolish and die, have I? Go and retrieve Toby, and I will be waiting here when you both arrive."

Mercy considered me for a moment before he fixed me with a stare, then stepped under the cluster of trees where the shadows linger, vanishing before my eyes as rain fell down more heavily.

Taking in my surroundings, I noted that Mercy was correct, and everything was so green. The grass beneath my feet crunched as I moved my booted feet, the leaves on the trees above me swaying in the sync with the wind. I could smell the dampness in the air, scent the clean crispness of the air a stark contrast to the humidity of the desert.

Time seemed to go by with agonizing slowness, leaving me standing in the middle of the vastness of an eerily quiet forest. I had expected more animals roaming the forest, or at least more sounds. The hairs on the back of my neck stood to attention as my eyes scan the forest.

A flutter of green caught my eye and my heart skipped a beat. Standing in an opening at the edge of my viewpoint, a hooded figure strode toward me. I stepped out into the clearing and watched as she came closer, shielded by the moss-colored hood.

I had formed her name on my lips, ready to call out to her, a massive grin on my face. Yet something, perhaps similar to my mother's sense of impending doom, made my stomach flip as the hooded figure came within striking distance and yanked down her hood.

It was not Rowan who stood before me.

Instead, the man who had manhandled her at the ball smirked at me like he was the cleverest of fellas, and I saw his intentions in the embers of anger in his eyes. My hand reached back, grasping the hilt of my sword and unsheathing it in one swift movement.

"Did you really expect her to meet you here, Montgomery?"

"That would have been her choice," I replied, circling my wrist to rotate my blade. "But I assume you or someone else has decided to make the choice for her."

The man tossed aside the cape that was so like Rowan's and withdrew two scabbards from his sides. We stared at each other, neither of us willing to look away first, and sized each other up. I could tell by his gait that he knew what to do with his weapon, and this territory gave him home advantage. But I had skill and magic, and I could harbor a guess that any magic he held within his flesh and blood paled in comparison to mine.

"She begged for days to be let out of her room. She even bargained with me to let you live. But Rowan is neither my queen nor my bride yet, so I do not bow to her will."

Rage, fiery hot and seething, spread inside me. I growled, thinking that this man thought Rowan was his. I wanted to make him bleed, wipe that smirk off his face, and present his carcass to Rowan in tribute.

And that scared me.

"Tell me your name," I demanded. "So that when I see Rowan again, I can tell her that I ended your life for thinking that you were good enough for her."

The man laughed at me, and this did little to temper the anger in my veins. "And you think that you are, Montgomery mongrel? The queen herself has sent me to kill you, to punish you for putting romantic notions in Rowan's mind. Oh, how she wept from the window of her tower, calling after me, begging me not to go. I will be sure to comfort her once she learns of your demise."

The rain began to pour down around us, soaking my clothes to my skin, clinging my hair to my face. But I readied myself to strike, as the man opposing me introduced himself.

"I am Paris, and Rowan is my future bride. My name will be shouted in glory when I tell the tale of how I felled the Montgomery heir."

Paris came at me with a battle cry, and as our swords clashed together, metal on metal, the sound ripped through the forest like the loudest of thunder. Even as we moved, blocking blows and strikes, I had to admire the artistry in his movements, the warrior instinct in him. However, he intended to take what was mine, and he would die for it.

Once Toby and Mercy arrived, he would be outnumbered, and perhaps he would surrender, but I doubted that very much. As I blocked a strike with my sword, Paris slipped one of his blades free of my block and drove the tip of his blade toward my stomach.

I sank to my knees, avoiding the wound to my stomach, earning a gash in my forearm. I could smell the coppery scent of blood in the air, felt the sting of it, but I ignored it. I released the hold that I had on my magic, summoning the air to me and pushing it in a firm shove toward Paris, sending him to the ground on his ass.

Rising to my full height, I waited as Paris got back to his feet and grinned. "You want to play it that way then. If you insist."

Before my eyes, Paris's image blurred and a moment later, there stood two of him, a mirror image with no way to differentiate who was real and who was not. Or even, if they were both real.

The two came at me with added vigor, and I did not get the chance to use my magic as I blocked each and every strike, my death visible in both of their eyes. I heard the sound of someone vomiting over my shoulder and almost breathed a sigh of relief. Mercy called out my name.

That was enough to grab the attention of one of the incarnations of Paris, with only one head turning in the direction of my companions. With as much strength as

I could muster, I kicked out, driving my blade up and into Paris' chest, the metal scraping the bone as I drove it between his ribs and up into his heart.

The second Paris disappeared, leaving a wide-eyed Paris glaring down at me. I withdrew my blade, and the dying man crumbled to the ground. It was only as his breathing stopped, and his lifeless eyes stared back at me, I realized with a start that I had killed a man for the very first time.

Mercy and Toby rushed over as I let my sword, still stained with Paris' blood, clatter to the ground. Mercy helped me to my feet and checked me over for any wounds, but apart from the slight gash, and the sudden guilt at taking a life, I was unharmed.

Toby, whose face was pale after his trip through the shadows, glared at me, punching me once on the shoulder before he stated.

"I knew you should have let me go bloody first."

chapter twenty
rowan

FOR ALMOST FIVE DAYS AND NIGHTS, I RAGED AND roared, screaming at my mother, at Emilee, even at Paris, to let me out. I tried in vain to escape through my turret window and leap onto the ground below, but my stubborn will was no match for the strength of Emilee's compulsion. I knew, without a shadow of a doubt, that every moment that I remained stuck here was another minute closer to Jules' possible death. My heart could not hold that much sorrow in it.

Food and water were refused. Servants who entered the room to assist me with bathing were swiftly encouraged to leave with the promise of a blade. On the third day, when I screamed for my mother and told her that I would slit my own throat if she did not answer me, a flurry of militia men entered my room and stripped me of my weapons, all apart from a dagger that I had hidden in the base of my boot.

My mother meant to keep me alive, and Jules' blood would forever stain my hands. Sleep claimed me numerous times over my imprisonment, but the dreams that seeped into my subconscious were not pretty dreams; they were dreams of death and destruction. Usually, I awoke in the morning and did not remember a second of my dreams. Yet, I remembered every second, every minute, every word spoken, as if I had lived this dream before.

I pace the room, my long moss colored cloak dragging along the ground as I listen to the men and women of my army inform me of the breach of our security. It seems that during the night, the king's assassin had crept into my castle with the intentions of kidnapping my most valuable commodity; my siren.

"Had I not explicitly ordered for the siren to be under constant supervision?" I growl at the man speaking, and everyone in the room bows their heads.

"Forgive me, your Sovereign, but the boy was young and fell asleep. He has been reprimanded. However, the siren is still where she should be and did not suffer any injuries during her ordeal."

I wave my hand, feeling the weight of the crown atop my head and shout for someone to bring the siren to me. The doors to the war room open, and my former best friend is almost carried in by the female soldiers by her side. Gone are her refined gowns, her plethora of jewels, and her face is pale now that it is free from any adornments. Her brown eyes are missing the light that used to sparkle in them, yet I do not feel any sorrow for Emilee; one cannot hold onto any emotions for a person who betrayed them as Emilee had me.

The soldiers stop inches from me and cast Emilee down to her knees. She bows her head and waits for me to speak. I indicate for the soldiers to bring her to her feet, and I look into the eyes of the person that I had loved like a sister and feel empty.

"Tell me what happened this eve." It is an order, not a

request.

"My Sovereign." *Emilee begins, a slight tremble in her voice. "I had just turned in for the night, my eyes closing as I drifted off to sleep, and that's when I felt him. The silver assassin reached for me, but I screamed even though he told me that he would not hurt me."*

I let loose a snort. "The last time you met, the shadow promised to kill you, even with just a murderous glare in his eyes. What makes you think that he would not hurt you this time around?"

Emilee clears her throat. "He said that his king would welcome me to his court, that I would receive far better treatment that I did under your care. He told me that King Julian would not ask me to do anything that I was not comfortable with."

"If he promised you the world, then why did you scream?"

Emilee's eyes dart around the room before they settle on me once more. A single tear slides down her cheek, and she rushes to wipe it away. "I am a Cambridge witch. I serve only one royal, and she is a queen. I will not bend the knee for any foreign king."

I admire her loyalty. But this weed of anger in me has turned bitter and twisted, and when I look at Emilee, it only serves as a reminder that I am indeed all alone in this world, and when I remember who I used to be, my thoughts go back to Julian, and the way he had made me feel. And my heart twists even more into darkness.

Lifting my gaze, I order the soldiers to take Emilee back to her room, to light as many candles as possible, and to try and reduce the chances of any shadows clutching to the corners of her room. They lift her up and lead her from the room, halting only when I utter an order to wait.

"The next soldier to fall asleep and risk her life will hang for it. Do I make myself clear?"

There was a rapturous sound as the entire room replied with: "Yes, my Queen."

Once Emilee has been escorted from the room, I turn my attention back to my most high generals. "What word have we on the rebels?"

One man, the son of the man who served as my mother's second in command, comes forward. "The latest news we have is that they have scattered to Saor, hoping that the walls and security of the Null territory will remain a sanctuary for them. They hope that you will not breach the walls for fear of shattering the truce."

"Saor already shattered the truce by harboring fugitives within its walls." My fingers unconsciously touch the scar that runs from my eye to my chin, a present from the man who had been a father figure to me before he tried to take the throne out from under me. "We will send in the strongest of our combat mages, and we will tear the city apart. The Friar is to be brought to me alive, as is Augustus Ashbridge."

The general waves away his consignment of witches, and I turn my attention to another branch of my army. Sometimes, I find it hard to believe that they take orders from a girl who has barely turned eighteen, but they do. My mother had been right; wearing a crown is a powerful thing.

Addressing one of the others who once served under my mother, I ask him about another mission, one that is personal and as vindictive as possible.

"How goes our spy within the Montgomery desert?"

The general, a small, well-rounded man who has not seen the battlefield in over a decade and would not hold his position if he did not have such a record of service. He once *fought alongside my father and spoke often of him. It seemed once my mother was out of the way, most of the men who were in my father's regiment have much to say about him.*

"It goes well, my Queen. My daughter has made herself a favored bedfellow of the King's general. It seems the general sometimes, after enough desert ale, converses in his sleep. She reports that the general has still not been able to shield more than a handful of soldiers during practice, and his frustration at not being more proficient with his magic only adds to his woes."

I turn away from the packed room and glance out the window. The forest, once my escape from a future that I had not wanted, beckons me toward it. It seems like an age since I lost myself in the scent, in the tranquility and the peacefulness of the rainforest. But a warring queen has little time for girlish needs and wants. I smile, an odd feeling as I close my eyes, listening as the rain batters the windows in front of me.

My plan is simple. I will take from Julian what knowing him has taken from me. I will garner as much information as possible from his general, and then my spy will slip a deadly poison into his ale. Julian is not bred for war; not like I am. He needs his general and his shadow in order to come up with a plan, whereas I can close my eyes, see all the possible outcomes, and know which plan will succeed.

In order for me to reign supreme over Vernanthia, I need to rid Julian of his support system. And when he is vulnerable, I will drive my sword through his heart, like he has done me.

"Sovereign, if I may. The Queen mother wishes to speak with you."

Turning slowly, I let a small smile creep over my lips. "Does she now."

"Indeed."

I step down off the dais and make my way toward the man who has spoken, Paris' father, and whisper, "Tell my mother that I have nothing to say to her. Tell her that I am the queen she always wanted me to be. And she will watch from her ivory tower while I burn Montgomery to the ground."

I stride from the room, leaving a flurry of activity behind me. And only when I am alone in the cover of the shadows do I allow myself to tremble.

The person in my dreams, I did not recognize. She was bitter and twisted. She was the queen I feared I would become under my mother's influence. Yes, I hated Emilee for what she had compelled me to do and despised her for not having enough character to come face me during my imprisonment.

It was Paris I detested the most. The man who had come to my bedroom door and gloated about how much he would enjoy killing Jules. He taunted that my mother had agreed to bring forward the wedding if he killed the Montgomery heir. I screamed at him, called him every vulgar name I had within my vocabulary, and all Paris did was laugh, telling me how much he would enjoy breaking my spirit each and every day of our marriage.

It was during that time that I could not help but wonder what the Friar thought about my absence. Had word filtered through to him that I was a prisoner in my own home? My mother's actions had only steeled my will and my desire to see her overthrown surged. Instead of pulling me to her side, my mother's vindictiveness had sent me marching in the opposite direction.

How could she have turned this evil? Nothing in her life had been so terrible. She was adored by her people by all accounts when she was a princess. With doting parents, a loving husband, and an heir borne shortly after she became head of the Cambridge coven, life was sublime. Perhaps the stories were true, and perhaps what they say was true. Power was the source of ultimate evil, and it corrupted all who wielded it.

The door to my bedroom opened slowly and I glanced away, feeling my best friend's aura reach out for me, so familiar that I almost knew it better than my own. I could smell the meaty broth that she had brought with her, my stomach rumbling as the scent assaulted my nose. Emilee's eyes were red and puffy as she sank down into the armchair facing my bed and tucked her arms around herself. She did not speak, nor did I, but after a lengthy silence, Emilee was the first to break the ice.

"I'm sorry, Rowan. So unbelievably sorry."

"If you are so sorry, release me from my compulsion so a boy does not have to die because he had the misfortune of being born a Montgomery. The same boy who kissed me when he knew I was his mortal enemy. A boy who spoke of freedom and snow as if it were magical. Have you no conscience? Do you care so little for me that you force me to stand idly by as Paris attempts to murder Jules."

"It's because I love you that I do this. Do you realize, Rowan, that when you speak his name, your voice softens, your eyes get this faraway look, and you speak of the Montgomery boy as if he has captured your entire heart."

Because he has.

A voice whispered in the back of my mind, and I realized that it was true; I truly loved him, which was madness.

"I simply do not want to see any bloodshed for no reason. You tell me that you want to serve me in future, but how can I ever trust you, especially when you promised as children that you would never use your magic against me."

"She is my queen," Emilee sobbed.

"And I am your friend!" I exclaimed, not caring that my voice has travelled. "You were the person I thought I could depend on the most, and now that is ruined. Do you think when I am sovereign that I will let you live as my mother does? I should avow it now, so that you know that I am utterly serious. You will be nothing more than a tool, a means to frighten an entire nation. You will compel at my will, and you will watch the destruction that you cause with your very own eyes."

Emilee clasped a hand over her mouth, but I am not finished unleashing my rage on her. "Be fearful if I do become sovereign, Emilee, because your hands will be stained by the blood I force you to spill. For every life I take because of your actions that led me here, you will also take a life. Anyone you love, you will be forced to watch them die, and know that simply saying "I release you" could have spared you this existence. If I am to know no peace, then neither are you."

I saw the tears well in her eyes, and it only fueled my pent-up fury. "I swear to you, by the old gods and the new, your actions here today have turned my heart cold. I will never trust you again, and I will never forgive you for forcing me to be a prisoner. If you were not so much a valuable trinket, I would shove you from this window and end your sniveling."

I stood, catching a glimpse of myself in the mirror behind Emilee's head. I no longer saw myself, but rather the scarred battle-hardened queen from my dreams with a cold, vicious heart.

And I welcomed her.

Emilee stood, wiping the tears from her eyes. "You do not mean that. Once you have had time to cool off, once you are no longer under the Montgomery heir's spell, then we will talk again."

I snarled, my lips curling up so that I bared my teeth. "You speak my mother's words as if it were her lips that moved. Go, Siren, and kiss the feet of your current master. And pray that I never become the one to hold your leash."

Emilee fled the room, and her reaction added fuel to fire of my rage. I grabbed hold of the bowl of broth and flung it at the door with a roar. I glanced around my room, my prison, and I snapped. Reaching under the bed, I flipped it over, sending the blankets and pillows off in a flurry. I swiped my arm across my dresser, sending trinkets and jars crashing to the ground, the contents spilling on the stone. I picked up my chair and smashed it against the door until the splinters of wood pricked my skin.

Slumping down to the ground, I buried my face in my hands and screamed into my palms, hoping that it would diffuse some of the rage in me, but it did little to soothe my soul. Right now, at this moment in time, Paris would be stalking the woods and lying in wait for Jules to appear. Would Jules think that I had set him up? Would he believe that I sent Paris to kill him? Would he die all alone in the forest with no one to hold him, or would he slay Paris and continue to hate me forever?

Over my shoulder, I heard a tweet and spun round, coming to my knees, to see a raven standing on the window ledge, his black eyes watching me with a human intelligence. We regarded each other cautiously for a moment, neither of us moving, as if the bird was waiting for me to speak.

"Hello," I said, spotting a rolled-up piece of paper in its mouth. "Is that for me?"

The bird bobbed its head, but didn't drop it. I held out my open hand and smiled at the bird. The raven tilted its head and dropped the small scroll into my hands. When I made to thank it, the bird let out a gurgling croak and flapped its wings, soaring into the air and leaving me alone again.

I stared at the tiny scroll for a minute, wrapped in a red string bow, wondering who could have sent it. Carefully unwrapping the bow, I sat it aside and rolled out the paper. My eyes widened as I read the message from The Friar, who had apparently heard about my imprisonment from a spy in my mother's kitchen.

The idea made me smile, and I read further into the note, The Friar asked me to stay strong. He was working on a plan to free me from my mother's grasp, and even if the rebels managed to free me, I was under no obligation to join them. My will was still my own.

I folded up the scroll and hid it inside my tunic, for fear that my mother would sweep into the room and figure out that her husband's best friend was behind the rebel group looking to take her throne from her.

And I would do as he asked; I would stay strong, and I would wait. And when I was free, I would help the rebels take my mother's throne, even if I had to sit on it to do so.

I would wait...

chapter
twenty-one
julian

WE REMAINED GATHERED AROUND PARIS' BODY FOR A while, trying to figure out our next move. My eyes refused to move from the sight of the blood staining the tunic Paris wore, while Mercy and Toby continued to squabble. Mercy, showing the signing of exhaustion from too many shadow jumps with extra passengers, argued that we should remain in the cover of the forest for a time.

Toby simply frowned at Mercy and stated that if Paris did not return to the Cambridge house, others would be sent in search of him. And once his body was discovered, House Cambridge would hunt them down like animals. I couldn't argue with either of their points of view, but considering that Paris had told me that Rowan was a captive within her home and tried to bargain for my life, I knew that I could not let her remain a prisoner.

I picked up my sword, using the end of my cloak to wipe the blood from the steel, and cleared my throat. "I'm going after Rowan."

Toby whirled on me, and I staggered slightly. "Are you mad? She set you up, Jules. She sent her freaky fiancé to gut you like a fish!"

"That's not true," I replied, shaking my head. "Rowan is being held captive, Paris himself said so, and she begged for my life. I cannot leave her to suffer."

Toby glanced at Mercy, holding out his hands. "C'mon Mercy. Back me up here. We cannot simply storm into House Cambridge on the words of a dead man to rescue the damsel from her ivory tower." When Mercy refrained from answering, Toby huffed out a breath and glared at me.

"Perhaps if you thought more with your head and less with your-"

"Enough!" snarled Mercy, his eyes darting through the forest. "We are not alone."

Immediately we went into battle mode, our backs meeting each other as we formed a defensive stance. Toby had unleashed his sword, with Mercy fiercely gripping his dual blades, ones eerily similar to Paris'. I shook my head to try and clear some of the rain dripping down my face to little avail. A chill crept over my spine as rain slid down the collar of my tunic and along my back.

"I never thought I'd miss the desert. That was until all this bloody rain."

I chuckled, surprised at how easy it sounded considering we might be facing an impending death sentence.

"There are archers in the trees, as well as bladed men stalking around the great trunks of the trees. They watch from the shadows, unsure of what to do."

"How many?" I question Mercy, wondering if they have the numbers to seriously defeat us.

"The shadows tell me two dozen men and women. They also tell me that some of the archers are not grown yet, so I assume some children are in there as well."

That angered me. Not even my father sent children into battle before years and years of training and molding into soldiers. What kind of monster was Kendra Cambridge?

I shifted my weight from one foot to the other. My eyes darted through the vastness of the tree branches, trying to discover the archers that had arrows pointed directly at us. I heard the familiar sound of an arrow whizzing through the air and lifted my sword to block it before it could find a home in my chest.

The arrow fell to the ground as we rallied together and braced ourselves for attack. For almost an eternity, the only sounds came from the elements around us; the wind whistling through the trees, the rain pouring down on us, the squelch of our feet as we tried to remain sure footed in the mud.

We waited for the full-on assault to come. But it did not. What we last expected was for a familiar person to strut from the trees as if this was not a battlefield.

Augustus Ashbridge came into my line of sight first, and when I let loose a surprised sound, Toby cast a glance in Ashbridge's direction. Ashbridge came forward with his hands held up in surrender, his voice carrying across the wind.

"Cease fire! Stand down. These men mean us no harm as of yet."

I heard Toby mutter 'want to bet' under his breath, and I couldn't help but grin. Mercy looked stunned for the first time in his life, and I felt a little sorry for him. Ashbridge came within striking distance, so I held out my sword.

"That's close enough, Ashbridge. Care to tell us what you are doing here?"

The High Lord of Saor grinned, his eyes twinkling with mischief. "Probably the same thing you all are doing here. We came to rescue the princess."

I waited for a moment and then lowered my sword, Mercy following suit, yet Toby still held a firm grip on his sword. Ashbridge glanced up at the sky, and then his eyes fell on me. "Perhaps we should take shelter from the coming storm, friends. Come, we have somewhere dry and warm where we can speak freely."

The three of us remained planted where we stood, refusing to move and go with them until we were certain we could trust them. Ashbridge whistled a small short sound and all three of us gasped in disbelief when Mercy's father came out of the forest.

Mercy and his father looked only slightly alike, considering it was hard to compare Mercy to either of his parents. Conrad had greying hair, though not of the pure silver like Mercy's, and the shape of their faces were quite similar. Conrad was a merchant by trade, his ability to find and source valuable items not a magic sought after, but a valuable commodity, nonetheless.

"Papa?" Mercy said, his voice full of shock.

"Yes, Mercuree. Please come with us. I will explain everything once we are stowed away safely."

Mercy turned his attention to me, awaiting instruction. I nodded, sheathing my sword at my back before telling Ashbridge to lead the way. We walked into the cover of the trees, Mercy walking in front of me, while Toby took up the rear. Ashbridge strode ahead, and slowly others came out of the forest and joined the short trek into the depths of the forest.

We walked for a little while longer until we come to what looked like a dead end. Toby opened his mouth, ready to fling accusations no doubt, but I held up my hand, which immediately halted him, earning a quirked brow from Ashbridge.

"This better not be a trap, Ashbridge." I warned, folding my arms across my chest.

"I assure you it is not." Ashbridge walked over to a wall of heavy vines and lifted the curtain to reveal a cave entrance. He motioned for us to go through, which we did in pretty much the same formation as we had during our journey here.

A small passageway illuminated by torches guided our path, and once the curtain was dropped into place, I glanced back and could not see any light from the outside. I continued to walk down through the cavern, my boots clopping against the floor, and the sound echoed and announced our arrival.

At the end of the corridor, the mouth of the cave opened up, and I stepped into what looked like a meeting area, with various tunnels leading out of this main area. Ashbridge removed his cloak and sank down onto a chair at the top of the room. Mercy's father stayed off to the side, and Mercy tried his best to focus on me and not his father.

But my attention was on the man seated at the top of the room, next to where Ashbridge had sat. The man, with greying hair, and a variety of scars on his face and neck, was in charge of this ragtag group of people. He had this aura about him, one that made people pay attention.

Our eyes met, and we glared at each other for a

moment before he gave me a small smile and inclined his head.

"You must be Julian Montgomery."

"Forgive me, sir, but I feel at a disadvantage. I know not who you are."

Rising from his chair, the man came toward me, and Toby inched closer, his sword still in his grasp, but I shook my head. The man held out his hand, and I hesitated before I reached out and shook it.

"My name is Lawrence Reinhart. But many know me as The Friar."

His name sounded familiar, but it took a snarl from Mercy to force me to remove my hand from his.

"The Friar is the leader of the Rebels. The traitors who want to remove the reigning heads from their thrones." He glanced at his father in utter disappointment, before coming to stand by my side, sending a jolt into my heart.

"Mr. Reinhart, what makes you think that your declaration has not just earned you a swift execution? No matter if you are a Cambridge traitor or a Montgomery one. Even thinking of slaying a ruler is punishable by death."

Backing away from me, Reinhart took his seat like I had not just threatened to behead him. He tucked one leg behind the other and rested his hands in his lap. He leaned in and whispered to Ashbridge, who got up from his seat and returned with a canteen of hot tea. Ashbridge poured five cups, picked a random cup and drank from it.

"So, none of you boys think we would poison you."

Toby grabbed one of the cups and lifted it to his lips before I could stop him. When he didn't keel over and die, he handed the cup to me and shrugged. I sat down on one of the benches, with Mercy and Toby joining me. I took a sip from the cup and shivered as the warm liquid crept down my throat.

"What if I told you, your Highness, that we wanted to remove the current monarchs from the throne and replace them with you and Rowan?"

Shrugging my shoulder, I replied. "That will happen in due course. Why push for it now?"

Reinhart closed his eyes, and when he opened them once again, I swore I could see a sheen of wet. "We have it under good authority that Kendra Cambridge is close to mounting a siege against House Montgomery. Rowan was sent after the same valuable item as you were. She has credible information that could lead to the destruction of the Montgomery line."

My heart pounded in my chest, but my face remained a mask of indifference, a trait I had learned from many years playing at prince.

"If this is true, then we have something the Cambridge sovereign wants."

Reinhart shook his head. "Kendra only wishes for more power. She can feel the time for her to step down and let her daughter reign, and she is loath to relinquish the crown, even to her daughter."

I sat the cup down and clasped my hands together. "And this has got something to do with the Montgomerys why?"

"Because I think you love the girl who is like a daughter to me and would hate to see her ruined by her mother's lust for ultimate power."

I froze, seeing this man in a new light. I could hear how much he cared for Rowan in the tenderness in his voice. However, any affection that he had for he did not outweigh what it was he intended to do... take the throne from my father, a feat Reinhart could only do if he pried the crown from his cold, dead hands.

"I understand that you have little recourse to trust me. There are many of us so called rebels. From both sides of the war. Would you not like to see peace, Julian? Wouldn't you like to live in a world where Rowan was not your enemy?"

And wasn't that all I ever wanted? The Rowan part was recently true, yet all my life I had wished to be free of this war. I did not want to hate someone because of their name, even though it had been ingrained in me since birth to hate those who remained loyal to House Cambridge. If there was another way that lessened the risk of innocent lives being lost, was it not the right and just thing to do to consider it?

Or would that make me a traitor as well?

"Rowan's father was one of our founders." Reinhart continued, and I tried to mask my shock at that. "He did not want this life for his daughter. He loved the little girl who smiled at the rain and hugged animals. Thomas sought a better way for his daughter to rule. And I think together, you and Rowan can achieve what the entire continent of Vernanthia has longed for, for centuries."

"And what is that?"

"Peace, dear boy. We simply long for peace."

Was I seriously considering siding with these rebels? How could pretty words entice me so? Or was it as simple as my heart's desire lay with a girl who under pain of death could never be mine? Could one act of treachery lead to a peaceful future for all of Vernanthia? And if so, who was I to think I could be the one to usher in this change? I was merely a reluctant prince who did not wish to be king.

Reinhart left me to my musings, turning his attention to Mercy, who looked like he was ready to commit murder. Reinhart then cast a glance at Conrad who shook his head, leading Mercy to heave out a breath.

"You have been watching me, Papa, from the corner of your eye since we arrived. Please, enlighten me as to why you took it upon yourself to betray the crown?"

Conrad's gaze flickered from Mercy to Reinhart, before he cleared his throat and began to speak. "I have watched my only child grow from a boy who laughed freely to a young man who shared more in common with the shadows he could control than his peers. Had it not been for the friendships that you had built with his royal Highness and Tobias, I fear that you might have delved far too much into the shadows."

"Papa, please." Mercy said sharply, uncomfortable with his father divulging secrets in front of strangers.

"Do you know how much your mother cried?" Conrad continued, anger in his tone. "Do you know how much she cried when at seven years of age, you came home covered in someone's blood? That was the night you stopped laughing. You stopped trying to be normal. Malcolm Montgomery used you, a child the same age as his own, and asked you to kill. And with each request he put upon you, my dearest Mercuree, we mourned the loss of our son."

"Enough!" Mercy exclaimed, shaking off my hand as he stood. "I did what I was born to do, and I tell you father, I am very good at what it is I do. But obviously you are a better spy than I, considering I had not a clue what you were up to."

"Please, Son, let us speak privately." Conrad begged.

"I have nothing to say to you, Papa." Mercy stated, putting his back to his father as he said, "May I take leave of you to cool my temper?"

Normally, Mercy would not ask me, he would simply vanish, but we were putting on a show, and the show, it must go on. I dismissed him with a wave of my hand, and Mercy stormed off down the tunnel. I saw Toby fight the urge to go after him, so I leaned in and said, "Go after him. I will be fine until you return. I am fearful for anyone who gets in his way when he is in such a mood. Please make sure he doesn't sully relations by devesting someone of their heart."

Toby laughed, and the tension from Mercy's outburst seemed to evaporate. Toby looked at Ashbridge and issued a warning of his own.

"If a hair on his pretty little head is so much as out of place, then I will hold you responsible."

Toby stalked off after Mercy and left me alone with the two men, Conrad having slipped away as soon as his son departed. Now, the real discussions could begin.

"It is admirable, to have such loyal men at your back." Reinhart said.

"Loyalty that is earned and not bought is the best loyalty to have," I said in response, and Reinhart bowed his head as if I have said exactly what it is that he wanted to hear.

"Before you continue, I have a few things that I want to say."

Reinhart nodded again, so I continued, hoping that my nervousness, the tremble in my clasped hands, was masked. I tilted my head slightly and spoke directly to the man in front of me, ignoring Ashbridge completely. He was not the one who could answer to my demands.

"While I agree to listen to your demands, it is by no means any compliance with your views or wishful actions against the crown. If no one attempts to injure me or my men, then we will not harm any of yours. Do you agree?"

"We do."

"If we enforce this truce, and we decide that we wish no further part of your rebellion, you will allow us to leave under the stipulation that we will not use any knowledge of your whereabouts, or those within your organization against you."

Reinhart regarded me with surprise. "That is amenable."

I inhaled a breath and nodded. "But before we go any further, our first course of action must be to retrieve Rowan from her captivity. Paris stated to me that she is under the siren's compulsion and cannot leave her tower. Either the siren dies and the compulsion is broken, or we must find another way to free Rowan."

"I can help with that."

I spun round at the sound of Mercy's voice and peered at my friend. "Rowan won't go with you easily. You have to make her trust you, considering you tried to kill her the last time you met."

Reinhart spluttered an indignant curse, but I ignored him.

"If you order me to bring her to you safely, your Highness, then I must obey your orders."

I rose and went to stand in front of Mercy, ignoring the eyes cautiously studying us. I put my hands on his elbows and said, "I would never order you to do anything that you did not wish to do. However, I would ask my friend to help rescue a girl being held against her will. If you do not wish to do this, then we will find another way. But would it not be better to use your power for good, instead of the murders my father asks of you? It is too much, Mercy, for one man to bear."

Mercy leaned in and rested his forehead against mine and whispered so low that only I could hear him, "And that is why you will make a great king."

Stepping back, Mercy vanished into the shadows, and I released a breath I did not know I had been holding. Mercy would get Rowan, and she would be safe.

I turned around and faced Reinhart, who wore a strange expression his face. His lips kicked into a smile, wrinkles crinkling around his eyes. Ashbridge also grinned like an idiot as Reinhart rose and bowed low at his waist.

"It is nice to meet you finally, King Julian. Very nice indeed."

chapter
twenty-two
rowan

PATIENCE HAD NEVER BEEN PART OF MY MAKEUP, AND A mere hour after getting the message from The Friar, I paced the trashed confines of my room, my eyes watching the window for further messages. I was dressed in my cloak, the sole dagger in my possession fixed to a sheath at my waist. My hair had been braided and rebraided numerous times out of boredom.

Despite wanting to continue to wallow in my anger and rage, I put my bed the right way around simply for something to do and for a place to sit. And now, as I sat cross-legged on the bed, I counted the seconds in my head, hoping that any attempt to rescue me would come soon.

My thoughts grew dark as night settled in, the moon casting shadows against the curve of my prison. I wondered who had been victorious in battle. Had Paris managed to sneak up on Jules, or had his bravado been his downfall, wanting to gloat in Jules' face about me. I knew little of Jules' skill with a blade. I could only assume that being the future heir, he had been trained somewhat to defend himself.

Even though I tried to have faith in that reasoning,

every time I closed my eyes, I imaged him lying in the grass, bleeding to death alone and thinking that I had betrayed him. I could hear the rain pelting off the roof, a steady thump, thump. With a quick glance out the window, I could see the darkening of the clouds, an indication of an impending spate of rainfall. Nothing unusual for the city of Cambridge, but I could not help but wonder if it was as ominous as it seemed.

"I like what you have done with the place."

Startled, I leapt from the bed and had my dagger in my hand a second later, braced to take on whoever had dared to slip into my room. But I could see no one, and my door had not creaked open. My eyes had been trained on the window, and not a soul had crept in that way. Then, I knew who it was who had ventured into my room without having to lay eyes on him.

"Have you come to finish off what you started?"

"Would you believe me if I said I have come to rescue you?"

I chortled, spinning around and trying to pinpoint where the voice had come from, to no avail.

"Do you promise to play nice?" The voice asked from deep within the shadows.

I gave a nonchalant shrug of my shoulders. "Sure, I'm game. My day couldn't get much worse. Death might be a welcome distraction."

As soon as the words left my mouth, the silver shadow emerged from the far corner of my room, and I felt envious of his power. My eyes widened in wonder at the seamless migration from shadow to man. The silver of his hair was pulled back into a low-slung braid, wisps hanging freely around his face as they framed his eyes.

And those eyes- it looked like the silver of the moon has been captured in those eyes. There were many that would consider him handsome, all coiled muscles and high cheekbones, with tattoos that curved up his arms and stretched across to kiss his neck.

I slipped my dagger away as I quirked a brow. "You are rather handsome for an assassin."

"And you are rather mouthy for a princess."

"You are not the only one to be disappointed by that."

"I am not disappointed. Simply perplexed."

We regarded each other for a moment before the assassin rolled his eyes and said, "Come, we haven't much time. Let me take you to Julian."

Now it was my time to roll my eyes as I folded my arms across my chest. "Oh yeah, and how gullible do you think I am? Even if I wanted to, do you expect me to just saunter out of here with you and trust you. You tried to kill me."

"I am sorry."

"Oh, you really sound it."

With a sigh, Mercy reached out and grabbed my arm hard. "I do not have time for this, little girl. We must go. Julian awaits us."

Mercy tried to drag me toward the shadows, and my head suddenly was pierced with an agonizing pain that dropped me to my knees. My arm burned from where he had gripped me. As soon as I scooted away from him, the pain in my head receded.

"What is wrong with you?"

I rubbed my temples as I slowly got to my feet. "Remember your little siren friend? Yes, well she used it on me, and I cannot leave this room of my own free will."

The assassin frowned, and I blew a hair out of my eyes as I said, "Thanks for trying. If you really did come for Jules, tell him I'm sorry. He's alive, right? Paris didn't kill him, did he?"

The smile that crept over Mercy's lips sent a shudder of fear along my spine. "Paris is dead, killed by Julian." Pride filled his voice and I searched inside myself to see if I would feel anything about Paris' death. I did not.

"Good riddance to him. Karma's a bitch."

That brought a strangled laugh from the assassin, but he quickly sobered. "Julian is in the company of a man you might know as The Friar. They have agreed to a truce until you have been rescued."

Jules was entertaining the rebels? For me?

"Tell me, princess, what exactly did the siren compel you to do?"

I recounted Emilee's exact wording, and then I repeated them for the assassin. "You will not leave this room of your own accord. You will stay here, until I release you from this order. You will only leave if your life is in peril, or you have no other choice."

A sly grin tugged at the silver haired assassin's lips as he said, "Do you believe that I would harm you, princess."

"In a heartbeat."

"Do you consider that your life would be in peril if you did not come with me?"

I could see where he was venturing with this, and my own lips curved into a smile. "Sure."

"Then let's make it so."

Mercy pulled a dagger from the array of weapons at his waist and came at me. The next minute, he had one arm around my waist, and another coiled its way like a snake around my neck. I felt the kiss of a blade against the flesh at my neck and prayed that I had been right to entrust my life to him.

"Riding the shadows has different effects on people. Some find themselves nauseous. Some experience odd symptoms. Just remember to breathe."

"Sounds wonderful." I said, my tone teasing, but the shadow did not seem to get my sarcasm.

Mercy backed us almost to the corner of the room, where the shadows seemed to come alive in his presence. The tattoos on his forearm also seemed to move before my eyes. We were almost to the corner, taking careful steps in case the compulsion kicked in and thwarted our plans, when the door to my bedroom was flung open. My mother stood in the doorway, murder in her eyes.

"Unhand my daughter, Shadow. Or there will be no corner that you can hide, no place that will be a haven for you. I will hunt you down and send Malcolm his prized spy's head in a box."

"Wow, Mother. With that speech you almost sounded as if you gave a damn about me," I blurted out, trying to give Mercy time to get us closer to the shadows.

"I love you, Rowan. I want what is best for you."

"And holding me prisoner proves that, does it?"

My mother chose to ignore me, focusing on Mercy once more, but I pulled her attention back to me. "What now, Mother? Will you hunt me down as well and drag me back to the castle? Will you find some other poor sap and convince him that marrying the princess will be his greatest accomplishment?"

"You know that Paris is dead?"

I grinned, and for a second, I see a flicker of real

emotion in her features before she remembered herself. "Someone beat me to it. Pity. I was looking forward to slitting his throat."

"Stop this nonsense now, Rowan. You have been compelled to remain here and will do as ordered."

I laughed, and it sounded cold and distant. "Oh, Mother, it seems that your siren did me a favor after all. She compelled me not to leave unless my life was in peril. And I assure you that the shadow here hates me more than I hate myself. He would sooner divest me of my head than save me. So, as my life is indeed in great peril, I bid you good night. Go, Mercy."

A second later, as my mother screamed for her guards, Mercy lurched backwards and we became engulfed in the shadows. When I raced through the trees, the wind in my hair, the grass beneath my feet, the animals surrounding me, I felt an absolute sense of freedom. But here in the shadows, there was no warmth, no sense of self, nothing but the utter darkness and I was terrified. The shadows felt as if they were reaching out to caress my skin, and I tried to struggle away from Mercy, if only to escape the overwhelming sense of emptiness.

Mercy held me tighter as I tried to stop the panic that had surged forth in my chest. I felt it the moment we left the shadows, but my eyes, my eyes only saw darkness, and I feared I had gone well and truly blind.

"Just breathe, Princess. It will pass."

I felt his arms leave me as I struggled to find my footing, my eyes unable to see.

"I can't see. Mercy. Why can't I see?"

Warm hands cupped my cheeks, and I almost cried, knowing whose hands touched my face with such tenderness. "Travelling with Mercy is an experience. You will be okay, Rowan. I am so very glad that you are okay."

"Jules, is it really you? Is this some sort of trickery? Some magic to fool me-"

My words were cut off as Jules captured my mouth with his, and I closed my eyes, losing myself in this feeling, this feeling that I was home in the arms of the boy who was supposed to be my enemy. It was rather sad, when you considered that I felt more at home with Jules than I would ever feel wearing a crown.

I felt Jules pull back from our kiss, and I opened my eyes, blinked a few times, and they eventually cleared. In front of me, I saw the boy with hair the color of the sand, eyes as blue as the ocean, and a smile that filled my heart with happiness.

"Hi."

"Hi yourself."

Our moment was ruined as throats cleared, and I turned to see the Friar watching us with satisfaction, as if all his plans were coming to fruition. Jules reached out his hand, and I took it, allowing him to pull me over to the benches, where I had sat a mere couple of days ago. We sat down, side by side, so that our shoulders touched.

Glancing at Jules, I nudged his shoulder. "So, you've decided to band with the rebels?"

"Not yet. I was waiting to see what you were considering."

"Well, right now I'm considering I need a warm bath and a decent meal. Thoughts of a coup can wait until I've been fed."

Jules laughed and squeezed my hand, as the entire room smiled at us like we were a pair of prize-winning mules. I leaned my head against Jules's shoulder, but my eyes lifted to meet the Friar's.

"I am so glad that you are okay, Rowan. When you did not return, we feared the worst. However, upon hearing of your captivity, we mounted a rescue mission. How fortunate we were for your young prince to arrive and bring his shadow with him."

"The shadow's name is Mercy and should be addressed as such. Does he not have enough people who treat him as a possession or a thing? At least see him for the human he is."

My eyes roamed over to Mercy, who met my eyes and inclined his head so briefly I could have sworn I'd imagined it. We might not like each other very much, but we were both victims of our bloodline. But he had saved me from my mother's clutches, and I owed him one.

"Forgive me. It is hard to see the person when all I have heard is legends."

"Try harder," I said.

The Friar chuckled. "Spoken like a true queen."

"If you say so," I grumbled under my breath.

Jules cleared his throat and asked, "What do you want from us now, Reinhart? We are both here, listening. Now is your chance to persuade us that your mission is the best course of action for Vernanthia."

My former father figure looked from me to Jules and replied, "I want this from you, an alliance between the two covens. A king and a queen who are not at war but can stand in the same room and speak freely. A king who will allow a rival queen to rest her head upon his shoulder and does not flinch."

"We want," Ashbridge interjected. "We desire to set

up a council, where any grievances will be discussed first, and a nonviolent resolution agreed upon. You can both rule your own covens, but still be open to discussions, and most of all, peace."

"But you want us to help you kill our parents?" I asked.

The Friar shook his head. "How could we ask you to help us find a peaceful resolution if we used violence to get it? We wish to arrest, or subdue, not kill. If we can remove them from power without any bloodshed, then we will do as much as possible to ensure that."

Ashbridge cracked his knuckles. "But we need something from Mercy before we can start to plan our next move."

"Indeed. The shadow..." The Friar paused as I glared at him. "I mean, Mercy. Mercy stole a very important scroll from Augustus, containing details of a curse that might be the final piece that we need. If Malcolm is able to translate the scroll and decipher its meaning before us, then all hope might be lost."

"Malcolm does not have the scroll."

We all turn to look at Mercy, who plucked the stolen scroll from inside his tunic pocket. Excitement lit up the Friar's eyes as he took a step in Mercy's direction, his hand extended.

"Not so fast, Reinhart," Jules said as he beckoned Mercy over. "Tell us what is in this scroll first."

Disappointment flooded the Friar's eyes, and I wondered what magic could be contained in the scroll. He folded his arms once more in his lap, taking a rather long pause before he began to speak.

"The scroll outlines the first war between the covens, and the curse inflicted on Vernanthia because of the coven's willingness to war with their kin."

I snorted, unable to help it. "A curse? Really? This is not a fairytale, Friar. This is real life. Do you expect us to believe that some curse is the reason why we hate each other? Give me a break."

"My cynical child," The Friar sighed. "I am saying almost exactly that. Why do you think there is no history of the first war? No written recollection? It is because each and every Monarch has erased any mention of it."

When none of us uttered a word, it was Ashbridge who continued with this vivid tale. "It's true, Rowan. When I was growing up, my mother used to tell me a story of a future king and queen who would be born to save us all. She told me about our ancestor who had been murdered by a Montgomery prince, a null who used the magic in the air to call out to the gods and ask for vengeance for her death. The gods granted it, and the curse implies that no coven would rest until…"

Ashbridge stopped speaking and looked to The Friar for guidance, like I had done so many a time before. Jules squeezed my hand as he asked the question that we were all burning to ask.

"Until what, Ashbridge? No point in playing coy now."

Ashbridge looked at us with such sadness that I wished I could cover my ears to stop from hearing the words that tumbled from his lips.

"Until love is possible between the covens. That's what my mother used to say, but we need the scroll to find out the exact wording."

I sat up straight and shook my head. I understood what they were alluding to, I *knew* what they meant. They saw Jules and I, the bond we had formed so quickly, and they thought that like in the fairytales, we would fall in love and end the war of the covens.

Isn't that what has already happened? You fell in love with him like magic…maybe you don't feel anything for him except for this wretched spell?

"Shut up," I muttered, and they all thought that I was speaking to them instead of speaking to myself. "You look upon us as if we are here to save you all. I say, what a ludicrous notion to have. You cannot expect all the answers to be contained in one little scroll. You cannot expect me to think that my feelings are not my own, and the result of some Null's curse from centuries ago. No, I will listen to no more to this foolishness."

I leapt up from my seat and yanked my hand from Jules. He looked at me with such pity that I wanted to slap his face to rid his eyes of the emotion. His lips began to form my name, and I shook my head.

"This is what happens," I told him, hoping he would understand. "You let people in, and they destroy you. That man, who was like a father to me, manipulated me my entire life. My only friend used her magic to force me into captivity. And now, these people use legends and myths to try and persuade me that what I feel in here is nothing but a spell, and that we have no choice in who we-"

I almost said the word, but it choked in my throat. I spun on my heels and fled the room, ignoring the sound of my name as Jules called out for me. My heart threatened to break inside my chest and break me along with it.

chapter twenty-three
julian

EVERY INSTINCT INGRAINED IN ME URGED ME TO FOLLOW after Rowan, to take her in my arms and reassure her that curse or no curse, the feelings we had for each other were real and true, and not a single word that they said could take that away from us. But I couldn't. Not when I had a niggle of doubt in my mind.

As I watched her flee, I closed my eyes, willing myself to stay and ask the questions that needed to be answered. When I opened my eyes, Mercy was looking at me with intense eyes.

"I will follow and ensure she is safe."

Before I could respond, Mercy had blended in with the shadows and vanished from the room. Toby, heaving out an exaggerated breath, sank down beside me and scrubbed his face with his hands.

"That was not a friendship I ever expected. Must have bonded over the shadows."

"Mercy will not forget that Rowan, despite her reservations about him, treated him like a person and not a thing."

Focusing my attention back to Reinhart, I turned the

scroll over and over in my hands. It was such a simple thing, this parchment in my hands. How could the contents of a single slip of paper convey a riddle and a response that could change our lives forever? Magic was a way of life for us all. But, I found it difficult to believe that the fate of the kingdoms could be delivered to us in a scribble of ink.

"What is it that you want from me?" I asked Reinhart, not even regretting the sharpness in my tone.

"I want you to give us the scroll and allow one of our crones to decipher the context. We need to see if the curse can be broken by you and Rowan. I understand that we are asking a lot from you both, but if there was any other way, we would have found it by now."

I considered his words before I spoke, trying to see sense and think with a logical mind. Yet I could not help but wonder if Rowan was alright, and if I could really trust the motives of the man who wished for me to betray my own father.

When I finished mulling it over, I turned to the man sitting beside me, my general and the person I trusted most with life. I looked into his eyes, and without Toby having to say I word, I knew he would back whatever decision I made. Even the slight twitch at the corner of his mouth was an indication of his agreement.

So, I rose, walking over to stand in front of Reinhart. I held out the scroll to him, refusing to release it when he grasped the other end. I held his gaze and tried to remind him that Rowan and I would not be used as pawns in his pursuit of power.

"I am choosing to entrust you with this, Reinhart. But I want to make it crystal clear that Rowan and I will make choices of our own free will, no matter what it states in this scroll. You will not force us to become part of this immensely futile path you are asking us to embark on. In the end, we both make our own decisions, and you will accept that."

I released my hold on the scroll and made my way in the direction in which Rowan went, Toby quickly on my heels.

"Julian."

I paused and peered over my shoulder.

"Do you not wish to know what is contained within the scroll?"

"Not particularly," I responded with a shrug.

In a quick few strides, I was out into one of the darkened passageways. Toby pressed a finger to his lips and inclined his head in the direction we were moving. After a couple of steps, he paused, glancing around to make sure that we were out of earshot before he shook his head.

"Well that was all kinds of wrong, was it not?"

"What is your opinion of Reinhart?"

Toby frowned, his eyebrows almost touching by the expression on his face. "He has more agendas than he is letting on. There is no way that he would wish to remove a monarch from the throne and not put someone else, someone like Rowan, who he felt he could manipulate into being his perfect sovereign, in her place. A puppet."

There was a reason why Toby would make an excellent commander one day.

"And?" I pressed him.

"And," he repeated before saying what it was that I suspected all along. "He sees what we all see. This undeniable chemistry between the two of you. I've never seen anything like it. It's like you two just gravitate towards each other like magnets."

"Do you think that this is down to some curse?"

Toby rolled his eyes and shook his head. "I do not know what to think. Maybe the fates have decided that you and Rowan, or the fact that you two are mortal enemies and still look at each other like you cannot stand to be apart, are the way to a peaceful resolution."

"That is very profound."

"I am not just a pretty face."

"Yes, sometimes he can be repetitively annoying."

We both whirled round as Mercy stepped out of the shadows. By the grin on his face, Mercy quite enjoyed startling us.

"I am so getting you a bell," Toby grumbled and I chuckled, needing the release right at this moment as my temples began to throb.

I opened my mouth to ask about Rowan, but Mercy cut me off.

"Rowan is off down that path, sitting by the fire and listening to stories being told to the children in the group. She seemed to sense me observing her and threatened to break my arm if I did not leave her be."

I smiled at the bemused expression on Mercy's face, and I felt compelled to explain Rowan's magic to him. "Rowan is a tracker, amongst other things. She sees auras and uses that to find anything she wants. I assume she could sense yours after you both rode the shadows."

"I see."

That was all that Mercy said in response, as if no further explanation was needed. I placed my hand on his arm in thanks for looking after Rowan, and then I walked away from my friends and went in search of her.

I could hear the crackle of the fire as I strode into the opening, felt the heat of it against my skin, and it reminded me of the desert sun. Had it only been a few hours since I had embarked on this mad task to find Rowan?

Like Toby's explanation, my eyes wandered over the room and bypassed everyone else until they land on Rowan. Huddled in the corner of the cozy chamber, Rowan sat with her hood up, her knees resting on a log in front of her and her chin resting in her hands. Against the flicker of flames, she looked breathtakingly beautiful. But ever since I first laid eyes on her, even when I could not see her face, when I had not known her name, Rowan had taken my breath away.

I stood watching her for a moment, listening to the woman weaving a tale of princes and dragons around the campfire to those young boys and girls gathered around, their eyes eager and captivated by the story.

I continued over to where Rowan was seated and sat next to her, surprised by how much my body relaxed once we were next to one another. She didn't speak, and I did not press her, allowing her to make the first move, but I was unable to deny that I was anxious to hear her speak.

"For once, I would have liked for someone to tell the story about the princess who saved the day. Perhaps, if there had been more stories about the princess who tamed the dragon and saved the kingdom, without the need for the handsome prince."

I suppressed a smile, continuing to watch the gathering of children. "Maybe you can create a story where the princess saves the day. Who knows, perhaps once we have decided if we are to save Vernanthia or not, they will tell tales of Rowan of Cambridge and her fierceness."

"Perhaps." That was all she said, but if I was not mistaken, I could hear the smile in her voice.

We sat in silence, listening as the children gasped and squealed as the woman told them of a giant green-scaled dragon, who breathed fire from its mouth, with teeth as sharp as a blade, and could melt the strongest of steel with just the steam from its nostrils.

"Is this all that we are, Jules? Is what we have nothing more than a convenient brush of cruel destiny?"

My heart, it threatened to break at the undeniable resonance of hopelessness in her voice. It struck me that perhaps Rowan felt as I did; that had we not been borne with royal blood in our veins, then would we have been forgotten unto the void of life, never to cross paths with those closest to us, or each other.

"I know little about destiny. I only know that since the very first moment that I laid eyes on you, dancing in the snow, silhouetted by the moon, I wanted to be near you, to surround myself in that carefree essence that seemed to leak from your entire being."

She tilted her head to peer up at me, a coy smile ghosting her lips, and I fought against the urge to kiss her.

"Some folk would consider it creepy, watching a girl from the windows, while she was completely unaware."

I felt a sense of pride well up in my chest, as Rowan's tone changed to that of a teasing one. I did that. Me. For the first time in my life, I felt that I had achieved something worthwhile.

"And what would you say of it, fair lady?"

"I would still say it was rather creepy, in a romantic sort of way."

Laughter rumbled in my chest, and I whooped with amusement, interrupting the story time and earning a glare from the storyteller, before I clasped a hand over my mouth, leaving Rowan to issue an apology on my behalf.

When I had composed myself, I reached out and took Rowan's hand in mine. I stared down at it, marveled by how easily her hand fits in mine, as our fingers interlocked. There was this hiss of electricity, or so I thought, as if we should never separate our hands again.

"What are we doing, Jules? What do we think can come of this… of anything?"

"At this moment, we are sitting in front of the fire, just Rowan and Julian, and nothing more. We do not have to think of tomorrow if you do not want to."

"That," she sighed. "would be a lovely idea. But tomorrow will rear its ugly head before we can blink. We are going to have to go back and face the music and decide if we are going to join the rebels and become traitors to our covens or return to our homes and become enemies once more. I do not think that I can consider either option."

And neither can I.

"Do you remember when I came to the stables in Saor, and I was rather angry."

"And then you kissed me?"

The way the corner of her lip kicked up made me want to kiss her again.

"Do you even know why, in the moment, I hated you?"

She made to pull her hand free but I grasped it more firmly in my hand.

"Because of my blood. Because of my name."

I lifted the back of her hand to my lips and pressed my lips to her skin before I answered. "No," I replied. "It was because you made me question everything they ever told me."

"Jules." Rowan sighed my name, and I knew deep down that no one would ever say my name quite like that ever again.

"Oh look, the young lovers! Have you come to save us all?"

We startled, our heads snapping up to stare at the person behind the voice.

Her hair was white as snow, her skin weathered and pale, with a crooked and misshaped nose as if it had been broken too many times to be fixed. Her eyes were as black as the night sky, and her spine was curved, causing her to hunch over and lean on a wooden walking stick embellished with a crow upon its head. And when she grinned at us, a handful of her teeth were missing.

Her black dress and shawl reminded me of a spider's web. Her shoes were shiny and pointed, as if someone had paid great attention to them. I could tell by the swell of magic around her that she was the crone Reinhart had been referring to. Crones were masters of deception and disguise, and using the guise of a haggard old woman was nothing more than an intimidation tool.

Crones could look like a devilish beauty one moment and a wrinkly old biddy the next. It kept them amused.

She lifted the end of her cane and tapped my knee once as she remarked. "Pretty enough you are. Not my cup of tea mind, but you will do."

"I am so glad you approve." I muttered, not trying to hide my dislike of the woman whose very presence made the hairs on the back of my neck rise.

"Do not give me sass, Julian Montgomery. I see what

is coming, and you will need more than sass to end this war."

Rowan jumped to her feet and grabbed the crone by the fringes of her shawl. "Tell us what it is that you know, old woman. Tell us now."

The crone muttered a word, and Rowan stumbled back as if she had been shocked. With a toothy grin, the crone shook her head. "So impulsive and quick tempered. It is not from Thomas that you inherited that nasty trait."

I glanced at Rowan and could see her blink back surprise as she asked timidly, "You knew my father?"

The crone completely ignored Rowan's question and turned her attention back to me. "Can you, Julian Montgomery, make the tough decisions when your lady love cannot? Will you be able to see past what your heart is telling you and consider that the head might know best? There can be no happy ending in whatever decision you make."

"I do not wish for happy endings, Madam, only peaceful resolutions. An outcome that will ensure those I care for are safe."

"Even, dear boy," the crone said with a sinister grin on her lips, "if that results in a grizzly end for you?"

I took the chance and looked into those empty black eyes of hers. In them, by gods, I swear I could see my death as clear as if it was happening in front of me. I consider her question, knowing the answer without having to dig deep enough for it.

"Even then." I replied softly. "Even then."

She cackled softly, and Rowan slipped her arm into mine and leaned into me. The crone's steely gaze roamed from me to Rowan and then she bowed her head.

"Good, good. There might be some hope for us yet."

She made to move away, leaving us with far too many questions. I opened my mouth to ask her to wait, to allow us to get some clarification about the scroll, but Rowan cut me off.

"Please, at least tell us what the scroll says. Or at least, if there is any truth to what The Friar is telling me; that we are tied up in some ancient curse that means only despair for us both."

The crone turned back to us and studied us for a moment. We said nothing, but I could feel the heat of Rowan's hand in mine, as well as the racing of my heart as the crone's eyes narrow.

"The scroll is real, as is the curse. It weaves a tale of the girl who on her last dying breath cursed the covens to fight. Until love is possible, there will be no end to the feuding. But it is not in the scroll what must happen for all of this to end, for peace to reign free upon Vernanthia and all to be well within the continent once more.

"Consider what it is for there to be only one heir apparent on either side. And for those two to fall in love, oh that is a wonderous thing. But, young lovers, for the war to end, when love is possible between a Montgomery and a Cambridge, it is only in their deaths that peace can be brokered, and the curse broken."

And with that, the crone was gone, vanishing before our eyes as Rowan looked up at me with fear in her brown eyes. I pulled her to me, felt the wetness of her tears as she cried, and I wished that I could say that the crone was lying. I knew bone-deep she was not.

"She cannot mean that, surely. What twisted turn of fate is this, Jules, that our love would lead to death."

In the end, it mattered not that myself and Rowan had these insane, immense feelings for one another. All that seemed to matter was that we were flesh and blood, easily slain in an attempt to break a curse that was bound to fruition by a dying girl.

Rowan lifted her head, and I wiped away the tears staining her face with my thumbs. "If my death ends all this pain and suffering, Jules, then so be it. But I want to die on my own terms, by my own hand. Can you promise me that?"

I had always thought that I would die one day, many years from now, decades into my reign as king. I dreamt of a glorious death in battle. But as I stared into Rowan's eyes, all of my fear slipped away by just the sheer strength and resolve in her eyes.

"I promise, Rowan. But we decide together."

She closed her eyes and wrapped her arms around me once more, and all I could hear was her simple response.

"Together."

chapter twenty–four
rowan

I TRIED TO USE THE STRENGTH IN JULES' VOICE TO STEEL my resolve, however I could not halt the sheer terror that had grasped a hand on my spine and refused to let go, tendrils of ice creeping up to fuse a hold on my heart. I did not wish to die, for selfish reasons, even if it meant that with our deaths, Vernanthia would have peace for the first time in eons.

When I had promised that we would do this together, I ensured that I pushed as much of the belief that we were doing the right thing into my eyes and voice, that I appeared unphased by our impending deaths. Now, my head resting against his chest, the comforting sound of his heart beating in my ear, I felt that resolve fading away.

Reluctantly stepping out of Jules' embrace, I brushed the hair away from my face and glanced up into the cobalt of his eyes. Despite the seriousness of our situation, my heart seemed to turn to mush whenever I held his gaze. It was something I had still to get used to, feeling this way about Jules. Especially considering we were meant to be mortal enemies with a future filled with certain death.

"If you keep looking at me like that then there is no

way I can go and face Lawrence or even Tobias," Jules said with an easy smile, as if he were trying to make light of the situation in which we found ourselves.

Heat flushed my cheeks, and I moistened my lips, wanting to feel his lips on mine once again with maddening need. When he kissed me, I forgot every single thing in the world and lost myself in sensation. It would be so easy, would it not, to indulge in this connection, this undeniable chemistry between Jules and I, even if only for a night.

"Rowan." My name on his lips came out in a husky but agonizing rush of breath. He closed those beautiful eyes of his as if he needed to jockey for control, and I stepped back to allow him to do so. In the midst of all the complications in our lives, we still had our own free will, and it was stronger than this so-called destiny etched on aged paper.

"I'm sorry to interrupt, but The Friar wants to see you both. The crone has deciphered the scroll."

Jules' friend Tobias stood in the mouth of the cave, his arms folded against his chest, and a grim expression on his face. Jules nodded his head in response, extending his hand to me. I knew what we were about to face, exactly what the mysterious scroll would tell us all. But as I slipped my hand into Jules', entwining our fingers together, I understood that I would not have to face it alone.

We followed Tobias silently, our footsteps and the sound of our breathing the only things to keep us company. We strode along the darkened corridor until I could hear the sounds of voices getting nearer and nearer. The voices sounded flustered, but none of them sounded as if they had been told that in order from them to get their utopia,

Jules and I would have to die.

As we entered the cavern, every gaze turning in our direction, and I shifted, slightly uncomfortable with the scrutiny. The Friar met my gaze, and his grin surprised me. The crone sat beside him, and as she rose and winked at me, I felt sick to my stomach. Mercy stood off to the side by himself until Tobias moved to stand next to him. Auggie lounged in one of the chairs, but his gaze watched Mercy before it shifted to look at them when they entered the room.

"The scroll has revealed more than we could have possibly imagined, Rowan. Our friend here has been able to tell us all about the curse, and how you both can break it."

The crone bowed at the Friar's words and made her exit from the room as if her presence was no longer needed. And it was not. She had delivered her herald of doom to us and had spun another story to the rest of them. Perhaps she meant to spare the others from knowing that this journey they embarked on would lead to our demise, or maybe the crone had a sick and twisted sense of humor.

You just never knew with crones, especially the older-than-dirt ones.

Jules squeezed my hand and pulled me closer to him. I could see the twinkle in my former mentor's eyes at the gesture. I lifted my eyes to meet the Friar's and frowned. He motioned for us to sit, but Jules shook his head.

"Just tell us what it is that you think we need to know."

The Friar leaned back into his chair and unrolled the scroll that he held in his hands.

"This very parchment tells of the death of the human who used blood magic to curse the covens. But that is not what is important. What is important is the wording of the curse, and how we can save Vernanthia."

He seemed rather proud of it, as if he alone had solved the riddle, and Vernanthia would be saved by him and his actions alone. How could I have not seen it before? How could I have not seen in him this need to be seen as a deity? He held the same look in his eyes as my mother had, the lust for power above all else.

"The words are as we once thought, that in order for peace to reign, love must be possible. The crone held the scroll in her grasp and felt its magic. This was inked moments after the girl died, when magic was still ripe in the air. The crone tells me that in order for Vernanthia to stop bleeding, love must be possible between the two houses."

I glanced at Jules and felt my heart expand as I caught him looking at me. I tried to banish the voice at the back of my mind, the one telling me that Jules only had feelings for me because he was cursed to do so. Was it the little girl in me who wanted Julian to love me for me? Had the fact that my mother had disdain for me because I wasn't what she wanted me to be colored my emotions and hindered me from thinking that Jules could feel for me because of who I was and not any magical tether?

"We believe that we have, with the crone's confirmation, found a way for this war to end."

The giddy excitement in his voice was not comforting. It was as if the man who had cradled me as a child, the man who had wiped my tears and cleaned scraped knees, valued power over my life. It left a bad taste in my mouth.

"We are of the consensus that you both should marry and align the houses."

That was not what I had been expecting and neither, apparently, had Jules.

"Excuse me."

The Friar smiled widely. "In order for peace to reign, the houses must be in sync with one another. A blessed union between you both is the catalyst for peace."

"You must be out of your minds!" I exclaimed, letting go of Jules' hand and lurching forward. "You cannot expect us to marry simply because an old woman said that it would be the only way to usher in peace."

"Do you not love him?" It sounded very much like an accusation rather than a question.

"How we feel about each other is none of your goddamn business."

"Rowan."

I wheeled on Jules and saw his answer in his eyes. He would marry me to save the continent, which made him a much worthier king that any queen I would ever be. Did I love him? In my heart and my mind, it was a roaring yes, but we hardly knew each other at all. How could I pledge whatever was left of my life to becoming his wife, when I knew it was not forever?

"Rowan," Jules uttered my name again, and I looked up at him, unashamed by the tears in my eyes. He came forward and cupped my face with his hands. The moment his skin touched mine, it was as if I was home and with the one I had been searching for my entire life.

"You do not have to say yes; no one will force it. But I need you to know that what I feel for you, it is not just about a curse or a country. I fell for you the moment I saw you dancing in the snow. I loved you when you danced and spoke of a freedom that could never be ours. And I loved you, Rowan, even when I hated you, when I thought you had been sent to kill me."

I could not stop the tears that now had overflowed from my lids and leaked down my cheeks. Jules brushed them aside with the pad of his thumbs and smiled a brilliant smile.

"But I do not need magic to know that it is I, Julian, who loves you. When you told me, as we danced among the shadows that you longed for freedom, I discovered that my freedom was you. You, Rowan Cambridge, set me free the moment you kissed me. If we were to only have one day left on this earth, then I want to spend it as your husband."

I heard the hidden meaning in his words, knew that he still intended for us to sever the weight of the curse by ending our lives. But just like magic, I heard the truth in his words and could not deny that I loved him too.

Jules brushed his lips against mine, as if we were the only two in the room. My hands fisted at the end of his tunic as I reluctantly pulled back and said, "Are we mad, Jules? We hardly know each other. Our parents will go to war simply for this perceived act of defiance. No matter what tomorrow brings, we do not have to go into it as man and wife."

"I know it is not the most romantic of proposals, but I do not want to wake up another day and not be tied to you, Rowan. Marry me."

I do not know if I had lost all reason and simply gone insane, but as Jules looked at me as if I was the light in the dark, I also found that I did not want to live another day and not be tied to him.

"Okay, Jules."

"Okay?"

"Yes," I breathed out. "I will marry you."

He kissed me again fiercely, and when we came up for air, Jules slipped his arm around my waist and looked at the Friar. "What happens now?"

"Now, we get you two married."

I glanced down at my attire, shrugging as I grinned at Jules. "This is a far cry from the dress my mother wished for me to wear for my wedding."

"I prefer this look on you. Although that dress you wore to winter solstice comes in a close second."

"Charmer."

Mercy strolled over and stood in front of us. His body language was tense, and his face a mask as he said to us, "Are you certain that this is what you want? There is no one that can force your hand in this."

Jules pressed his lips to the top of my head. "I want this, Mercy. More than I have ever wanted anything in my life."

"Then allow me the honor of standing by your side."

"Hey! Me too!"

Jules chuckled as Tobias stood beside Mercy, and I could not suppress the desire that Emilee might have been the one to stand beside me. I felt so alone in the world.

Auggie strode toward me and held out his arm. "Allow me the immense honor of baring witness to your union, Rowan."

In a flurry of movement, we were positioned in front of the Friar, and even as my brows narrowed, I figured that the man who had found religion after he retired from the army was going to marry us. I turned to face Jules, and my heart kicked like a drum in my chest as I reached for his outstretched hands. It comforted me that his palms were as sweaty as mine, and at least I was not the only one who was nervous.

"We will skip the ceremony and just bind you together."

A look must have crossed over my features because Jules glared at the Friar before he leaned his forehead against mine and whispered, "I know this might not be the wedding you dreamed of, and I am sorry for that. I wish one day, we could have a wedding in front of all the people who care for us."

I gave him a small smile and whispered back, "I think we already are."

Turning our attention back to our officiant, I swallowed down any reservations as the Friar produced a red ribbon, took our joined hands, and wrapped the ribbon around them. I swear I felt a buzz of magic as the ribbon kept our hands locked together.

"With this ribbon, I bind your lives together as husband and wife. May your love be strong enough to weather any storm. May your love survive anything that can be thrown at it. And last of all, may your love bind your hearts and souls together in this life and the next."

The Friar produced a knife and unbound our hands, turning them over slowly and slicing through Jules' palm first and then mine. He placed our palms on top of each other. As soon as our blood connected, I gasped with the sheer strength of it. It almost brought me to my knees.

The scent of magic flooded the room as the Friar continued on, his words becoming more powerful because of the magic and blood. "May this union be one of peace and love, spoken of through the ages."

Magic fizzled and popped in the air. "By the power given to me by the gods of old and new, I now declare that you, Julian Montgomery, and you, Rowan Cambridge, are husband and wife. Let not even death tear you apart, for you are now one body and soul for eternity."

Jules kissed me then with a ferociousness that I eagerly met, slipping my hands up and into his hair, holding him to me as the magic began to rescind, and I could see clearly once again. We broke apart, both breathless.

"Hello, wife." The look on Jules' face was of pure love, but his eyes were filled with lust.

"Hello, husband," I replied with a throaty laugh.

We had little time to enjoy our first moments as man and wife, as people began to filter in through the passageways and offer their congratulations. Soon enough, we were separated. Music struck up, and joy filled the rebel encampment. Food was brought out, as was wine and ale, the ensuing party could not have been more rapturous if we had won the war already.

Mercy offered his congratulations with a brief nod of his head, his gaze holding mine for a moment before he turned back to converse with his father. Tobias, on the other hand, grabbed me by the waist and twirled me around the makeshift dance floor, until I laughed so hard that tears watered my eyes.

When the music slowed, and Tobias stopped spinning around, he glanced at Jules, who was deep in conversation with Auggie, and brought his lips to my ear.

"If I could have picked someone for him, then I would have chosen someone like you. Brave, strong, smart, as well as being beautiful. Out of us all, Jules deserves a happy ending."

I moved to thank him, but my husband ensnared me from behind and pressed his warm lips to the curve of my neck. Tobias fisted a hand over his heart and backed away.

"Want to get away from all of this?"

I nodded as Jules grabbed me by the hand and led me from the party, moving down one of the passageways until we came to an area that was more secluded from the rest. Shielded by a curtain that Jules pulled back, he slipped inside and I followed, a startled cry leaving my lips as I saw what awaited me.

The small room was littered in candles, illuminating the space with orange flames. My eyes drifted to the makeshift bed on the floor, and I arched a brow at Jules, delighting in the reddening of his cheeks.

"I am not assuming anything, Rowan. Mercy and Toby planned all this. If all I do tonight is hold you as my wife, then I will be quite content in that."

I glanced back to see if the curtain had fallen back into place, and we were as cut off from the outside world as we could be. Jules studied me with an intense gaze. I walked up to him and pressed my lips to his.

All my life, my decisions had been made for me, but this was one choice I did not even have to consider.

"We are not really man and wife until we consummate the marriage, right?"

Jules shrugged, even as I slipped my hands under his tunic and rested them on his ribs. He shuddered, leaning into my touch. He captured my mouth with his, his hands fumbling with my own tunic as he lifted it over my head and looked at me like I was the most precious thing in the world. I knew I had made the right choice in marrying him.

"I have never done this before," he blurted out, his cheeks now colored with embarrassment.

I yanked his tunic over his head and pressed my lips to the planes of his chest.

"Neither have I," I said in reply with a grin. "We will be each other's first and last love. One that even death cannot taint."

"Let us not speak of death tonight, Rowan. Let us only feel our love."

I did not know who acted first, but our lips came together in an almost feverish clash, hands and mouths touching skin to skin. This love between us was so pure, it would smolder within our hearts for all eternity, long after we were no more.

Jules gently lowered me to my back, his lips like fire against my skin. I arched into him, never wanting this feeling to stop. He murmured in my ear that he loved me, and I had a second to say it back before he joined us together, and the world held its breath.

chapter twenty-five
julian

I AWOKE IN THE EARLY HOURS OF THE MORNING, A WARM feeling in my chest. Rowan was sprawled across me, her head resting in the curve where my shoulder and neck connected, one hand on my cheek, and her leg cast over my torso. With her hair down and her features relaxed, she looked almost content.

If a man could be blissfully happy, then I was pretty certain that I was feeling that way. After an initial clumsiness as we got to know each other intimately, our night had been filled with passion and love, something I had not thought possible before.

I now knew why I had not settled for simply being with someone else like Toby suggested. My body had been made to be Rowan's, as hers seemed to be made for me.

Last night had been one of the most amazing nights of my life. When I ran my fingers through my wife's hair, I tried to block out the overwhelming sense of doom that lingered on the edges of my happiness. I wanted to parade Rowan through the desert and proclaim her as mine. But that would never happen.

I lost track of how long I lay there, simply holding her

in my arms and wishing that every single morning could be like this. Then, I remembered once more that this was the last morning I would be alive.

Rowan stirred in my arms and stretched, freezing for a moment as she recalled where she was and whose arms she lay in. Lifting her head and rubbing the sleep from her eyes, she brushed the hair away from her face and gave me a tired smile.

"Morning, husband."

Oh, how I loved to hear her claim me like that.

I kissed the smile on her face and wrapped my arms around her tighter.

"Morning, wife."

Rowan shifted, putting her most feminine parts against my male parts, and I sucked in a breath. That only caused her smile to deepen.

"You look very smug this morning, Rowan."

"I married the hottest guy on the entire continent of Vernanthia, and then he claimed me for the better part of the night, melting my bones. What's not to be smug about."

Laughter rumbled in my chest as I shifted my weight, flipping us so that Rowan lay beneath me. She linked her arms around my neck and lifted her brows. "Melted your bones? And never in my life have I ever been told that I was the hottest guy on the continent."

Rowan pressed her lips to my shoulder and I shivered, wanting her with every fiber of my being. Like a moth to a flame, I could not stop myself from touching her, from kissing her. I could not stop from molding us together as Rowan dragged her hands down my spine and dug her fingers into my flesh.

When we were both sated, I flipped us back over to our original positions, and we lay in silence for an age. If time froze in this moment, I would gladly stay like this, in the arms of the woman I adored.

As if she sensed me watching her, she rested her elbows on my stomach and smiled at me in a way that ensnared my heart. In her smile, I saw the universe, I saw the future, and I saw the end. I knew without a doubt that I had been placed on this earth to stand side-by-side with her. We were destined to meet, undoubtedly set on a path that would change us forever.

And if the stars lived on through infinity, then so would she, burning brighter than the night sky, with her smile a beacon of hope in the dark. I felt so lucky to be given the chance to love her and utterly overwhelmed to be loved by her.

"Hey, where did you go?" Rowan questioned as if she had felt the tension in me.

I shook my head, pressing my lips to her forehead. "It's nothing. I just feel lucky that our paths crossed now, and not in the future when life had turned us bitter."

"The crone said you had dreams of the future. I did also. The hate I felt in my heart for you... I cannot imagine ever feeling that for you, no matter what."

Before I could reply, Mercy appeared inside our cavern and Rowan squeaked, pulling a blanket up over herself as I growled. "Mercy! Get the hell out!"

"I would not be standing here if it was not for a very good reason. Get dressed. The war drums have sounded."

We scrambled from our makeshift bed and dressed quickly, halting when we were fully clothed, hair less mussed and bed riddled. Rowan peered at me, a sense of desperation in her features as I pulled her to me.

"I wanted to waste the day away with you in my arms. I wanted to make every second count. I am so terribly sorry that I cannot have this day with you."

Rowan hugged me tightly, her tears wetting my tunic. "I did too. In the mere time that I have known you, Jules, you have given me so much that I can never repay you for. The last day has been the happiest I can remember being. I know what we have to do, Jules, but I wish with all my heart that we did not."

I tried to think of something poetic, words that could sum up exactly how I felt about her, but I struggled to find the right ones. There was nothing I could do or say to make her understand that my life had begun the moment I laid eyes on her. No words would make what we had to do to save our covens any easier, so I chose to say three words instead.

"I love you."

"I love you too."

I kissed her once, maybe twice, before we gathered ourselves and followed the din of noise into the main epicenter of activity.

We stood in the entranceway as men, women, and children rushed about arming themselves with knives, bows, and anything else that was handed to them. Auggie, Mercy, Tobias and Reinhart were positioned off to the side. From the fury in Tobias' stance and expression, this was not a planned movement.

"You couldn't just wait one bloody day, Reinhart! One bloody day before you threw it in the faces of the most powerful witches in Vernanthia. All these people are unprepared for what is coming. Their deaths will be forever a stain on your hands."

With Rowan by my side, we rushed over. Toby and Reinhart faced off against each other, and I stepped in front of them to stop them for coming to blows. I looked from one to another and frowned. "Does one of you want to explain to me what the hell is going on?"

I felt the waves of anger roll off Toby as he snarled at Reinhart. "Ask the illustrious leader of the rebels. He who thought it would be a great idea to send word to Malcolm and Kendra, telling them that he had convinced the pair of you to get married, therefore unifying the covens. He also explained to them that he was in charge of the rebels, and we were coming for their heads!"

I faced Reinhart, not waiting to hear his response because, in his expression, I read the purpose of his letters to our parents. "You wanted this. You kindled the sparks to ignite the war. You did not want us to marry because you wanted peace. You wanted us to marry so that you could incite violence and bloodshed."

Reinhart did not deny it, even as Rowan's palm connected with his cheek. The entire gathered forces stopped whatever they were doing and turned to watch them. I placed my hand on the small of Rowan's back, not stopping her from raging against the man who once was like a father to her.

"How dare you? You bastard. Is the scroll even real, or was it just some ploy to twist us into being exactly where you needed us to be? Goddammit, I should have seen it. It's exactly the best possible maneuver. Enrage the royal houses by marrying off their children and gain the upper hand. How could my father ever have followed you or trusted you? How could I?"

"My father," I interjected. "My father will send his army across the continent, even now I assume they are on their way. These are not your average soldiers. I have trained with them, and they have been waiting for this war their entire existence. These men, women and children will be no match for their training and for their magic."

"Kendra will not accept this insult lying down. She will send in her best magic users, those who sneak up on you and snap your neck before you can even blink. What you have done is not unite the covens, Lawrence, you have become the catalyst for the war."

"And so, what if I have!" Reinhart roared, his being trembling from head to toe. "Those two who sit on the thrones do not deserve the crowns on their heads. The scroll is true, I swear upon your father's grave that it is, but this war needed to happen so that the poison that is the covens is eradicated from this world."

He laughed then, a sickening sound that turned my stomach. "And how easy it was, you were both so overtaken with forbidden lust that I could sway you to marry, because you both wanted to be the heroes."

"Lawrence, this is not how we planned it. You swore that we would not blindly send our people to be killed. This is not the future we discussed."

Reinhart made to swing at Ashbridge, but his wrist was captured by Mercy, whose lips curled into a feral smile as he addressed Reinhart. "Please, do something that warrants me slitting your throat."

Two armed men came up and grabbed Reinhart by the arms, yanking him out of the room and down a hallway. Ashbridge put his head in his hands and sighed before he chanced lifting it again. Looking directly at Rowan and

I, an aura of sadness leaking from his pores, he shook his head. "I am utterly sorry. If I had known, if I suspected, I would not have encouraged you in any way. This is not the future we want for Vernanthia."

I believed him. Not a single person in this room wanted to be faced with a war. Everything we had done was to prevent it.

I clasped Ashbridge on the shoulder and said, "You are now their leader. I would suggest that you appoint someone to take one of the tunnels and ferry the children away from any fighting. You will need the young to usher in a new generation, and they cannot do that if they are dead."

Turning to Toby and Mercy, I said, "It will take my father days to get here, but Kendra could be here by morning. Asses the skills of the able-bodied men and set them to task to form a wall between the encampment and our enemies."

Toby did as asked, but Mercy stood where he was, even as Ashbridge ordered a middle-aged woman to usher the children out. When they had disappeared down a darkened tunnel, I looked at Rowan and knew our time together had ended.

Suddenly, my wife took off at breakneck speed, and I chased after her down one of the pathways and into the cavern where we had sat only last night listening to stories. I skidded to a halt when I saw Rowan hoist the crone up off her seat and push her against the wall.

"Will our deaths stop this? If we die, will it spare those inside these walls?"

The crone grinned, the gaps in her rotted mouth turning my stomach. She raked her eyes over me, and then Rowan, as she shrugged. "Everything is as it should be. Death is the only answer. For you, for him. If not, then for everyone. Grief is a more powerful emotion than vengeance. Love is the most powerful of all."

The crone flashed before their eyes, transforming into a midnight feathered raven. She flapped her wings and flew out of the cavern before either of us could stop her.

Rowan turned to me, steel in her gaze. We would go now. This was it. We would not have a lifetime, or even an hour. Death had crept up on us, and I was not ready to say goodbye to her, let alone my closest friends.

As if reading my thoughts, Rowan shook her head. "We won't tell them. It will be better once they know why it is that we have sacrificed ourselves. For them. For Vernanthia."

"And what if we did not wish for you to sacrifice yourselves for us."

Mercy's voice shattered the illusion that we could sneak off. My silver-haired friend slipped from the shadows he called his own, his expression grim.

"We simply wished to save you the burden of watching us die, Mercy. You have seen enough death in your life to bear witness to mine and Rowan's."

"Death is who I am, Jules. Ask it of me, and I would make it quick and painless."

I strode over to my friend and embraced him. "This is something that I would never ask of you, Mercy. But it must come to pass. Look after Toby when I am gone. I fear that he will not understand. I love you, brother."

"And I you, my King." Mercy inclined his body toward Rowan and fisted his hand over his heart. "My Queen."

When Mercy slipped back into the shadows, I held

out my hand, and Rowan slipped his dainty fingers into mine. I loved the little callouses she bore from wielding a bow and arrow. We walked hand-in-hand up and out of the rebel camp, both of us pausing to take in the beauty of the rainforest.

"I understand why you love it here. It is rather tranquil."

"I would have been so happy to traipse through the desert as your wife, Jules. Oh, so very happy."

Rowan began to walk then, and all I could do was follow her lead. Branches crunched beneath our feet, the scent of pine and wet leaves stung my nose as Rowan maneuvered us through the forest of her birth. In the distance I could hear the gushing of water and wondered if that was what Rowan wanted us to do.

Having spent my entire lifetime in the desert, drowning would never have crossed my mind for how I would die. Rowan slowed her pace as the sound of the water grew louder, until we stepped out into a clearing and what seemed to be the edge of the world.

Before my eyes, I could see nothing but the blue of the sea, the white of the foam as the waves that curled crashed against the cliff we stood upon. Rowan cleared her throat as if to speak, but remained silent, her fingers clutching mine ever so tightly.

Peaking over the edge, I looked at the jagged rocks below and knew that a person could not survive an impact against them. Rowan released a sob, and I pulled her to me, offering what little comfort that I could, considering we were about to plunge to our deaths.

I had to kiss her one last time, so I lifted her chin to tilt toward me and pressed my lips to hers. She opened her mouth instantly, and we lost ourselves in a frenzied clash of tongues and teeth. It was the kiss of a dying man, and the desperation of a dying woman.

When we broke apart, I rested my forehead against hers as I told her, "I love you, Rowan. I will find you, wherever our souls end up. In the next life or the life after that. There is no force in this world that will stop me from finding you."

"Oh, Jules. I love you too. And I will kick your ass if you don't find me quick enough."

I smiled, not finding it in me to laugh as I whispered, "Are you ready?"

Rowan shook her head. "I will never be ready to say goodbye to you, Julian."

We inched closer to the edge, heard the impact as a wave came closer and slammed against the cliff wall. I could taste the salt water on my skin, and I licked my lips, drinking in the sight of my beautiful wife so that her face would be the last thing I saw before I died.

The wind suddenly picked up, whipping against us as it screamed through the trees. The cold harshness of it bit against our skin, but neither of us seemed to care about it. It began to drizzle again, and I thought with amusement that this place must never have drought, never feel for lack of rain. It reminded me that I would never feel the sand between my toes or feel the sun at its hottest against my skin. I would never kiss my mother's cheek or drink ale and play cards with my friend.

But one glance at Rowan, and I knew that I would not have altered the choices that brought us here. Rowan too had lost so much in a short space of time, and I wondered if there was someone she would have wanted to say goodbye to.

Neither of us uttered a word, as we came as close to the edge as possible. With interlocked fingers, we were ready to set in motion our real destiny, to die so that others might live. With one final glance at each other, we mouthed our last I love you.

With a deep breath, we stepped over the edge and plunged to our deaths.

playlist
julian

Where's My Love - Alternate Version - SYML
Lose My Mind - Acoustic - Dean Lewis
Lost on You - Lewis Capaldi
Need You Now - Acoustic - Dean Lewis
Be Your Man - Rhys Lewis
Perfect - Ed Sheeran
Change It All - Harrison Storm
Waves - Acoustic - Dean Lewis
Leave a Light On - Tom Walker
Found What I've Been Looking For - Tom Grennan
Beautifully Unconventional - Wolf Alice
Wherever You Will Go - Charlene Soraia
Can I Be Him - James Arthur
Please Keep Loving Me - James TW
This Year's Love - David Gray
Sleep On The Floor - The Lumineers
Let Go - Dean Lewis
Water - Jack Garratt
Someone To You - BANNERS
After Rain - Dermot Kennedy
Moments Passed - Dermot Kennedy
Mr. Sandman - SYML
terrified - isaac gracie
Particles - Nothing but Thieves
Sober - Tom Grennan
Zombie - Bad Wolves

rowan:

Particles - Island Songs VI - Ólafur Arnalds
Maps - Freya Ridings
Can't Help Falling in Love - Haley Reinhart
Only You - Acoustic - Sarah Close
Dream - Bishop Briggs
Evergreen - Broods
This Is How We Love - Daena Jay
Looking Back - Claire Guerreso
All I Ever Do (Is Say Goodbye) - Zak Abel
Battlecry - Jordan Mackampa
Play – Marmozets
Like I'm Gonna Lose You - Jasmine Thompson
Take Me Home - Jess Glynne
Take A Bow - Rihanna
Save Myself - Ed Sheeran
World Gone Mad - Bastille
Imperfection - Evanescence
26 - Paramore
Are You Ten Years Ago – PVRIS
Hearts - Jessie Ware
Wicked Game - Lydia Ainsworth
While My Guitar Gently Weeps - Regina Spektor
Are You With Me - nilu
Beautiful Trauma - P!nk
What About Us - P!nk
All The Stars (with SZA) - Kendrick Lamar

other songs of note:

These are songs I listened to when channeling other characters, like Toby or Mercy.

You Don't Know - Katelyn Tarver
The Best You Had - Nina Nesbitt
Night So Long - HAIM
I Dare You - The xx
The Punisher Main Title - Tyler Bates
Devil Inside Me - Frank Carter & The Rattlesnakes
Vanity - Big Terrible
Tell Me You Love Me - Demi Lovato
Lose My Faith - Gold Brother
Beat The Devil's Tattoo—Black Rebel Motorcycle Club
Bloodstream - Tokio Myers
Can't Do - Everything Everything
Vale - Bicep
Homesick - Dua Lipa
Broken - Zak Abel
Rock Bottom (feat. Wretch 32) - Zak Abel
World Away - Tonight Alive
In My Arms (feat. Jamie N Commons) - Grizfolk
Bloodstain – Wrabel
Me And My Friends Are Lonely - Matt Maeson
No Mercy - PVRIS
Nightcrawling - Saint Raymond
Chemicals - Dean Lewis
Holy Ground - BANNERS
Cringe - Stripped - Matt Maeson
Grave Digger - Matt Maeson

Aggression - Palisades
Burns - George FitzGerald
Lemon to a Knife Fight - The Wombats
Fake ID - The Academic

about the author

SUSAN HARRIS IS A WRITER FROM CORK IN IRELAND. AN avid reader, she quickly grew to love books in the supernatural/fantasy genre. When she is not writing or reading, she loves music, oriental cultures, tattoos, anything Disney and psychology. If she wasn't a writer she would love to be a FBI profiler or a PA for Dave Grohl or Jared Leto.

acknowledgments

To the amazing girls over at CTP, Rebecca, Courtney and Marya,

Marya, what words can I use that will justify just how gorgeous the cover for Tale is?
This book is a dream come true and your amazing talent created a cover that is Shakespeare worthy. Thank you so very much!

Jamie, my trusty beta reader!
Thank you for being so awesome and I'm lucky to have you.

Sláinte, Kelly Risser, for teaching me so much and making sure Tale is battle ready!

My Parents,
Who taught me to work hard and never give up on my dreams. I love you both so very much.

LJ and Taylor, To Infinity and beyond x
My circle is small, but it is mighty.

To those who are always in my life, no matter what.
Sláinte

To MELANIE'S MUSERS,
An awesome bunch of people and I am so blessed to be
even a small part of our little community.
Oh, and GREG…for his terrible Irish accent and love of
Irish pub songs!

Special thanks to KAREN for coming up with Vernanthia
for me to use!

WILLIAM SHAKESPEARE, thank you, good sir, for
providing this author with such inspiration.

And finally, to you, THE READER, who has picked up A
Tale of Two Houses to read. Thank you, thank you, thank
you a thousand times over.